THE PREVAILING DARKNESS

The Chronicles of the
Raven Clan

THE PREVAILING DARKNESS

CHRISTOPHER LEE BAIRD

Published by Tate Publishing & Enterprises, LLC
127 E. Trade Center Terrace | Mustang, Oklahoma 73064 USA
1.888.361.9473 | www.tatepublishing.com

Tate Publishing is committed to excellence in the publishing industry. The company reflects the philosophy established by the founders, based on Psalm 68:11,
"The Lord gave the word and great was the company of those who published it."

Cover design by Rodrigo Adolfo
Interior design by Jake Muelle

Published in the United States of America

ISBN: 978-1-62854-166-3
1. Fiction / Fantasy / General
2. Fiction / Action & Adventure
13.10.23

SPECIAL THANKS

I would like to thank all of the friends and family who helped make this project possible. It has been a long time coming and without your help this project would not be what it is today. Thank you to, Stephanie Durham, who helped review and make strong suggestions on the development of the story. To a dear friend and theological think tank, Neal Fox, who helped edit and straighten out any serious issues in my thinking. And then to my mother, who has encouraged and fought for me along the way. Thank you to all of my friends who have picked me up and helped me push forward to see my dreams come true.

WILLIAM'S NARRATIVE

In a place closer than you think but farther than you could ever reach is a wondrous land known as the Outland. Originally from the Inland, or better known as our world, I found myself stuck there, learning the art of war from a great Guardian known as Amos. Before long, I did not even want to go back home. I had learned so much there, and I felt important. As a member of the Guardians, it was my job to protect people from the evils of the world. It was a better life than when I was back home in New York. I was just a little punk back then. In the Outland, I gained purpose and power.

Not even a year had passed when a new friend came into my life. His name was Lee Christian, and his arrival marked a new dawn for me. That was the time when the Black King marched upon the land, killing everyone in his wake. We all fought valiantly against his army and tried our best to end his tyranny. There at the end, I could feel the castle breaking up around me, falling into the great canyon that sat just beyond its walls. Furniture slammed against me, pinning me to the wall. I was blinded and couldn't see anything.

Now I've awoken in a familiar place, lost in despair. The darkness is rising against me, trying to stay alive by snuffing out what little light is left. But I'm not going to give up. I've been fighting too long to just let the darkness win. I will overcome my challenges and destroy the hurdles that stand before me. I have no choice but to overcome if I ever want to get back to where I belong.

As a point of advice to whoever may be reading this, never trust a demon when they tell you something. It was a hard lesson in my life, but I learned that they will tell you half-truths, lies, and whisper things in your ears to distract you from what is real. Even a hardened warrior struggles with the devastating blows that demons throw at you. They will try their hardest to drag you down with them.

OUT OF THE FIRE

William Knight's eyes began to flutter as he started to wake up. He found himself lying on the floor of a monastery. He slid his hands through his shaggy, sandy-blond hair. He had been waiting two years to get a decent hair cut but never got one. William yawned, stretching out his arms. He had no idea how long he was out, but he sure felt good now. William sat there for a moment, stretching out his limbs. After getting all of his kinks out, he studied the layout of the room. It was a large chapel lit with candles and soft lamps. Surprisingly, the people were able to gather enough for a well-lit room. Most of the pews were chopped up and used to board up the beautiful stained glass windows. William got to his feet in order to get a better look around. That was when he noticed that he was wearing a hospital gown.

"What the?" he said to himself. His eyes scanned the room again. They had turned the chapel into a triage unit. Sick, dying, and dead people littered the floor. There wasn't any rush since most of the people were dying a slow death. All that could be done for them was to make them comfortable. William reached down to his right hand and rubbed a leather bracelet, which was strapped to his wrist.

"Thank God in heaven," a nun cried, rushing over to William. "I thought for sure that you had died."

"What? Why?" William asked, bewildered.

"You poor thing," the nun said wrapping her arms around him, helping him up and leading him to a seat. "I'll fetch you some good clothes to wear."

William grabbed her arm as she walked away. "What happened here?" The woman started to choke on her tears as she walked quickly away. "What happened here?" William asked himself.

"Nothing good," a familiar voice said behind him. William spun around to be greeted by his friend, Lee Christian. Lee too was lost in the Outland with William as they struggled to find their way home. Lee was leaning against a wall with his hands halfway in his pockets. His jeans were ragged and worn and so was the rest of his clothing.

"Lee! Where are we?" William asked excitedly. William rushed over to him in a nervous manner. "I mean, the last thing I remember was us fighting with the Black King." William was talking a thousand words a second.

"Calm down," Lee said with a chuckle. "We'll get to it. You've been out for some time."

"How long?" William asked.

"Longer than me by about three days at least." Lee smiled. "You're going to need a set of clothes." Lee pointed at William's gown. William felt the draft coming in the back and quickly clasped the gown shut as a few nuns walked by, giggling. "I'll show you everything once you're ready."

"Here you are," the nun said, returning with a pair of clothes for him. The sight alone made William cringe. "Is everything okay?" she asked.

"Yeah, no problem." William was less than convincing. William lifted up a pair of tan corduroy pants that looked as if they somehow barely survived the fifties. The shirt read, "*I live for Rock.*" William rolled his eyes.

"Hey, at least it's something," Lee said, trying to make him feel better.

"Be grateful that the Lord gave you what he did," the nun said walking away, disappointed at William's ungratefulness.

Lee led William to a closet, out in the hall, for him to change in. "Don't get me wrong," William started as he was getting dressed, "I am thankful, but this is just wrong." William paused, investigating the scars that covered his body. Along with the scar above his right eye, there were two new scars. One from the last battle at the End of the World and the one he received on the road to Mear, where he had lost his fight with a group of soldiers. Mear was the oasis to the east of the desert, which had been invaded because Lee was uncooperative with the King of Ram. Even though the people were able to push back the army, many people lost their lives there, including a dear friend.

Lee leaned his back against the door as William asked the tough questions.

"What happened here?" William asked. "It looks like we're home, but the place is in shambles."

Lee held his breath for the moment, sorting out the answer in his head. "It seems like the Outland seeped into our world too. Creatures have been sighted all over the world."

"How long ago?" William asked. "How long have we been out?"

"I don't know," Lee answered. "It seems like it's been a while though. These people have been here for quite some time. I was informed that we were in a coma ward during the last attack. We're lucky they were able to get us out."

"We need to get answers," William said as he opened the closet door, shaking his head at the state of his wardrobe.

Lee chuckled. "Don't be so hard on these people. Most of them are wearing dead men's clothes." Lee placed his arm around William's shoulder and started down the hall. "Don't worry though. I'll make it up to you." Lee removed his arm and pulled away from William.

"How?" William asked.

"I'm going to get you a gun," Lee said, imitating a hillbilly's accent.

"Really?" William's face brightened. "What kind? You know, I'm pretty particular about my firearms."

Lee handed William a plastic bottle with a clear brownish liquid in it. "Drink this."

"What is it?" William asked.

"Tea, it'll help," Lee said. William took a swig. It was very bitter with a strong kick.

"That's nasty!" William said, gasping. "It tastes like a pair of old socks."

"It's better when heated up, but it'll keep you healthy."

"Who made it?" As the words left William's mouth, a loud crash came from down the hall.

Lee chuckled. "I almost forgot. You have to see this."

William followed Lee down the hall and through a door that led into the kitchen. A boy stood there holding on to the edge of the counter, his knees shaking from underneath him.

He was about fifteen years old with light brown hair. "I can't see how it's possible you people can walk around without tails. Your bodies are so unbalanced."

"How's the training going?" Lee asked.

"Fairly bad," the boy said. "I see *he* finally woke up."

"Who is that?" William asked.

"You don't recognize him?" Lee teased William with the question, purposefully holding out on the boy's identity.

"Of course not," the boy said. "Why would he? I'm in shambles." William looked the boy up and down trying to figure it out but he couldn't. William looked into his eyes as he continued to ramble on. "I need to go to the armory today so I can be issued a weapon. I won't be left unable to defend myself."

"You can't even walk in a straight line," Lee said. It was harsh but the truth. "What makes you think you can handle a weapon?"

"I'll manage," he said. "I always do."

"Warren?" William said with unbelief.

"Well, good for you," the boy said. "Lee needed two hints before he got it right."

"How?" William asked. "You're not supposed to be human." In the Outland, Warren was a hybrid creature known as a Warrian, made up of several different animals. As a Warrian grows, their overall appearance changes. They start off taking on a wolflike form, then to the likeness of a large cat, and ultimately into a humanoid creature with wings on their backs. The first stage after being a pup is called a Missions level. This is the age where they go out on missions and engage the people. The next level is the Trial's level, named because of the difficultly that they have with the transformation. As they grow, their bodies resemble more like a saber tooth tiger with large leathery wings. With heightened senses, they have a difficult time interacting with others, and most do not survive the process. Lastly is the Elder level, where they take on a form like that of a gargoyle. These are the elites. Warren was known as one of the best warriors that the Warrian people had. Born with a special ability, he was able to transform into each level at will. The gift of transformation is not that uncommon for Warrians, but it did place him in a position above the rest.

"You don't need to tell me twice," Warren said. "That last blast changed me somehow."

"What blast?" William asked, looking over at Lee who shook his head.

"Don't worry about it," Lee said. "Both of you need to go to the armory, so we better get going. The doc should be back soon."

"Who's the doc?" William asked.

"A friend of mine," Lee said. "He's been working on figuring out why the Outland is crossing over. I'll introduce you later."

The three of them slowly made their way to the armory located on the third floor. Lee rattled on about the history of the building and filled in what he could about what had happened while they were out. Warren walked three paces behind William and Lee, using the wall to steady himself.

"This building was built over one hundred years ago as a church. Just over fifteen years ago, there was a campaign to build a hospital here, so instead of tearing down the old building, they just built around it. We are currently on the far west side of the hospital. This was such a historical place for the town that the people couldn't part with it, so it's gone unchanged. Even though they rebuilt most of the structure, the entire inside still resembles the original church. Five years after that, they decided to add on a medical school to the west side, placing the church in the center of the building."

"Why is everyone here?" William asked.

"They're hiding," Lee answered. "Apparently, while we were in the Outland, it was starting to invade our land. Currently, most of the people outside are infected with a dangerous disease. It resembles something in the fashion of rabies, but as far as I can tell, it is only happening locally."

"So we can't leave?" William sounded concerned.

"We'll have to look into it. I didn't bother before because you were still in a coma," Lee said.

"So how long have we been out?" William asked.

"From what I was able to gather, it was at least nine years."

"Nine years!" William exclaimed. "How?"

Lee shrugged, not sure what to tell him, because he did not know. "Eight years ago, a man by the name of Scott Edwards was named president of the United States of America. He brought peace and prosperity. He raised wages, brought jobs back into the country, lowered taxes, and he made our foreign relations better than ever before. Science and technology went through the roof, and our country was on the rise. The next election, Edwards won by the biggest landslide in this nation's history. He had every state backing him up. The man running against him only got three hundred votes throughout the entire nation. In the next four years, he made the people even happier, but it was at a cost. He made the people so happy that no one was watching the ball, letting Edwards go unchecked. He weakened the infrastructure of our government to the extent that we had an abundance of military arsenal but no troops to use them. Just before the end of his term, he turned the government over to someone who called himself The Trepidation. He swept over the nation like a flood. The people didn't even stand a chance. After he destroyed most of the resistance in this country, he moved on to the other countries. The Trepidation left behind groups of people he called Temps. They're the ones ruling the country now."

"Why Temps?" William asked.

"Probably to let us know that they are just temporary and that he's coming back," Lee said, stopping at a door. It was a bi-level door. Lee knocked on the top part of the door, and it slowly swung open. Sitting inside was an older woman who was wearing a nun outfit. On her lap was a shotgun. "Hey, sissy, what's up?"

"I heard you a mile away," the woman openly mocked Warren and his inability to walk correctly. "People are going to mistake hop-along there for one of *them* someday, banging into walls and making such a racket." The woman had a fire in her spirit that everyone liked. She was sassy yet refined. "So what do you want?"

"My friends here need weapons," Lee said. "What do you got?"

"Well, thanks to that idiot who crashed into the hospital last week, we've got plenty of weapons, but I'm not sure I want to trust a firearm to someone who can't even stand on his own two feet."

"Hey, you just wait. I'll show you what I can do," Warren said, pointing at her.

"I'm sure you will, sonny," she said sarcastically, standing to her feet.

"Give him a break," William interrupted. "I'll get him in shape."

"Fine," the woman said as she grabbed two belts off a hook. She laid them down on the shelf in front of them. The two belts had a .9mm Glock pistol in their holsters, four clips each. One of the belts had a knife with the sheath attached. The nun laid down a second knife on top of that. "Since Lee won't need it, you can have it."

William looked over at Lee with a puzzled look on his face. Lee turned his back to William and raised his shirt. Attached to Lee's belt were the two Guardian knives that Amos had given to him back in the Outland. Resting on top of the sheaths was a holster with a gun in it. Lee dropped the shirt and turned back around.

"A Desert Eagle. That's a nice gun," William said. While Lee was showing off his weapons, Warren was strapping the two belts that held the Glocks.

"So you know your guns," the nun said.

"I should," William replied. "My dad's a cop. He taught me everything I know."

"Well, what kind do you want?" the nun said, opening the door. "We've got more than we need, so take what you want."

William stepped inside the door and went straight for a ten-gauge shotgun. *That'll make a hole*, William thought to himself, but he laid it back down after a moment. *I might need speed. A ten gauge might be too much.* William moved down the line looking at all of the firearms. "You know your guns too," William said. "You've categorized them from strongest to weakest."

"An old habit I learned from my dad. He used to collect guns," she said.

William picked up a twenty-gauge shotgun. He smiled knowing he had the right one. William opened a case for a long-range rifle that was lying on the shelf next to him. He pulled out a shoulder strap and hooked it to his new shotgun. Slinging it onto his back, he turned his attention to a sawed-off shotgun lying on an upper shelf. He grabbed the gun and threw it into a brown leather pouch along with a large number of shells for it. He tossed it at Warren. "You might need that." William turned to the other end of the room where they kept a large assortment of swords, knives, and other close combat weapons. A lot of their weapons came from what they could scavenge from around the block, like the pawnshop down the road and the hunting store next door. However, their biggest contributor was the truck that crashed into the hospital the week before. The truck was packed with all kinds of weapons that were now being used for their benefit. William saw a beautiful double-edged sword. As he took it down, he knocked over a brown cardboard box. When it hit the ground, several shurikens (throwing stars) scattered all over the floor. That's when William had an epiphany. William scooped up the shurikens and took the other two boxes. He thanked the nun, and they went on their way. "Lee, I need an empty room."

"Why?" Lee asked.

"To help hop-along," William replied.

Lee took William and Warren to a room on the second floor. It was a bare room with only a card table sitting off to the side. William placed the shurikens on the table and opened the boxes. "Okay, pal. This is what you need to do." William walked to the other end of the room, which was about twenty feet away. He took a marker that he found on the table and marked an X on the wall then drew a circle around it. "Okay, take five of the stars and throw them at the X. If the stars land inside the circle then you can leave them there, but if they don't, then you have to take them out of the wall and use them again. Once you've filled a circle, make a new one."

"Why?" Warren asked.

"You said you were having trouble with your balance. Throwing these will help you find balance," William said. "We'll be back to get you after we get done at Doc's." Warren gave his first shot at the X on the wall. As the shuriken left his hand, Warren's weight shifted, and he toppled over onto the floor. The star also hit the floor two feet shy of the wall. William and Lee left the room and started for the stairs to go to Doc's laboratory.

"Do you think that'll really help?" Lee asked.

"I know that he'll get plenty of practice walking back and forth picking up the stars."

The horizon of the sky was at a permanent dusk. The purple and red hues reached past the mountains in the distance, giving the land a red tint. Soldiers gathered around their camps, listening to the distant roars of cannons and gunfire. A sobering presence was felt in the camp. Everyone knew what was on the line.

Captain Harper stood in front of a map in his staging area, investigating the movement of enemy troops. His Allied World War II uniform was neatly pressed and polished. He was always concerned with the details, which made him perfect for this assignment.

Harper's finger gently traced the lines on the map, following them to the place where the enemy had made their encampment. "Jonathan!" He shouted, waiting on him to come running. Once he had taken his place, he continued, "Take your men down to the southern ledge. Don't let the ratty demons pass."

"Yes, sir," the soldier replied.

"How are things on the front?" a familiar voice asked.

Harper turned only long enough to confirm that it was Amos speaking to him. The scruffy beard hanging from his chin was all Harper needed to see. With a shift of his eyes, he returned back to his map. Standing beside him was a younger soldier with short blondish hair; it was a traditional military cut. Both of them were in their Outland Guardian uniforms. They were similar to that of a Yankee uniform during American Civil War but fashioned more in the design of the British soldiers of the Revolutionary War.

"It's been a long time, Amos." Harper started off with the pleasantries. "Been well?"

"Not particularly," Amos replied.

"Your job was to secure the Warriors in the Outland and usher them directly home, back to the Inland." Harper preferred getting to the point of things. It was rare for him to make friends with this approach, but it was more efficient. "Instead you allowed the enemy to drag them here."

Amos took responsibility for his failures in the Outland, refusing to make excuses. His original job was to keep the world in proper flow, not escort a group of Inlanders through the Outland. On top of that, the Black Queen had interfered, dispatching his body at the Temple of Light. He focused his mind to the problem at hand, asking, "How are the gates holding?"

"Terrible." Harper pointed in the direction of the enemy camp. "They're not making it easy on me. Every time we defend a gate, another one goes down."

"How many have gone down?" Amos was concerned. "I want to limit the Warriors exposure to this world as much as possible."

"You're not going to be happy." Harper pointed out the chart. "Out of one hundred and eighty-nine gates and portals that were opened, they've closed down ninety-three, almost half."

"Have they closed down the essential ones?" Amos studied the map more closely.

"The ones in the hospital are gone, the one next to the bar has been taken over, the one next to the bakery and the three in England have also disappeared. Personally, I think it would be better this way. It will certainly reduce the trauma to their psyche. Spending prolonged periods inside of the gate will drive them off the deep end."

"Maybe so," Amos started, "but if they spend too much time fighting with the Temps of this land, they will grow a taste for battle. Besides, they will also grow more accustomed to using their supernatural abilities, which is why the demons brought them to this place."

Harper took time to glance over at his partner. "Is this your new apprentice?" he asked Amos. "Are you training for a new assistant?"

Amos shook his head. "This is Cecil. He's the one in charge of the master's plan."

Harper's eyes widened. He had heard the name before. Cecil was well known for his insight and tactics against their enemy. He was a high-ranking officer that was skilled with his blade as well with the ability to plan ahead.

"You transformed into a Warrian cub in the Outland, didn't you?"

"It was important to observe the group locally and to gain their trust," Cecil explained. "I guided their progress for as long as it was useful. After that, I disposed of the body and observed from behind the scenes."

"I heard that *that group* also cloned your body using a Jelly Mold." Harper chuckled at Cecil's expense.

"That body is playing its own part in this event," Cecil rebutted. His face remained unchanged, serious about the role the Jelly

Mold would play. "Everything has been accounted for. The rest is up to them to make the right decisions."

Amos decided to change gears, saying, "Raven's Clan is eccentric at best. Though they have no experience fighting demons or those things that truly matter, they do cling to their friends as if they were family."

"Raven's Clan?" Harper asked.

"The group was formed under Tobias Raven," Amos informed, "so it has been suggested by my former student that they be named after him."

"That would be William Knight?" Harper asked.

"Correct." Amos shrugged his shoulders, relaxing in the moment as he explained that "William had mentioned it merely on a whim, but it seems to have stuck."

Harper nodded, glancing to his left at the main briefing tent. He noticed the door flap in the wind, signaling that the person inside was ready for him.

"Come with me," Harper said, waving them to follow. "The General, Michael, has sent another officer to give you a hand on your journey. Apparently, things are getting interesting on the frontlines."

As they opened the flap to the tent, they saw another angel standing in front of the briefing table. He looked as if he was in his late thirties with long black hair. Even though he smiled and greeted his fellow comrades, his eyes were still fierce, those of a seasoned warrior.

"Good evening, my name is Jonas." He extended his hand to them.

"What brings you here, Jonas?" Amos asked, shaking his hand in return.

"You mean other than you allowing your charges run all over the land as they please and allowing the enemy to take them within their camp?" Jonas did not spare them of his criticisms, and they could not refute them.

"We do have a plan," Cecil offered. "Hope is not lost for them yet."

"I am interested in hearing about it." Jonas was having a difficult time seeing the plan that Cecil spoke of. It all seemed as if the enemy was winning. "I hear that you were some kind of genius in the field of strategy, but I have not seen that yet. You had to drag two uninvolved people into this, one of whom is still in the enemy's service. The only ally we have in this Raven Clan is still immature. Even he is walking down the enemy's road."

Amos raised his hand to stop Jonas, defending the decision to bring Lee to the Outland. "We could not have brought a seasoned Christian into the Outland. It was hard enough to keep Lee Christian there. The enemy chose two warriors from the group to side with them as the False Prophet and Beast of the last days, so we needed two Guardians to defend and protect them from that end."

"But they are still weak, and they are walking down a road that will lead them to destruction," Jonas countered. "How do you expect them to fight the enemy the way they are now?"

Cecil used this question to explain part of his plan. "Right now, they are trapped in this dreamlike world unable to comprehend the illogical and irrational things going on here. Once they wake up, they will realize how strange this world really is."

"You're not going to erase their memories of this place?" Jonas asked. He leaned forward, shocked at the suggestion. "Standard protocol dictates that we erase their memories of the Outland, not to mention their time here!"

"But that's what the enemy wants." Cecil extended his hands, trying to explain. "Erasing their memories will defeat the purpose of bringing the two Guardians here."

Jonas shook his head, unconvinced that Amos and Cecil should have involved the Guardians. "They will have a hard time coping with reality if you leave their memories intact. It will leave them vulnerable to enemy attacks."

"They're already open to the enemy!" Amos shouted, pounding his fist against the table. "That's how they got here in the first place. That is why the enemy uses the Outland as a recruitment center."

Cecil stepped forward, calming his voice as he said, "We need this opportunity. Through this experience, they will be bound together. They will seek each other out and reunite. This world *is* doing damage to them, making them violent and destructive, but we will have the greater advantage once we are back in the Inland, once we are back to their home. There we will have many more mature Christians to call on. But we'll need the Warriors to find our Guardians in order to have that take place."

"I don't like it," Jonas said, backing away from the table.

Harper finally joined in on the conversation, asking Jonas, "More importantly, why were you brought here? Surely Michael has more important things for someone such as yourself."

"I've been tracking down a demon by the name of Baccale. It seems that Satan has employed him in this fight. He proclaims himself to be a god of chaos to those he ensnares. Over the years, he has been giving strange abilities to men. We believe that once the Warriors return home, he will somehow grant them the powers that they possessed when they were in the Outland."

"Is there any reason they called him in?" Amos asked. "Surely there are other demons that can grant the same kind of power. Why Baccale?"

"I have no idea," Jonas admitted.

THAT NIGHT

William and Lee went to the seventh floor of the building, traveling down eerie halls where the fluorescent lights flickered as if they had come straight out of a scary movie. Six doors down on the right hand side was the door that led them into a large lab. Standing at a microscope, which sat in front of a window, was a man in a long white jacket. "Hey, Doc," Lee called out.

"Good evening, Lee. How was your day?" the doctor asked.

"Pretty good. My pal woke up today," Lee said excitedly.

The doctor spun around, lowering his glasses from the top of his head. "Oh my. I had no idea we would be having guests." The doctor rushed over quickly to shake William's hand. He looked like the type that didn't have a life outside his work. The goofy expression on his face as he shook William's hand confirmed that the doctor was a nerd. His hair was matted, and his fingernails were wildly untrimmed. The man had grease stains on his clothes, but despite his appearance, he smelled pretty nice. William shook the man's hand and smiled, greeting him as politely as he could. "Are you going to show him Joe?" the doctor asked Lee.

"Of course," Lee said, directing William toward a large white sheet. Lee pulled it back to reveal a startling sight, one that William never thought he would see again. It was a zombielike creature. Joe drooled, letting his saliva drip to the ground as he leaned against the chain that held him to the wall. The sight of William and Lee didn't seem to faze him as he stood there. "That's odd?" Lee said, opening a notebook. "Normally he gets excited when he sees new people."

"It looks like you guys broke his spirit," William said, taking a step back. "You're telling me these things are roaming the city?" William started to feel claustrophobic.

"They could be roaming all over the country," the doctor said. "I don't know."

William shook the edge off. "When are you going to kill that thing?"

"I remember you saying that they had their usefulness, back when we were planning our attack on the Black King." Lee focused back to his book.

"That was when we had someone to control them," William demanded. "I almost lost..." William paused. "My team?" The thought was a little foggy but still painful. It seemed as if it had happened so long ago.

"If we can cure them, we can save the city," Lee said. There was a hopeful undertone in his voice as he smiled. William remembered how warm that smile was, always piercing through the darkness that surrounded them. That was the hope that got them through the Outland.

"Yes, well I think that it might be easier said than done," the doctor said. "From my calculations, the people might only have six to seven days at the most before it becomes irreversible."

"How so?" Lee asked.

"One, the first day of infection, no symptoms are seen. On the second day, they show a slight decrease in temperature and perfuse cold sweats. On the third day, they show signs of an increase in temperature. The fourth day out, they experience numbness in their limbs along with debilitating muscle cramps. On day five, their face begins to sag, and they lose their sense of taste. The sixth day is when they turn violent, like a toddler with a hangover."

"Brain damage," Lee said softly.

"Right," the doctor concurred. "It's a toxin that eats away at the brain, turning them violent and irrational."

"Do they eat people?" William asked, staring at Joe.

"No, if they do bite, they don't do it to chew. It's only on a maiming basis. In fact, that's the reason they die. They don't eat. Despite their appearance, they are actually alive. Their heart is beating, but it's like something ate away at their consciousness."

William was still holding his chest. "Can you get infected by a bite?"

The doctor chuckled, patting William on the shoulder. "No, whatever is causing them to be this way, it is not contagious, which makes it even more puzzling."

The next morning, William was awakened by the sweet aroma of fresh coffee. William opened his eyes to the sight of a cup placed on the table in front of him. He had spent the night with his feet up on the counter, pushing himself back in his seat. The doctor was sitting across the table from him, reading his notes on the molecular structure of the blood samples he took. William groaned as he pulled his feet back, trying to sit up.

The doctor laughed. "I've spent many nights like that before. You slept very well for having that thing in here with you."

"I knew Lee was here," William said, reaching for his cup. "So do you have a name or should I just call you Doc?"

"Doc will do, but my name is George."

"Good to meet you, George. So how long were we out for before yesterday?" William asked, assuming that he had the answer.

"No one knows. A nurse remembers seeing *you* a week ago, but she didn't remember seeing you before that." Doc made sure to point out that it was William who was seen, not necessarily the others. "Hey, you're probably hungry. Let's go meet Lee downstairs for breakfast."

"Okay," William said.

Together, William and Doc went down to the third floor where the dining hall was located. The tables were set up in rows like the Weremore dining hall. Both William and Doc gathered their morning's ration of food, eating in silence, until Lee approached them with his plate. Lee sat down, patting William on the shoulder. "How'd you sleep last night?"

"Like the dead. Cold and stiff," William tried to joke, but there was more truth in the statement than he would have liked to admit.

"Well, I was thinking that we should have Warren help us with the cure," Lee suggested.

"What does he know about modern medicine?" William asked.

"Nothing really," Lee said. "But most Warrians are botanists. He knows all about plants and how they can affect people. He might be able to come up with something."

"Hey, have you seen Warren today?" William asked.

"No, but he usually skipped breakfast back in the Outland," Lee said.

"Yeah, but he can't be doing that now that he's..." William paused for a moment, moving his eyes toward Doc. He wasn't sure how much he knew about Warren being a Warrian, but he did not want to blow his cover. "Since he has *that* condition."

"What condition?" Doc asked.

"It's nothing, really," Lee said. "Do you think he wore himself out? He's as stubborn as you are."

"Yeah, okay," William said, nodding in admittance. "Let's check out his bunk after we're done with breakfast."

"Hello there," A woman said, setting her tray down beside William.

"Hi," William replied, shaking her hand.

"This is the nurse I was telling you about," Doc added. "The one who found you."

"Oh." William shook her hand again. "Thanks."

"That was a terrible night," she said, picking up her fork.

"If it isn't any trouble, I'd like to hear about it." William was being genuine, but it was a little overbearing for poor Maria.

Maria swallowed hard, making room for the bile to come up. She thought about it for a moment before she started. "The first night of the invasion was the scariest. Troops from an unknown militant group had started their invasion. For the most part, no government had put up much of a fight. They all allowed the group to run through the streets, seizing power over the people. Many fought back, dying in the name of their ideals. Others hid themselves away. Those who embraced the coming of the titans were sent to lavished cities to be served by slaves that were captured. Only a few of these cities exist throughout the world.

"It was only six months after the raid when the first wave came—the mindless masses marching through the streets, ruling both night and day. We had originally set up this hospital to care for the people wounded during the invasion, continuing to run it for the sick and impaired. It took them four weeks, after the initial attack, to break through the barriers. We lost several people that day, unable to move all the patients. You were lucky enough to be in that group. Some people don't like to call them zombies, but I cannot think of a better term for them. They may not actually be dead, but they seem like it to me."

It was starting to become a long shift. Three of those things were able to make it into the hospital, and three men from the construction crew went missing. The security team was conducting an inspection of the barriers, ensuring there were no more holes in their defenses. The sun had been down for a few hours, but the lights in the hospital were still on. Thankfully, the Temps who took over the area did not cut the power.

"Nurse!" a doctor yelled. "Who are these patients?" The doctor leafed through his paperwork. "I don't have anything on them." He was not even out of medical school yet, but times were tough. Being low on the totem pole, he was stuck in the triage unit.

The nurse shook her head, leafing through her paperwork too. "Neither do I. That will make of a total of four people that have no paperwork."

"When did they get in?" The doctor glanced around the room, overwhelmed with the amount of people flowing into the ward.

"Last I checked, these beds were empty."

"Well, let's write up something on them. I'll be back in ten minutes to perform the physical examination."

The doctor excused himself, completing his rounds for the day, leaving the information gathering for the nurse. There was not much information to gather on them. Between the three bodies that lay in front of her, two of them had scars. The other looked as if the body was well sheltered. The young teen didn't have as much as a scratch on him.

She gave them an once-over, making note of their scars, hair color, height. and all the rest of the identifying markers. It was a quick examination. She finished with the three of them by time the doctor returned.

"Well, how are the patients doing?"

"I have their identifiers written down, and they seem physically sound on the surface." She looked over her notes as she spoke.

"Any idea of where they came from?"

"A dozen or more people came in the other day. With that plague wreaking havoc out there, who knows where they're from."

"Well, you should ask that group if they remember seeing any of them."The doctor went back to examining the boys. The nurse turned, frustrated with the doctor. She had her own rounds to do.

A crash came from the back of the triage center. Everyone turned to see what the commotion was. One of the construction workers broke through the flimsy drywall that blocked off the triage center from the construction wing. One of the mindless zombies was clawing at him. Screams filled the air as more of them took advantage of the opening in the wall.

The nurse grabbed one of the gurneys in front of her, pulling it back to the triage center. Everyone was running for the same exit. "Grab a gurney!" she shouted. "We need to save as many of them as we can!"

"No!" people screamed, pushing her out of the road.

The nurse pushed the gurney through the door, letting someone else catch the survivor as she ran back into the room to grab more people. She was not alone in her efforts though she thought that she was. More people came back for the survivors, beating off the invasion of attackers.

"Watch out!" the doctor shouted, smacking one of the zombies with a heart monitor. "We've got to go!"

"I won't leave them!" The nurse shouted as she pulled on one of the gurneys.

"We don't have a choice!" the doctor shouted back, helping her push the last gurney though.

"Help me!" a woman screamed. Everyone turned to see. She was an amputee. Her legs had been taken from her by the very things that were there to claim her life. "Don't leave me! I don't want to die!"

The nurse's heart was crushed. The zombies were already at the foot of her bed. The inevitable was already nigh. Three mysterious figures appeared in the doorway, covering up the fate of the woman. All three were dressed in nice suits, untouched by the war erupting outside. Each of them carried one of the newly admitted boys.

"Where do you want them?" the older one asked. His beard was neatly trimmed, sporting the air of a warrior about him. The nurse pointed to the location of a pew, laying down blankets for him.

"Close that door," one of the other men ordered. "You don't want them getting in here." The man seemed arrogant and bold.

A nurse laid the three boys in the pews of the old sanctuary of the church. She draped blankets over them, placing pillows under their heads as the others boarded up the doors. All was silent, nothing stirred.

The doctor came over and sat next to the nurse who had admitted the three boys, holding her as she shook.

"We're all going to die," she cried.

"We've already died," the doctor countered. "We're in hell now." The words made her sob harder.

Once they had finished with their meal, Lee and William went to the resting area. Since there weren't enough beds for all of the people that were being housed in the church, they made one common sleeping area. No one was actually assigned a bed. The rules were first come first serve. William and Lee searched all the beds looking for Warren, but they had no luck. Worried about where he might be, the two went back to the room where they had left him.

William came up to the door fast, plunging into it. What they saw was surprising. Warren made twelve more circles on the wall.

"What?" William's words fell short as he entered the room. Warren was standing in the center of the room with perfect posture holding three shurikens in his hand. With one throw, all three hit the circle he was aiming for. "You mastered shurikens in twelve hours?"

"Forget the shurikens, look at him," Lee exclaimed. "He seems to be walking fine."

"And there's more," Warren added, picking up two more. With his elbows pointing down, he raised the shurikens to eye level. William noticed that Warren had the same kind of silver bracelet on that he did.

"Where did you get that?" William asked.

"You didn't notice?" Lee said, raising his hand too. "We all have them." Lee stretched his hand out toward William. Lee's bracelet was the same type of leather bracelet.

"Wow," William said. "What are they for?"

"I think they are linked to the Outland," Warren said.

"What makes you say that?" William asked, turning sharply back toward Warren. In Warren's hand were the two shurikens, but this time they were on fire. William jumped back. "I still have control of my phoenix power," Warren said.

"And I can still transwarp," Lee added. "I think Warren has a point. I think the bracelets connect us to the Outland allowing us to use the powers we acquired there."

"Too bad I don't have any powers," William said, composing himself.

"You never know," Warren said. "After all, you weren't given a bracelet for no reason." William sighed.

"Let's assume that we need them for something," Lee said, pressing on through William's negativity. "I assume we're not planning on staying, right?"

"I can't stay cooped up in here," William replied.

"I need to get home and back to my body," Warren said.

"Right, so the only question is when." Lee crossed his arms waiting for a reply. "I already know how we can get out. They have the front door, along with all other doors up to the third floor, barricaded. However, the fourth floor has the least amount of activity on it."

"Right, and I've heard that at eleven, until three in the morning, the zombies all gather back in the city in one particular area," Warren added. "There are rumors that between those times they don't even attack," Warren finished, giving them a window of opportunity.

"We shouldn't go tonight," William demanded. "We should get plenty of rest first. We need to stay up tonight and sleep in the morning. Tomorrow we can leave."

"Are you sure we should so soon?" Lee asked. "Maybe we should wait a bit longer."

"No," William said. "We have all we can get from these people. If we stay any longer, we're just going to get attached. Since Warren is doing so well, we need to go get in some target practice."

With their plan set, the group sprang into action, readying themselves for the next evening. After lunch, William took Warren and Lee to the swimming pool, on the lower level, to teach them everything he could about the guns that they picked out. William taught them how to fire, clean, and maintain the firearms. The day ticked by as the two learned from William's extensive knowledge about weapons.

William's father always taught him about the important balance that people should maintain with weapons. To have proper balance with a weapon, you must have respect for it as well as a respect for the person on the other end. Yet as long as the people on the other end were dead, evil, or not human, William didn't really care about having respect for them. William had a skewed view of the world, feeling that good things with good hearts deserved to live, but he was not clear on his own definition of what good was.

After the sun went down, the group went up to Doc's laboratory to help him with his research. Warren and Lee went back to looking through documents, and William sat down far out of Joe's reach, tossing little kid's toys at him, watching Joe react as he tried to smash some of them and tried to play with others. It wasn't until four in the morning that Doc came to the lab. As he entered the room, he saw William asleep on the floor with Warren and Lee still hard at work.

"Hey, Doc," Lee said. "Where have you been?"

"I was wrong," Doc said. "It's not a virus or bacteria. We've been looking at it all wrong." Doc tossed a large stack of papers onto the counter where Lee was sitting. "It's not a disease."

"It's not?" Lee said, straightening up to look through the paperwork. "Then what is it?" Warren didn't bother looking up although he was paying attention to the situation. "It's a narcotic?"

"That's right, and this little bugger has been cleverly engineered. It's a bit too advanced to be from around here," Doc said. "It carries a chemical that acts with the same qualities as LSD and Novocain. It also carries trace amounts of several other drugs. I believe the so-called zombies go back to the source of the drug that feeds them. For some reason, their refueling time runs around eleven o'clock. That probably means that they lie around in a comatose state for several hours until the high of the drug wears down, that will be when they can move again."

"So we wipe out the source in order to stop this abomination from continuing," Lee said with conviction.

"If we can find it," Warren replied.

INTO THE WILD

At the appointed time of departure, the group assembled on the fourth floor of the hospital with Doc, gathering by the exit door, preparing to venture out. "Here you go," Doc said, handing Lee a brown leather bag like the one Warren had. "It's some food I was able to smuggle out of the cafeteria."

"Thanks," Lee said. "Stay safe."

"You don't need to tell me," Doc replied. "There's usually some of those drugged-up zombies caught in this corridor, so be careful. They're pretty fast too, so watch it."

William removed the boards placed to barricade the door. "What are you talking about?" William asked.

"Oh, yes," Doc started. "When the drug is running through their system, they move quite slowly due to their nerves going numb and all. Once the drug leaves their system though, they seem to get much faster, but they lose most of their dexterity."

William pointed to the door while raising his gun. Warren removed one of the pistols from his holster while reaching for the handle. The old knob creaked in his hand, showing the age and abuse it had taken. Warren pulled the door open. It released an awful screech as the hedges turned. William could see down the forty foot hallway to the end where it hit another wall, teeing off from there. Warren turned his back and headed for the two backpacks and his leather satchel, which were sitting behind William. William lowered his weapon and turned toward Doc. "Nothing. You had me worried. I thought we might have had—"

William stopped, hearing the sound of footsteps approaching quickly from down the hall. William spun back in the direction of the hall where one of the zombies barreled toward him. William barely had time to raise his gun to chin level when the brute tackled him to the ground. The man tried to wrestle past the gun William was using for a barrier. Before Warren had a chance to react, Lee tore the hem from around his sleeve and wrapped it around the man's mouth, using it as a gag. Lee placed his foot between the man's shoulder blades and pushed while pulling back on the gag. Warren dropped the bags and rushed to Lee's aid, but his feet were caught in the straps of the bag. He fell to the ground. The man stopped attacking and became calm as Lee pulled back. Slowly, the man rose from the ground with Lee pushing hard against his back. The man spun around, knocking Lee to the floor. He lunged for Lee with his mouth wide open. Lee managed to get the gag across his mouth. Lee held his hands up high using the man's weight against himself. Lee kept his hands up as the man continued to pound on him without mercy. William tried pulling the man up, but he wiggled too much to get a solid hold. Doc pushed William out of his way, handing him a small vial. Doc plunged a syringe into the man's neck. He squirmed for a moment before going limp like a dead fish. Lee rolled him off and hopped to his feet.

"I hope we don't have to fight too many of them," Lee said, chuckling.

"Next time shoot him," William said.

"He's still a human being, and he's alive," Lee demanded. "It might have been a little different if he was just a zombie. Besides, why didn't you shoot?"

"Are you kidding? I've got a shotgun."

"Well, if you knew how to shoot—," Lee started.

"You guys! We should get going before the rest of the welcoming committee comes," Warren said, handing William one of the packs.

"You're still going?" Doc asked. "After what just happened?"

"If we stopped every time we were attacked, we would have never gotten this far," Warren said. "Besides, I'm not planning on dying here."

"Sorry, Doc. It was nice meeting you," Lee said, taking off behind Warren.

"Can you handle him?" William asked, pointing at the unconscious zombie.

"Not a problem," Doc said.

"Don't forget to lock this door behind us," William said, closing it as he stepped through.

The three made their way down the hall, the tile creaking beneath their feet. The shadows on the walls trickled, confusing their senses. Darkness shrouded them from the world. The only light that could be seen was coming from the streetlights and the moon. The hospital had been a war zone, a life-versus-death struggle. It had been the site of a serious conflict that would scar history itself.

Once the door was closed, William found it to be a good opportunity to discuss Lee's actions from their previous encounter. "What was that all about?"

"What?" Lee asked.

"Are you going soft on me?" William demanded, slinging the backpack that Warren passed off over his shoulders.

"Are you talking about that freak show back there?" Lee asked.

"I don't think this is the time or place," Warren said as his words fell on deaf ears.

"Yes, you need to be willing to make sacrifices," William demanded.

"They're still living human beings," Lee insisted. "I won't just *kill* anyone! Not as long as there is another way."

"They're gone, buddy. The lights are on, but nobody's home."

"You're a heartless fiend," Lee insisted, pointing at him. "There might be a cure out there. How can you just say that they have to die like that?"

"Their brain is fried from whatever drug they're on. Even the doc said that after so many days they can't be brought back because of the damage," William shot back.

"So you would shoot a mentally challenged person just because they're not all there either?"

"I would if they had the will, and the means, to kill me," William said, scoffing. "No, scratch that. All they would need is the will to want to maul me and then I would make their passing as quick as possible."

"You're sick." Lee was furious with William's view on the subject. As William and Lee continued to argue over the lives of the so-called zombies, Warren continued down the hall with one of his pistols in his hand. He was still a Warrian, concerned for the mission at hand. He had no intention on debating moral quarrels over the well-being of the enemy. He needed to stay focused. The job was still to get the two of them home, safe and sound. He would have to deal with getting himself home later.

Warren came to where the hall branched off into two directions, and he leaned against one side of the wall, listening down the hall for labored breathing, footsteps, or any sign of a living presence. The more he concentrated, the more he felt like a Warrian again. He was able to tune out the argument between William and Lee, focusing on the sounds echoing on that floor. He heard two sets of dragging footsteps around the left and back about fifty feet back. With each step, he could get a sense of the building's layout. Down the hall to the right, he heard a raspy breath coming from the floor. One of the zombies wasn't too far. Warren could tell from the weight of the breath that it was a man, fifteen feet away, and he was lying facedown on the floor.

Looking back at William and Lee, Warren found himself disgusted with their arguing. He was surprised that none of the zombies came running at the sound of their voices. Taking a breath and listening once more to make sure that there weren't any that he missed, Warren stepped out into the hall and shot the dying zombie, finishing the long struggle that it had. *That should settle the argument*, he thought to himself. *William was right. This is still a war, and all of our survival is on the line.* His mission was to get the boys home despite the odds. However, William's lack of remorse for the dead and dying was still disturbing to him. This was a war, but innocent people were infected and dying from this evil drug.

Warren held his breath as he heard something stand on its feet behind him. The creature's breathing was so low and steady that Warren overlooked it. Warren spun around with his gun raised. The man was running at him with full force. Warren pulled the trigger, hitting the man, but he continued forward. Warren pulled out his knife, and as the man came in close, Warren ducked, sliding his blade between the ribs. Warren waited for the man to pass before spinning and stabbing the blade into his lung. As Warren pulled the blade out, the man fell over. All life had left him. Warren looked down at his blade. It was glowing as if it had just been taken out of a furnace. His phoenix fire heated his knife during the excitement.

"What in the world are you doing?" William demanded. "Are you trying to get yourself killed?"

"It had to be done, and you two weren't doing anything about it," Warren said in a hurtful tone. "This is war, and death is necessary." William gave a small victory smile toward Lee. "But we can't forget that these people are sons, fathers, and mothers. They're just regular people. Not devils."

"I just don't want us to kill them unless it's absolutely necessary," Lee said.

Warren nodded, giving his approval. He turned and continued down the hall, leading to the right. As the other two followed, William decided to continue the argument.

"So what is this holier-than-thou attitude? What about the humans you killed back in the Outland along with the other creatures?" William jabbed. "Don't they count?"

"It's not a holier-than-thou attitude." Lee was obviously hurt by the comment. "We didn't have much of a choice back in the Outland because that was war. I'm just saying that we don't have to kill every infected person we see. The field of battle is something different than just killing innocent victims here."

"Innocent?" William spat. "None of them are. It's dog-eat-dog out here."

Lee was getting tired of this argument as was Warren.

"If you're such a pacifist, why don't you throw that cannon away?" William asked, pointing at his pistol.

"You might want to stop," Warren said. He was standing five feet behind them, directly in front of a large window. The moonlight poured in on him, casting his shadow over them. They both turned to look at him as he motioned them to look forward. A zombie moaned as he lurched forward. William raised his shotgun for the man as he staggered pathetically for them.

Lee grabbed the gun. "William! We don't have to kill him!"

William jerked the gun away. "I thought we went through this already!"

"You better hurry and decide," Warren said almost sarcastically. "He's getting pretty close."

"Fine!" William said, taking a few steps forward. William raised the butt of the gun and knocked the man across the nose, toppling him over. Several footsteps echoed from a stairwell down the hall. "Oh now what?" William whined.

Warren took a step back from the window, firing three consecutive shots into the glass. "Come on!" Warren said, jumping out.

"Warren!" Lee and William yelled together as they ran for the window. They looked out the window in terror. They were on the fourth floor, and Warren didn't have wings anymore.

As they looked down, they saw that Warren made it safely down to the next floor. The hospital extended farther out in a stair-step fashion. With the sound of footsteps getting closer, William and Lee climbed up onto the windowsill and jumped out too. The fall was only ten feet, so the landing didn't affect them.

"Let's go," Warren said, taking off for the next landing.

The three of them made it safely off the hospital's roof and onto the ground. Once they made it to the ground, there were not any other people. The entire town seemed to be empty. Only a few cars were on the side of the road and only a few streetlights were lit. It was a ghost town.

Warren brushed passed both William and Lee. "I hope you're finished."

"So where are we?" William asked.

"Somewhere in the Texas Panhandle," Lee answered. "We'll have to pick up a map on the way."

They walked for about four city blocks before William saw a sign of hope. "Look!" William shouted. "It's a Super Sammy." William trotted toward the large sign that had a depiction of an old man in a cowboy hat on it.

"What's a Super Sammy?" Warren asked.

"It's a large department store," Lee said. "We might be able to stock up on supplies while we're here."

Lee and Warren caught up to William on the other side of the parking lot. There was one car parked in the massive parking lot; its windshield was smashed in. As the three of them made it to the doors, they found the keys to the building still in the lock. Lee looked in the windows.

William pulled on the doors. "Someone was able to lock up. I doubt any of them got in, so let's go shopping."

"You mean looting," Lee corrected.

"Come on, man," William said. "It's cold out here. If we're going to survive, we have to get provisions."

Lee crossed his arms. "I didn't say I wasn't coming, just call it what it is."

With a smile, William unlocked the doors and stepped into the building. He made his way in as far as the light took him. Even with the skylights above, William could hardly see around the store. "I can't see a thing," William said, turning to his friends. When William made eye contact with Lee, he gasped. Both Lee and Warren's eyes seemed to shimmer in the dark as if they had cat's eyes.

"What's wrong?" Lee asked.

"Your eyes," William said, taking a step back.

"Even now, he's still part Kalymor," Warren said, taking a look. "They have the ability to see in the dark."

"And you?" William asked.

"I must still be Warrian after all," Warren said with a smirk on his face. "I see just fine."

"I'll go find a flashlight for William," Lee said. "Warren, take him over to the clothing department so you guys can change."

"Okay," Warren said, taking William by the arm.

Warren pulled William over to the clothing department, placing him in one spot while he fetched some new clothes. Warren took careful notice to the specific size that William asked for. Before Warren brought William his clothes, Warren changed into the same outfit. Warren picked out a black pair of cargo pants and a navy-blue T-shirt to better mask them in the cover of night. Once William got changed, they went to find a pair of good hiking boots. In the shoe section, a nightlight gave William enough light to help Warren with the selection. Once they were done, William grabbed a fresh pair of socks and a pair of good boots for Lee.

Warren and William met Lee back in front of the clothing department. Lee had already grabbed himself a clean pair of jeans and a black T-shirt. After Lee was done putting on his boots, the three of them went to find proper jackets for the weather. Lee grabbed a thin black leather jacket. William picked up a brown leather coat that had a white wool collar. Warren found a black button-up long-sleeve shirt to wear under his charcoal gray trench coat. When Warren appeared, Lee and William wanted to laugh.

"What are you doing?" William asked. "What's with the coat?"

"All black?" Lee added. "Who are you trying to be?"

"You laugh now," Warren said. "But I'll be the one saving you latter. I'm going to find some medicine." Warren brushed past, pushing them out of the way. "And you're reflecting too much light."

Lee shook his head. "I guess we should be thinking covertly."

William rolled his eyes. "He's going to attract trouble dressed like that."

"I'm going to look for some extra food," Lee said, picking up his small satchel.

"Yeah, and I'll go look at picking up some extra ammo." William dropped his backpack next to Warren's. Lee watched William walk away, holding his pouch close.

Warren sifted through the medicine bottles in the pharmacy, making sure to reference the book that he got from Doc's lab. Only one in every ten medicines he found was useful. He tossed the good ones into his satchel, rummaging through the rest. After he was done with one full shelf, he leaned against the wall flipping through the pages of his little reference book. *What am I doing?* he thought to himself. That was when he heard a bottle drop to the floor to his left. Warren turned his head sharply toward the sound. There stood a man, staring at him. The man's face was creepy with a twisted grin stretched across his face. Even with it being blacker than night, the man still looked directly at Warren's face. Warren knew there was trouble.

This man was not one of the zombies that they had faced before but something different. The man raised a cleaver to the side of his face and chuckled lightly. Warren's eyes darted from the left and to the right, looking for the best way out.

"What's wrong?" he whispered. "Don't you want to play?"

"No!" Warren yelled, jumping over the counter.

The man rushed out of the medical center, chasing after Warren, swinging the knife wildly. Warren rolled and dodged the man, trying to evade the blade.

Lee was crouched down in the middle of the food aisle. He had just finished looking through the canned products on the shelf. He couldn't make up his mind; what would be best for a long trip? There wasn't much sitting there that looked good to take on the road with them. Lee shook his head, thinking it over, when he heard feet scuffing across the floor. Lee sat still only turning his head. A group of zombies had made their way into the building and now were shuffling their way to the back of the store. Lee slowly got to his feet. Lee picked up a can of corn and chucked it down one of the aisles. Sure enough, Lee was right, the zombies scuffled toward the sound in the hopes of clobbering whatever it was. Two of the mindless creatures walked right passed Lee, thanks to the cover of the dark.

William was behind the gun counter, pulling out shotgun shells and ammo for both Warren and Lee. "Nothing says I'm sorry like a bullet," William whispered to himself with a silent chuckle. He began to sift through the other guns and ammunition in hopes of finding something special. William heard something echo far off. He turned off his flashlight and slowly poked his head up over the counter to look around. Without his light, William couldn't see ten feet in front of himself.

"William," Lee whispered. He was kneeling down at the open end of the gun counter. William jumped.

"What?" William started.

"Shush," Lee said in a soft whisper. "We've got to go." Lee took William by the hand and led him to a fire exit nearby. Lee pulled out his gun and waited for a moment. Gunshots rang out in the store. Warren was in trouble. Lee raised his gun to point at the center of the ceiling. Lee squeezed off two rounds with three seconds between them so Warren could find his way to them. Almost instantly, Warren popped out of an aisle and ran for them. Lee opened the fire door and made his way outside with William in tow. A few seconds later, Warren joined them, closing the doors behind him. Warren rested against the doors keeping them closed, but to his surprise, a zombie was waiting for him outside. The man lunged at Warren. Before he could react, Lee wrapped a cloth around the zombie's mouth and tossed him to the side.

The sound of something heavy slammed against the door as the hoard tried to break loose. "Help!" Warren called out. William saw a chain lying against the wall, running for it while Lee helped hold the door.

"What is that?" Lee asked. "Those zombies don't have that kind of strength."

"Whatever it is, I shot it at least three times," Warren said as William tied the door closed with the chain.

"No," Warren said, exhausted.

William turned around to see an angry mob of zombies enclosing on their position. "We're surrounded," William said. William pulled his shotgun off of his shoulder and pumped it. One of the unspent shells flew out of the chamber. "What do we do?"

Lee drew his gun. "We fight."

As the words left Lee's mouth, a bell sounded. The bell tolled twice, filling the streets with its sweet yet strong ring. The time was now two o'clock, and moaning echoed throughout the city. The faces of the zombies went from anger to sadness. A deep, emotional depression filled their faces. The zombies looked as if they had just lost someone irreplaceable. A loud sad moan came from them as they started to turn and walk away. The parade turned into one of death and grief.

Lee glanced at William and Warren. "Uh, what just happened?"

"Got me, but it was probably a good thing," William said. Quiet resumed through the streets.

"Maybe we should follow them," Warren suggested.

"Are you crazy?" William said.

"They're probably going to get drugged up again," Lee said. "They might be vulnerable, and we could find whoever's behind this."

William rolled his eyes. "If you say so."

Warren stayed behind for a moment, picking up the unspent shell that landed on the ground.

The group slowly followed the mob. More zombies filed into the streets, all channeling in one direction. None of them acted hostile toward the three; they just shuffled to their destination. The final destination was a bar with a bright neon sign sitting above the door. The name *SAL'S* was glowing deep in the night. It was the only sign that had life for miles. It appeared to be a classy bar with a nice and polished look on the outside. The bar was overshadowed by three large warehouses. Several zombified people were lying around the street in a comatose state, gripping onto empty 64 oz. pitchers that once held their ale.

"Well now what?" Lee asked.

"I don't think I want to go in there," William said. Suddenly, one of the oncoming zombies wrapped his arms around William and Lee and staggered toward the bar. He didn't want to harm them, so the two obliged. Warren followed, shaking his head in objection.

Once they entered the bar, the zombies seemed more like helpless drunks than the undead. The man clinging to William and Lee released and stumbled over to the bar to take an empty pitcher from the counter. After retrieving his mug, he stumbled over to a tap that was protruding from the wall. Warren scanned the room, counting at least fifty people. The sounds of incoherent moaning and babbling made the bar feel alive with excitement.

"Like lost puppies," the bartender said, looking over at the man. The bartender looked like he was in his late forties with slicked-back hair. He was a well-groomed man, dressed as if he were a bartender from back in the thirties. William, Lee, and Warren walked over to the bar where no one else had wanted to sit. "What would you guys like?" The man turned, taking particular interest in Warren. His smile sent chills down their spines. He placed his hand on the bar in front of William. Just as soon as he placed it on the counter, he pulled it back as if he had reached into a fire. "You don't look old enough to be drinking." The man made a half attempt at smiling.

"What's wrong?" Lee asked.

The bartender raised his hand to his chest, trying to cover it. "I…I burned it on the grill earlier today. I was foolish."

"Do I know you?" William asked. "Ripley?" *That's it!* William thought. *He's not as pale, but that's Ripley.*

"I'm afraid not, stranger. The name's Sal. I'm the owner of this bar." Sal placed a pitcher of green ale on the counter as one of the zombified men came over. "Who is this Ripley?"

"A friend from a town called Daniel," William said. Daniel was known as the city of the dead back in the Outland. They had been cursed and became an immortal army. Ripley was their leader, who had befriended William after a little adventure they shared in the mineshafts under the city.

"Just outside of Ram?" Sal asked. A surprised look came over both Lee and William. Ram was a desert city that was unique to the Outland. It had to be more than a coincidence. Unfazed by the comment, Warren looked away from him and started to study the room again. "What do you want to know?"

"What happened here? When did it start?" William asked filled with excitement.

"Well," Sal started, "it all started about eleven years ago when Senator Scott Edwards was running for president of the United States of America. One man was backing his entire campaign. His name was Almond Henderson. I believe he was a European man from somewhere near Transylvania. Almond was a powerful politician that took Edwards straight to the presidential office.

"A few years after Edwards had been elected into office, the Trepidation approached Almond in hopes to strike an accord with him, but Almond was consumed with greed and the lust of power, so he declined.

"In the end, Almond's own bodyguards killed him to gain favor with the Trepidation. As a result, he made them his leading Temps. The Trepidation brought peace and prosperity to all the lands, stomping out hunger, disease, and even war.

"Meanwhile, Edwards was crippling this country, preparing it to be invaded by the Trepidation's armies. The people didn't stand a chance. When it came time for Edwards's reelection, Edwards won by a landslide. Only about a few hundred people voted for the other guy. It was in Edward's last year in office when the Trepidation made his move. He took all of the untouched countries with almost no effort, and to this day, only a handful of rebels defy him, and even *their* resistance is crumbling."

"What about the Temps?" William asked.

“It’s a hard job ruling the world,” Sal said. “You need someone you can trust to watch over your property. That’s why he chose the Temps.”

“That just goes to show you how arrogant the man is,” William said. “He still wants to own the whole world so he only refers to his second-rate rulers as temporary.”

Sal gave William an odd look. Sal was confused by William’s statement. “So you don’t know—,” Sal started and then quickly paused. “I overestimated you.”

“What do you mean?” Lee asked.

“He’s a Temp,” Warren said without moving.

“Maybe I didn’t,” Sal recanted. Sal raised his glass to gain the attention of everyone in the bar. “My friends, these people wish to close my bar. If they have their way, I’ll lose my life and you’ll lose your delicious drinks.” Silence fell upon the bar as several of the zombified men dropped their glasses.

William started to go after Sal, but Lee stopped him. “Don’t play into it,” Lee said. He pressed himself against the bar as the men stood out of their seats. Sal made his way through a back door, locking it behind him. “I’m out of ideas,” Lee said, watching the zombies close in on them.

“Me too,” William said, pulling his shotgun around.

“We can’t blow through them all,” Lee said.

“Get back here!” Warren yelled from behind the bar. Warren had slipped behind the bar without William or Lee even noticing. Warren was pulling out all the tap hoses from behind the bar, tossing them onto the counter. “Drinks are on the house!”

Lee and William hopped over the bar as Warren cut the tops of the hoses off. The drugged ale spilt onto the floor. The zombified men tripped over each other, trying their best to drink the poison off the floor.

“Look!” Lee said, pulling open a latch hidden in the floor. “Let’s not stick around here.” Lee was the first to jump down into the basement. It was old and rustic cellar with dim lights illuminating the room. The ale dripped through the floorboards, and Lee could clearly hear the people scrambling to get every drop.

William jumped down second landing behind Lee with Warren hopping down last, closing the door behind him. Warren landed on his feet with no problems.

"Not bad for barely being able to walk yesterday," William commented.

"Look at that." Lee was staring at a large clear tank with the green ale sitting in it. The tank looked like something out of a sci-fi movie with lights shining through the bottom, lighting up the entire tank. The glass tank was big enough to fit all three of them in.

"Look over there," Warren said, pointing to three more tanks in the corner. William cocked his shotgun, and Warren caught the unspent shell in midair. "There's no point in that."

Lee walked over to the compressor that was feeding the tubs to the taps. "Let's get out of here," Lee said as William lowered his gun.

The three of them found the door that led up to the alley in the back behind the bar. As they surfaced, they came out behind a dumpster. Lee peeked around the side, looking for enemies. He could see Sal sitting calmly at the corner of the building, smoking a cigarette. *Cocky brat*, Lee thought. Lee returned around the dumpster to report his findings. "He's sitting over there right now waiting for us to kick the bucket."

"That isn't going to happen today," William said. "Let's throw him a little party," William said, cracking his knuckles.

"Not yet," Warren demanded. "He's too far away, and if he calls for reinforcements, we'll be done for."

"Then what?" William asked.

"Hello, Addiction," a female voice said.

"It took you long enough," Sal replied.

William, Warren, and Lee peeked out to see who was there. All they could see was a tall shadow cast upon the wall.

"Cornel screwed up. They're here." Sal kicked at the dirt on the ground.

"Who, the Warriors?" the voice asked.

"Yes, Morygon, the Warriors and their Guardians. Cornel failed. He was supposed to keep the Guardians locked up over there. I can deal with the Warriors."

"The Guardians are a liability, but not even Cornel could have kept them there forever. Harper and his band of merry men would have eventually busted them out."

"Why did we even recruit Cornel if he couldn't delay them?" Sal tossed the cigarette to the side.

"You cannot blame Cornel for all of it. When Emmit crossed into the Outland, he gave Amos a chance to bring that Christian into our midst," Morygon said.

"We needed him to cross over though," Sal insisted, pointing his finger in her direction. "He was the trigger for the antagonist. Without her, the plan would fall through. She needed power in order to control the Warriors. Without Emmit, she'd still just be human."

"I understand your point, Sal." Morygon's voice sounded understanding, but Sal's actions spoke louder. He jumped to his feet, backing against the wall. "But you've become somewhat of a liability."

"No, I—" A long green arm flew out from behind the wall that was masking the female voice. The hand jabbed into Sal's stomach. Slowly his body began to turn into sand. It only took about ten seconds before he turned completely into a pillar of his own image. Once he had completely turned into sand, Morygon shifted her hand, pulling it back out of view. The statue of sand collapsed into dust. One piece didn't turn to sand though. Sal's earring sat on top of the pile that used to be his body. This was the sin that gave him his power. It allowed him to control those who had been intoxicated and to produce the toxin. However, without it, his life was drained from his body.

"Too bad, Sal," the voice laughed as it left the alley.

"What was that?" William whispered.

"I don't know," Lee said.

"Me neither," Warren added. They stood there for a moment not sure what to do when they heard the sounds of moaning coming from behind them. The ale had been drained, and the zombies were back to being hungover and mean. "Time to go." As the three of them were about to go around the dumpster, a group of zombies came up along the other side surrounding them.

"Back inside!" William ordered.

The night moved on slowly. Rest was something to be desired for most. William nervously paced the floor of the cellar while Lee sat on the dusty wooden steps leading outside. Warren leaned against a support post while they all pondered about what had just happened.

"He turned into dust," William said, talking to himself. "*Poof*...and gone."

"What was she?" Lee chimed in. "Was she an Outlander? With arms like those—"

"She wasn't any species I've ever heard of," Warren replied. "They were talking about Dr. Emmit. Like the doctor from Ram. Maybe she's one of his hybrids. Maybe she's a chimera."

"That's possible," Lee said.

"So Emmit was from here," William said.

"And did she say something about Amos?" Lee added.

"Not that I heard," William replied.

"I wonder how Lily is doing," Warren said, straightening up.

"I forgot about her." William shook his head, so caught up in the problems of this world that he forgot about his other friends.

"How about Toby and Naven?" Warren said with a smile.

"No one could forget those two," Lee said, chuckling. "I wonder where all of them are."

THE WHITE WARRIOR

The sunlight poured through the basement windows onto Warren's face. The gentle glow and warmth of the sun slowly brought him back from his sleep. William was already awake, franticly looking out every window he could, trying to see where the zombies were.

"Maybe they've all died without the drug," William said.

"Not a chance," Lee said half asleep, sitting in a chair. "Remember Joe? He went a week without the drug."

"Then they might be asleep." William was fishing for explanations. "We should make a break for it."

"You haven't slept, and I'm still tired," Lee said. "The only one who would make it is Warren."

"We can't stay down here. We lost all of our supplies back at the Super Sammy Store," William insisted.

"He's right," Warren said, getting up off the floor. "If we have a chance, we should make a break for it."

Lee exhaled deeply as he stood to stretch. "Are you sure they're not out there?" Lee asked William in a whining tone.

"Yes," William reassured him.

Lee picked up his jacket off the floor and dusted it off. "All right, let's go find out." William grabbed his shotgun. The three of them made their way to the exit and unlocked the latch. The light rushed in, blinding them as the door opened. William kept his gun up and ready for a fight while the other two covered their eyes from the sunlight. The alley was clear of enemies, and the streets looked clear too. They stood their ground for a moment making sure that everything was safe before walking away.

"Well, it looks good," William said.

Suddenly, a white flash overwhelmed them, engulfing them all. Inside the bright flash, a large creature landed on the ground with a thud. The light seemed to linger for a moment before passing away. Left lying on the ground was a large furry creature curled in a ball. William pointed his shotgun at it while Lee and Warren stood behind him as if he were a shield. The creature lifted its head to look around. It had thick hair, pure white as the December snow, with deep blue eyes. Its body was like that of a Raptor, but the creature's muscle structure was thicker. The three of them recognized who it was immediately. It was Naven only with white fur instead of red. Naven stood to his feet without saying a word.

"Naven, are you okay?" William asked, lowering his weapon. A loud moan came from the back of the alley. One of the zombies had seen them and was staggering toward them. William raised his shotgun and fired off a round. The bullet missed its target.

"We don't have time for that!" Lee insisted. "We need to go."

Moans continued to grow closer from the main street. The commotion had drawn the attention of the entire group.

William reached for Naven, touching his side. "Naven, we have to get back inside."

Naven turned toward the street, growling at the unnatural fiends entering the alley. Naven grabbed his muzzle as if he was starting to have a headache.

Out in the street hundreds of the zombielike people were staggering toward the alley, wanting to see what caused the commotion. With a bright flash, a white pillar of light shot straight up in the air. After a few seconds, the light dissipated. In a loud crash, bodies and bricks from the buildings flew with an incredible force out into the street. Naven crashed into the open road, towering over the street by two stories.

Naven's body had changed into his larger form with the head of a tyrannosaurus rex but a body that was made to walk on all fours. With a white mane that flowed from his neck, he had more of an appearance like a horse than a dinosaur.

Lee, Warren, and William were sitting on Naven's back with their hands wrapped around and through his hair. Lee had timed the jump into the light perfectly so that they could land on his back. Warren and William naturally followed after him.

Naven roared, shaking the buildings around him. Then he took off down the street, heading out of town, tearing through the power lines that got in his way. The lines snapped like threads as his massive body moved through them. Blindly he ran through the streets, crushing cars underfoot and running into the sides of buildings.

"What's wrong with him?" William shouted over the wind. He moved in close to Lee, pressing against his back so he could hear the response.

"He seems like he's in pain!" Lee shouted back. Turning his attention back to Naven, he shouted, "Are you okay? What's wrong?"

Naven grunted, shaking his head as he picked up speed. His movements were not very coordinated, and his whimpering was a giveaway that he was in pain.

"He's not talking," Lee replied.

"Where is he taking us?" Warren asked.

"Does he even know?" William could tell that Naven could not tell where he was going due to whatever was bothering him.

"Should we get off?" Warren looked over the edge, judging the distance to the ground. He did not want to make the jump, but he wasn't sure where Naven was taking them either.

"If we do that, then we may never catch him," Lee said. "We should just stick together."

It was not until dusk after Naven had exhausted himself when he began to slow down to a walk. His breath was labored, and all three of his passengers were tired and sore. They had held on for their lives, doing their best not to fall off his back.

Naven's direction turned to the left, taking out more power lines as he made his way off the road. Naven growled as the lines zapped along his side, stumbling into the flat, barren lands.

"Are you okay now?" Warren asked, rubbing Naven's back.

"It hurts," Naven said. His voice sounded odd. It was as if there were two voices entangled in one. "They won't get out."

"Who are you talking about?" Lee asked.

"It's hard to think."

"Toben?" Warren asked, confused for a moment. "What happened?"

"We're stuck, merged together." Toben lowered his head, shaking it. Toby and Naven had merged together, like they did back in the Outland, but now they did not seem to be able to separate. "It's so hard to think. My head hurts."

"What do we need to do?" William asked.

"How would I know?" Toben asked in frustration. "I'm not a rocket scientist." Toben sighed and started to mumble numbers under his breath. He was trying to get both minds to concentrate on one thing, focusing their attention.

"Okay, we can work with that," Lee said. "Where are we heading?"

"Downhill," Toben said exhausted. "I need to rest." Toben collapsed as he came to a stop, tossing the group off his back. He decided to lay down where he had landed in hope of getting some rest.

William, Lee, and Warren picked themselves up off the ground, looking around at the landscape as they wiped the dust off of their clothes. The land was barren, the road was the only sign that intelligent life had been through there. Naven groaned as he rubbed his head into the dirt, trying to rub away the pain.

"He's in no shape to move," Warren said, looking at him with compassion. "Whatever happened, it's tearing him apart in there."

Lee nodded, patting William on the shoulder. "It doesn't look like there are any enemies nearby, so we're going to survey the area up ahead. Warren, why don't you stay here and watch over Toben."

Warren nodded, still tired and stiff. Though he was becoming accustomed to walking and running in his new form, his body still felt as if it were new and not yet been broken in. Taking a seat next to Toben's head, Warren leaned against him, staring up at the stars in the sky.

Lee and William walked a few hundred feet away from their friends before they started to strategize about their next move. Toben had taken them off course a bit, but now that they had recovered a new member of the group; Lee assumed that the plan would change.

"Now where to?" Lee asked, surveying the empty wasteland.

"Well, we're heading west, and if we continue going in this direction, we'll head into New Mexico." William was holding a map that he had picked up from Super Sammy's. "I don't know exactly where we are, but if my suspicions are correct, then we might be somewhere near the Colorado border."

"I don't know if that's a good thing or not," Lee said. "Home is in the other direction."

"Do you think there is anyone left?" William asked.

"It doesn't seem right, does it?" Lee turned to William, squinting his eyes as he thought. "I can't quite place my finger on it, but something is off, like we're still in the Outland."

"I feel it too, but it's probably just because so many Outlanders have passed over to our side already."

Lee exhaled. "You're probably right. I just get this feeling like we're not home yet."

"We've fought through worse," William reassured him, closing the map. "It's time to make these people accountable for their actions. We should start by eliminating the closest threat."

William stared off into the distance as though his mind had wondered for a moment. Lee watched him carefully, slowly moving so he did not call attention to himself. After waiting for a moment, he snapped his fingers, calling William back to reality. William's head jumped alert.

"Are you okay?" Lee asked. "You seem distracted."

"I'm fine," William said, flashing a smile to reassure him.

"I don't think we should be looking for a fight at least for right now." Lee was having second thoughts about fighting against the Temps. Toben was stuck in a painful merged state, Warren was trapped in a human form that he was not used to, and William was starting to daze off. Lee was the only one that seemed right in his mind and body.

"What are you talking about?" William asked, shrugging his shoulders. He placed his hands on his hips and glared at him with contempt. "This is what we do. It's like our job."

"We fought one war!" Lee threw his hands up in the air. "We're not experts at it. We nearly died!"

William turned away, his face flushing. It was almost as if he were hiding something.

"What is it?" Lee asked.

"Nothing." William turned away, waving for Lee to leave him alone.

Lee swallowed his curiosity, knowing that there were more pressing issues at hand. "We need to reconsider our position and come up with a different plan. Going on the offensive is not the right thing to do now."

"But we need to strike while the iron is hot!" William gripped his hands together, emphasizing his point.

Lee raised his hands in defeat. In a quiet voice, he replied, "But the iron isn't hot." Lee turned away, thinking about the situation. "We need to pray about this."

Lee sat alone praying for direction, having been left behind by William, who was not interested in such activities. In the stillness of the night, everything seemed lost. He grew up hating violence, not wanting to hurt others; but in the Outland, he had no choice but to fight. Now, here, this was his home turf. Lee didn't want to kill people. The zombified people had no clue as to what they were doing, and many of the other people probably had no choice but to follow the Trepidation.

"What do I do?" Lee asked. "How am I supposed to proceed?"

Amos looked down on him, saddened by the pain in his heart.

"He still hasn't learned about why he's here," Jonas said. "The boy will be a liability."

"No, he won't," Amos argued. "His presence alone will be enough to turn the tide. Our master will use him as an instrument against the enemy." Amos placed his hand on Lee's shoulder. "You will be all right. Follow the path that God has laid out for you, and let your friends see your light so that they may see God's hand in your life."

"The Warriors are a liability," Jonas continued. "If the boy is not up to the task—"

"He is up to the task," Amos insisted, pulling his hand away from Lee's shoulder. Jonas had touched a nerve by writing them off so quickly. "He will spread the seeds that need sown."

Jonas glared at him. "Good."

"Where is Harper on securing the Gates?" Amos barked. "The Warriors are not supposed to be subjected to any combat."

"They're not doing that great. This is the enemy's land after all. Besides, exposure to the gate isn't good for them either."

"I know the limits of their psyche," Amos repeated calmly. "We need them to pass through here quickly."

Warren sat against Toben, speaking in a soft, calming manner. He spoke of the beautiful things from the Outland, about all the places and things that brought him comfort and joy. "Do you remember the Kyron flats, the green grass and the smell of the flowers in the spring? I would always go there with Cecil and Kyra."

"It was a nice place." Toben relaxed, remembering his time there; it was a warm sensation. "The feel of the sands at Cam beach and the smell of Granite." Toben exhaled deeply, looking back at him. "You seem tired. Why are you always pushing yourself? You're so serious all the time."

"I need to press on." Warren sank back against Toben, his hands folded on his stomach. "There are people who are counting on me, and I don't really have the time for playing around." He looked away, hiding his eyes. "I'm still a Warrian. I still have a job to do."

"I'm always here for you. Don't worry about slowing me down if you need a shoulder to lean on," Toben said.

"Thanks." Warren saw William coming closer. He stood to greet him. "What's going on?"

"Lee's stopping to pray," William said annoyed, shaking his head. "We're going to keep heading out in this direction. Hopefully we'll find out something about what's going on."

"I thought we knew," Warren said. "There is a bad guy terrorizing the neighborhood, and we're going to go have a little chat with him."

"I doubt it would be that simple. We're just going to head in this direction until we either find a lead or till we hit the Pacific Ocean." William had made up his mind without Lee's consent. They were going to be hunting down the Temps, serving justice on their own terms.

"Okay, Toben's getting some rest now so we can head out in an hour."

"Maybe you should get some rest too," William said.

"I'll be fine," Warren said. "Someone needs to stand guard. Besides, you haven't slept for a while yourself."

William shook his head again. *But I'm used to a human body, you're not*, he thought to himself. Warren was still wearing down his body like he did with his Warrian form, but the human body would never hold up like that. He decided to let Warren stay awake as long as possible and then let him crash later. Eventually, he would have to catch on.

It was in the middle of the night when Warren woke from a deep sleep in the desert. His mind was hazy as he stood to his feet. His thoughts were all closed off, unable to penetrate the cloud that surrounded them. The overcast on the horizon was red, like a sunset in summer, but the land was so dark that the sky didn't look real. Warren scanned his surroundings and saw that he was alone. "William? Lee?" Warren called out hoping that his friends would answer him. No one came. Warren lowered his head looking around the area, but there were no answers to be found, no tracks or signs of life either. Warren rubbed the back of his neck, trying to sort out the confusing situation. He turned his attention back toward the horizon. There about thirty feet out in front of him stood two little children. The one standing on the right was a boy who looked to be eight years old and the other was a girl about the age of six. They both looked homeless and sad.

"It was with desperation that wrath begot abuse," the boy said.

"And it was with desperation that wrath begot neglect," the girl added.

"And it was with desperation that wrath begot vengeance," the boy continued.

"Inside vengeance there was a hole."

"But the king of the Highland wanted to come and filled the hole with hope and strength."

"Doing so will kill vengeance, and with it, our brother."

"Don't let our brother die. Run away from the king of the Highland. He will lure you in with soft words and comforting thoughts, meanwhile, He will strike our brother down just like He has done in the past. Don't let him take our family away again!" Tears were streaming from the children's faces. Warren was moved with compassion for them. He did not want to see them cry.

Just then a snarl came from behind Warren. It was about fifty feet out. Warren spun around to confront them. Four imps approached on all fours. The Imps were humanoid-like creature with their limbs twice the length that of a normal person. Their noises were elongated like a rat, its ears were pointed with skin as black as soot, and its eyes glowing red.

"We are the guardians of the tunnel," the leading imp said. "We are the protectors of the way. You are not supposed to be here."

"What are you planning on doing about it?" Warren asked.

"Send you back!" it demanded.

Warren stretched out his hand. A thin flame shot out about seven feet and hung in the air till Warren grabbed the end. Once Warren grabbed the flame, it dropped to the ground like a whip.

As the flame hit the ground, the four imps froze in fear, watching the flame. Even though he didn't let it show, Warren was surprised that he was able to make the weapon. The only weapon that he was able to make with his phoenix power was a sword, and that was back in the Outland. He felt strength here. Power unlike anything he had felt in the Outland.

"You have no authority here," the leader said, leaping toward him. Warren raised his whip in the air spinning it in a circle. The whip wrapped around the imp, turning him to dust. The wave of dust crashed over Warren. As the second Imp rushed, the whip snapped, scratching the creature across the forehead. Warren didn't wait for the other two to take the opportunity to attack. Warren swung the whip down from the right to the left, a wave of fire launched from the whip in the form of an arch. In the same motion, he swung the whip in the other direction. Warren stood his ground for the moment, making sure there were no more enemies in the area. Once he was sure that there were no more, he tossed his whip away. The whip burned away into the wind before it had a chance to hit the ground.

Looking down at his hands, Warren could feel his power growing.

"Don't take my brother!" the little girl shouted, charging Warren with a knife. He felt the edge sink into his side. His legs quaked as they started to give out. Tears ran down her face as she screamed, but he could not hear her cries. Looking down at her, he still felt compassion for her; her sadness overwhelming.

Warren shot up with such a force he nearly knocked Lee off Toben's back. Warren's body was so exhausted that his mind was lost in a fog. Warren moaned as fell back asleep against Toben's neck.

"He's been pushing himself too hard," Lee said. "He hasn't eaten since we left the church."

"Do we have any food left from that lunch Doc made for you?" William asked.

"No, we ate the last of it for lunch yesterday," Lee said.

Through the darkness of the night, William heard growling off in the distance. "What's that?" William asked.

"Imps," Lee said. "I can't pick up on where they are, but they're not close."

"We have Imps roaming around here?" William asked.

"I've been looking for them for ten minutes, but I can't see them," Lee answered.

"I can't smell them either," Toben answered. "And sleeping beauty is drooling down my neck."

"Can you tell if there's a town nearby?" Lee asked. "We need to get some food in Warren's belly."

"Yeah, I can smell gasoline a couple miles from here," Toben said.

The town was once home to more than a few thousand people, quiet and quaint for its time. Now it was reduced to a dark and desolate place, a ghost town. Dust rolled in from the wilderness, covering the cars that were left abandoned on the street, leaving behind trails on the sidewalks and windowsills. Occasionally, a car would drift through the small town, stirring up the dust, but there were no other signs of life. Many of the towns in America were reduced to this state, abandoned and ruined.

Toben walked down Main Street until he came to a small convenience store. He stretched out in the middle of the street so the rest of the group could jump off. Warren was barely conscious and not responsive. His exhaustiveness had taken its toll. Sleep was in control now. The human body that he wore was much larger and used up more energy than his previous Warrian form. He had not yet learned the limit of this new vessel.

Before they had an opportunity to enter the store, Toben started to groan once again. His body was engulfed with a bright light as he began to revert back to his smaller Raptor form, back to the way they found him in the alley. Toby and Naven were still locked in the same white body, trapped in an unnatural form.

Lee entered the store through the broken shop window. The store was once a nice deli/bakery in its time. But looters had had their way with the place, taking their toll on the building and the merchandise. Not much was taken though. It was the work of vandals, destroying what they could. Lee unlocked the front door, letting the rest of them into the store. Once inside, Toben took off for the back room where the deli was located.

"Toben, be careful. You don't—," William called after him, but he was having difficulties keeping Warren up on his feet, so he gave up. "Why do I bother?" William said, knowing that Toben wasn't listening.

"Let's just get some supplies and get out of here," Lee insisted, looking over his shoulder. "This place gives me the creeps."

"Okay," William said, helping Warren to the floor. William and Lee went scouring the store for food while Warren slept with his back leaning against the wall.

"Hey, I found some peanut butter!" William announced with glee. The two of them began to stick their fingers into the jar and eat it off their fingertips.

"Hey, I've got something," Lee said stopping long enough to grab a couple of boxes of saltines from a counter. The box sat close to the window where he came through.

"Good thinking," William said. After they devoured their first peanut butter cracker, they heard a gut-wrenching sound. A group of motorcycles were approaching from up the street. "We've got to hide," William said.

"What if they're looters?" Lee asked. "Warren's out cold. He can't defend himself. Maybe we should go out and confront them. If they are hostile, then we can at least make a break for it. They won't even know Warren is here."

One of the motorcycles pulled in front of the store and pointed a flashlight inside. "Is someone in there?" he called. "Hey, guys, I think we have some looters."

"Don't shoot!" William yelled. "We're coming out." Lee and William came out of the store with their hands in the air. Seven men on motorcycles were waiting for them as they exited the store. The men were the very definition of a motorcycle gang. Each of them looked like they could tear the two of them limb from limb.

"You think it's cool to steal stuff that isn't yours?" a man said. He seemed like the leader of the group.

"We were hungry. We just wanted something to eat," William said, getting a sense that they might be okay. After all, what bad guy worries about people looting from other people?

"That doesn't answer my question," the leader of the group said. "Do you think you can just take what doesn't belong to you?"

"This store was abandoned," Lee blurted out. "And we were only eating enough to stay alive. We weren't running off with all of it."

The leader laughed at the explanation. "You might be all right. We're called the Iron Hammer. I'm Kyle, the leader of the group. There's been a madman on the loose just south from here. He's been attacking my men. Have you seen anyone like that?"

Lee and William shook their head, not sure what to make of the development. They had just gotten there, and as far as they could tell, everyone had gone mad.

Kyle grinned, thinking of how he could use these two to his advantage. He needed some new blood to fill the ranks after he lost so many people to the person hunting them. "I'm going to need some extra hands." Kyle tossed Lee and William a couple of candy bars. "If you help, I'll feed you and look past this little misunderstanding." Kyle pointed to the window of the store, trying to use the situation as leverage. "Sam here is busted up, and he's not going to be much of a help in a fire fight."

"And if we refuse?" William asked.

"I'll shoot you for looting." Kyle was more than serious, willing to kill them if they would not help. Their options were limited.

"That's a wonderful offer," William replied. "But we have a friend who is exhausted, and he can't be moved."

"Sam," Kyle said, waving the man to go inside, "stay here and watch their friend. You know what to do."

Sam got off his bike and headed for the store. He was in his late forties with a serious limp, carrying a sawed-off shotgun. "I'll protect him with my life." Sam nodded toward Kyle as he passed by.

"Right," Kyle answered.

"Let me get my gun," William said, running back in the store with Sam following slowly behind him. William knew that there was no talking their way out of this fight. Besides, this was an excellent opportunity to figure out what was going on. William picked his gun up off the counter. He approached Sam as he entered the store. "When he wakes up, make sure you tell him that we'll go to the Empire State building. We'll all go there once he's up to it. Okay? I don't want him to think we've abandoned him." William knew that Toben was hiding in the store and that he could hear the message. They had never talked about what to do if they got lost before because they never thought they would be separated. The Empire State building was the first thing that popped into William's mind, and though it was a long ways away, he felt it was necessary to establish a rendezvous. Toby should have known where the Empire State building was even though William wanted to make it back before Warren woke up.

"Yeah, I'll tell him," Sam said.

William made a slow jog out of the store over to Sam's bike. "Lee, you're riding with me," William said, getting on the bike. It had been some time since his father taught him how to ride on a motorcycle, and he never really had too much practice, but he was sure it would all come back to him on the road.

William followed Kyle and his group down the highway on the motorcycle with Lee sitting behind him. They had been on the road for twenty minutes following behind Kyle to his hang-out. A cold wind blew across the plains. Creatures of the waste-lands welcomed the cold. They knew that the sun would only bring severe heat. The icy air engulfed William's face as Lee used him as a shield. William could feel Lee trembling from the cold. The more Lee shook, the more the cold bothered William.

"Why'd we leave him?" Lee asked. "We should have stayed to protect him."

"Did you really think we had a choice?" William said, turning his head to the side.

"No," Lee answered.

"We didn't. Warren has Toben to look after him. If Sam has anything tricky up his sleeve, Toben will deal with him."

"I'm just worried." Lee squeezed his eyes shut, concerned about the safety of his friends.

"It'll turn out for the best," William said. "I promise." Lee took a deep breath trying to let the facts settle.

Kyle pulled off the road into a dirt parking lot, just outside of a small roadside bar and turned off his engine. "We're here," Kyle said. "We'll get you guys properly equipped and then we'll head off to find that scum."

"Right," William said, getting off the bike. William followed them into the bar leaving his shotgun behind, hoping that they weren't going to spend too much time at the hangout. If they got back to Warren before he woke up, then they wouldn't have to worry about him trekking across the land with only Toben to guide him.

The bar wasn't much more than a shed with power hooked up. A bright neon sign was lit above the door, welcoming people in.

"Hey, you guys want—" Kyle stopped abruptly, shocked at what he found inside. Sitting at the bar was a tall and slim fellow in his late twenties. He was wearing an old pair of blue jeans with a white T-shirt under a black leather jacket. Pulling off the James Dean look was easy for him. "Who do you think you are?" Kyle shouted at the man.

"My name is Alex. I am of a race known as the Multaroe. We are few and far between. We contain powers far beyond your wildest imaginations."

"Multaroe!" Lee said, taking a step back.

"What's up?" William whispered.

"I remember that," Lee said. A man named Kale once mentioned that he was a Multaroe along with his brother, but Lee wasn't sure if this man was him or not. "Kale, from the Temple of Light was a Multaroe."

"That's right." William remembered the cloaked man from the temple. "He said that he had all of the abilities of the Outland creatures."

While Lee and William were talking to one another, Kyle was having his own discussion with Alex. "So what do you want?"

"I am here to take out the garbage," Alex said. "You're the Temp Anger who works for Wrath."

Kyle's face dropped. "What did you say?" His voice was filled with anger and confusion.

"You see, your problem is you use your anger to fuel your powers, and you neglect to see the things around you. In your ignorance, you brought about your own demise. The two boys you brought along with you are Inlanders, Guardians of the Warriors whom your master wishes to use in these last days."

Kyle's face became pale. "Not a chance. Cornel was supposed to make sure that they couldn't come through the gate." Kyle turned back to William and Lee who were watching him.

"He failed," Alex whispered in Kyle's ear. Kyle had just enough time to turn before he became a statue of dust. The other men that had followed him stood in shock at the display. In sheer panic, they all turned and ran like cowards, speeding away on their motorcycles. Alex laughed. "All you have to do is destroy the source of anger to relieve the pressure." His voice had a ring of irony.

"Who are you?" Lee asked.

"You were right the first time. I'm Kale's little brother," Alex said, moving down the bar, shaking his finger at them. "But the Multaroes do not have the abilities of the creatures of the Outland as much as we possess powers equal to them. I do not carry any of the physical characteristics of a Raptor or Dogen, so I cannot breathe fire or control wind like they could through their natural abilities though I possess power that allows me to do the same."

"He told us to be careful of you. He said you were dangerous," William said.

"Well, isn't that just like Kale?" Sitting down, Alex poured himself a drink. "He never approved of my methods."

"How long has it been?" Lee said. "How long since we left the Outland?"

"It's hard to say," Alex answered. "I'm not a rocket scientist, but maybe three hours or so." Alex giggled as he drank a dark brown liquid.

"What are you talking about?" William asked with agitation. "We've been here for four day's already."

Alex laughed. "What, you actually think you've been lying in a coma for eleven years while the world has been ripping itself apart around you? Wormholes are a semilogical explanation, but it is so much simpler than that."

"I don't understand," William said.

"Your home is much closer than you think," Alex offered. "Yet farther than you can ever imagine." Alex grinned, taking a drink from his glass. "I'm not supposed to ruin the plot for you, but I'll let you in on a little secret. There's a two-part story involved with your being here. One side of the story is the Warriors and the other is the Guardians. You see, the Guardians back in the Outland have a secret legend about the Black Heart. A Tyrant King shall be born of the shadow through sin. He devours and destroys everything that he touches, and he will conquer the Outland."

"What do you mean, sin?" William asked.

"Hasn't he explained it to you yet?" Alex was pointing at Lee. He chuckled again. "Are you a sinner?"

William looked at Lee for support, but he could not read any clues. "Yeah, I guess."

Alex scoffed at the halfhearted answer. It was almost as if William did not believe he was a sinner. "You've got blood on your hands, anyone can see that. But the Eternal King, the King of the Highland, He said that hating someone is just like killing them. You've hated, envied, and literally killed people. You've lied and stolen, knowing that it was wrong. You have no idea how much you've sinned."

"What's your point?" William was getting tired of this conversation.

"That is what the Tyrant King will be made from, sin." Alex drank the last of the brown liquid. "Darkness thicker than slime will cover the Outland, and they will do their best to escape into your world. However, the Warriors must first be made ready primed to fight. And that's where you come in. The Guardians are supposed to stop the rising of the Tyrant King."

"How?" Lee pushed for the answer.

"That's part of the plot," Alex said. "But don't worry. You already know how to stop him. But I can tell you haven't even started yet." Alex stood to his feet, brushing off his jacket. "You'll want to continue east from here until you reach Mississippi."

"Where are you going?" Lee said, stepping forward to stop him. "We have more questions."

"And you haven't even given us any answers," William added, pointing at him as he spoke.

"Like you, I have my own job to do. The enemy has a diabolical plan in order with several key players involved. I can see which ones will be a problem, and I am making arrangements to take care of those radicals."

"What radicals?" Lee asked frightened of the potential answer.

"The devil has planted certain people in your group to distract you from your goals. The Warriors will be antagonized by them, causing them to fall away. It is my goal to remove these distractions."

"Are you planning on hurting our friends?" William asked skeptically.

"Not if they are really your friends," Alex reassured him. "I am only after the traitors that have been placed among you. For now, you need to worry about getting home. The quickest way there is to confront the Trepidation, but you also have to worry about his Temps." Alex walked over to the remains of Kyle. He grabbed Kyle's hand crushing it, causing the pillar of dust to crumble to the ground. Alex opened his hand to reveal a ring from the ruins. "In order to destroy them, you must administer a killing blow by taking the special item that feeds them their power." Alex lifted the ring. "It's usually is a piece of jewelry, but it could be any item that they hold close to them. The only thing they have is the power that feeds them. Take it and remove them from this world." Alex moved past them, heading for the door when he stopped to give them one last piece of advice. "Each Temp has their own special attribute, a special power that makes them unique, different from the others. They are extremely dangerous."

THE ENEMY

Standing alone in an elevator overlooking New York City was a prominent demon named Baccale. He did not care about a general's seat or even the accolades of his fellow demons. He found pleasure in the deeds he preformed, watching God's creations willingly walk down a twisted path away from Him. It was entertaining to see them fall so easily into his traps. God would call for them to come to Him, but they would follow Baccale's voice instead. He found people so easily manipulated.

An important event was starting to unfold here in this world, and Satan himself had invited Baccale to the party. He had special talents that would prove useful to his plans. The elevator bell tolled and the doors opened. A demon dressed in a dark cloak of shadow and darkness stood in the opening for a moment, staring at the well-groomed body that Baccale was dressed in. Currently he was dressed in the form of a human man in his early twenties. Unlike most of the demons in this world who wore cloaks of shadow and darkness, Baccale found his human form to be comfortable. It was a unique prize he had acquired and proved to be a convenient tool at times.

"Are you getting on?" Baccale asked.

"Sorry," the demon said sheepishly. "For a moment there, I thought you were an Echo." Echoes were artificial beings made here to populate this demon's training ground. With the Echoes in place, it made the world seem more real, giving the humans trapped here less of an opportunity to realize where they really were. The Echoes used in this world were complex in design, having intricate personalities and emotions. Most demons could only build one Echo and give them the simplest of emotions. That was all they usually needed them for, to play a single role, usually of a family member or friend used to confuse and manipulate people not to actually interact.

Baccale grinned at the thought, already sick of his presence. "What's wrong with Echoes? Without them, people would realize this world is merely a dream and wake up or, at the very worst, recognize what we are doing."

"I guess you're right," the demon said.

"You don't seem like you're from around here?" Baccale observed his uneasiness. "Where are you from?"

"I have recently been transferred from the Department of Temptation."

"A tempter?" Baccale acted like he was impressed, crossing his arms and tilting his head to the side to get a better look at him. "You know, without tempters, we couldn't do our jobs either." That was a lie. Baccale could not stand such shortsighted people. In his eyes, tempters were even more of a tool than the humans they hunted.

"Are you with Logistics?" the demon asked.

Baccale nodded. "I've been temporarily assigned here to the training grounds."

"Really? For the Warriors?" the demon asked.

Baccale nodded.

The demon was now intrigued. "Where were you before?"

It was starting to become a challenge for Baccale to hide his contempt, but he managed to pull it off. Turning away, acting shy about his accomplishments, he said, "I'm with Supernatural Affairs. I started off working with the occult and cults generally. You know, performing unexplainable phenomenon. I even helped start a major cult once. But I've been freelancing on independent missions lately."

"Wow," the demon said, "I've never met a supernatural caster before. You know, you guys make my job a lot easier too."

Baccale did not like the sound of that. It implied that he could not finish a job; that by some chance, he only weakened a human's resolve, never crushing it. To his own account, Baccale had always shattered his prey's resolve, making sure that they would never turn to God or at least to the true maker of the universe. The suggestion that he could not was outrageous. Baccale recovered quickly, smiling with the response. "How so?"

"Well, I know a lot of people who I have tempted that would not budge until they experienced something supernatural and then they go running willingly to our master."

It was all milk and water to Baccale; being a simple truth that a lot of the younger demons thought was groundbreaking. This demon had no imagination. He was a sap who could not see past his own experiences. He probably could not tempt a husband into going bowling, leaving his family at home when they needed him, let alone convince a pacifist to pick up a gun. Baccale could do both in his sleep.

Just then the door opened on another floor. Another demon stood in the doorway. He too wore the cloak of shadows and darkness, but his hood was down, revealing a handsome face with short black hair. His name was Bysoul, and he was the demon in charge of the training grounds as long as the Warriors were there. A strong, dominating presence emanated from him. Though he had the feel of death surrounding him, little was actually known about him. He was the lieutenant of the logistics department, and the chief had given his full support to his appointment. He was a figure that Baccale could relate with; a fiend that hid away in obscurity unseen by people.

"Evening," Bysoul said, waving them off the elevator. "I see you've met Ripoll." He pointed to the other demon. A smirk flashed across his face as he motioned them to follow. "I know that he might not seem like much, but he is a master at his own craft. Our master chose him for the design of the Temptations and the Sins that rule over them."

Baccale flashed a warm smile, disgusted at the thought that this "sublevel" demon would hold such an important role. *Oh well*, Baccale thought to himself, *I'm not interested in having that kind of fame. It's not like I want that position anyway. My role is much better.* "Congratulations, you came up with a fascinating world."

"This world was actually set up by Morygon," Bysoul said. "Ripoll inhabited it with Echoes and developed the interactive players, but that is all."

"But the master was quite pleased with how my minions turned out," Ripoll added, trying to remain in good favor. The little weasel was searching for praise among the elite demons, but all it brought was ridicule and spite.

"Indeed." Bysoul did his best to act like he was commending him. It was true that Ripoll was an expert at making Echoes, developing more than any other demons could and with complex emotions and personalities too. However, he was still a lowly demon from the Department of Temptation. That was all he was, and that would never change.

The three of them approached a large set of double doors together. They were antique in design with delicate carvings etched into the woodwork. It gave off a naturalistic feel, almost Celtic in origin. The waves and curves of the craftsmanship were inspiring.

Bysoul pushed open the doors, letting them swing softly. He stepped to the side, letting the other two demons enter the room first while he closed the doors behind them. The room was a large auditorium. Most of the seats were covered with a heavy canvas as if the room was under construction. Only a few lights were on, adding an eerie touch to the room. Shadows shifted and the canvas moved as though other demons waited in the darkness.

"Good evening," a feminine voice said from the shadows. Morygon was wearing yet another one of the cloaks of shadows and darkness, watching them as they entered the room.

"Is our master here yet?" Bysoul asked.

"Not yet," Morygon answered, "but he is on his way."

"Who is that?" Ripoll asked Bysoul, pointing at the shadow Morygon was hiding in.

"This is the architect of this training ground," Bysoul replied, grinning at the memories he had of the demon. "Morygon prefers a feminine voice."

Morygon raised his hands to shrug off the comment. His hood was still raised, covering his face. You could not see the manly figure that was hidden behind the soft womanly voice. "I find it to be a convenient distraction. Mankind can sometimes be swayed easier with a soft utterance than with a loud declaration." He pointed to Ripoll. "My mask is not so different from yours."

A cough came from the back of the auditorium. A well-built man with a shaved head stood there, waiting for the demons to finish their insignificant conversation. From the expensive sunglasses to the designer jacket that topped off his outfit, the man's appearance was the very essence of "cool." No rock star or actor could ever compete with his charisma or good looks. Fame and popularity clawed after him.

"Master!" Bysoul shouted, bowing down as he approached. The other demons followed suit, giving a bow in his direction.

"It's a busy season," he said with a grin. He motioned to another demon following him, "This is Cormon. He's going to be your Conductor on this little excursion."

Bysoul extended his hand, taking Cormon's in return. "I am Bysoul, the director of these training grounds. I'll be influencing the Warriors path while here in this world."

Their master pointed to Ripoll. "And that is the creator of the Echoes here. He created almost everyone on this side."

"Ripoll, at your service." He smiled, which made Cormon a little nervous. He did not like this demon. so clingy and attention-starved. An attitude like that always attracted mistakes and shortsightedness. Dependence on the approval of others was an emotion best left to the humans.

Their master pointed to Morygon, who remained where he was, across the room. "Morygon is the architect of the training grounds, and then we have Baccale. Baccale will be adding the fuel to our fire once we get rolling. Let's get this meeting underway." He pointed to Bysoul, letting him start with his report.

"Well, the enemy has been able to infiltrate the training grounds, setting up gates and portals to reduce the interaction that our boys have with this world. There are four angels in charge of the attack. The guardian angel of the Outland, Amos, has joined the frontlines of the group, along with Harper. Also, General Cecil, whose expertise is found in antisupernatural tactics, is leading the charge. Lastly, we have Jonas, who has just joined up with the group."

Eyes shifted to Baccale. The rivalry between him and Jonas was well known. He simply picked at his teeth, waiting for the briefing to be over. It seemed to be a waste of his time.

"The Echoes are doing their job, providing a distraction for the Warriors and their Guardians. The Temps and their Sins have offered reasonable amount of fight, giving the Warriors some combat experience. Since they have not all been reunited yet, we are letting the enemy progress them through the land at a swift pace. Once we reunite them, we will slow their efforts."

"And how are things coming on your end?" Their master raised his hand toward Baccale, expecting good news from him.

"I have completed the item you have requested," Baccale said with a twisted smile. He raised a small vile of mysterious clear liquid. Gazing through the vial, intrigued with the golden tint and simmering oil, he was captivated by his work, well pleased with his accomplishment.

He quickly snapped back to reality, turning to address his master. "We'll need to anchor their gates here in this world. Once this happens, the Warriors' powers will slightly manifest themselves in their own world. However, their gates will need to be opened from the other side. Once it's all said and done, they will be able to have complete control over any powers they received here or in the Outland. Though it may become troublesome, I suggest we anchor everyone in the group, Warriors and Guardians alike."

"Excellent," the master said. "Then the plan is developing exactly as anticipated."

"Excuse me, sir," Ripoll asked, raising his hand sheepishly. The master pointed at him with a smile, giving him permission to speak. "What is the purpose of transferring their powers to the human world? How does that help our cause?"

The other demons lowered their heads, backing away, expecting some kind of outlash from their master. With a gentle smile, as if he were speaking to a child, he explained himself. "What is the one thing people love to hear especially in America? Now? What is the story that everyone wants to hear?"

"A hero who fails?" Bysoul asked.

"How about a story where the bad guy wins?" Cormon offered.

"One where the hero becomes the villain?" Morygon suggested.

The master chuckled at the guesses. "The idea that the villain, who is despised and hated, who has so many sins on his head, can rise above the hardships and hatred to become a hero—that is the story people want to hear. They want to see this villain become a hero by his own power, transformed not by a supernatural being that changes them from within. That way, the villain never has to actually change in order to be good. It already lives within him. It gives them the hope that they can rise over their own sins by their own power. That is the purpose of transferring their powers, to give them the confidence that they can save, not only themselves but also save those whom they love. With that, they will never want to ask for our enemy's forgiveness because they will have no need for it. Or at least that is what they will think. Then I will step into the picture, and become their savior. I will show them how to save themselves."

"But they have a Christian in their midst," Ripoll exclaimed, concerned with the outcome of his master's plan. "Won't he tell them the truth?"

This made the master laugh. "The only reason Amos was able to drag that Christian to the Outland was because he was so immature. I have reviewed his case, and by the time he understands what we are doing with his friends, it will be too late for him to convince them that they are wrong. Besides, Christians have been dropping the ball for centuries. Thanks to biblical illiteracy and the absence of accurate teaching, we've been able to convince people that normal Christians have it all wrong, that their Bible is inaccurate and untrustworthy. We tell them that they need our secrets to understand God's will and salvation."

"We have been able to increase our deception in these last days," Bysoul added. "It has been an exciting experience. People fall easily to our persuasions."

"Sir," Cormon started, "my minions are on the move. They should be splitting up the group as we speak."

"Good," their master said. "What about this Alex? I have heard some disturbing news concerning him."

"Alex is a Multaroe who has gone rouge from the Outland," Bysoul answered. "He was able to open a portal and is now running wild here. We suspect that he is causing just as many difficulties for our enemy as he is for us. It is to our advantage that he has a flawed logic, turning from our enemy's plan. He will surely act as a destructive force, giving our Warriors much needed fighting experience."

"Well, we cannot allow him to go running around on his own accord. I don't care how they are split up. Just send one of the groups after Alex. I have a feeling that he will be a thorn in our side if he goes unchecked. Cormon, go pick up the boys and take them to the alternative gate that Alex is using for his base of operations. Let them fight it out there."

"Alex has taken a valuable piece of the puzzle from the Outland using it as collateral to lure the Warriors in. Can we use that to stir on the conflict?" Cormon asked. "They are particularly fond of their friends from the Outland. I'm sure they will rush to their rescue."

"That is fine. And if the collateral is not enough, go ahead and add some incentive on top of that." Their master stopped for a moment, thinking about how the plan was unfolding. "On second thought, I need to make an appearance. I know exactly who I want to dispatch the Multaroe. I will find the boys and lead them to you. Just point them in the right direction."

JOURNEY TO THE GATE

Sam stood in front of Warren with his shotgun resting in his arms. Sam was watching out the door, waiting for Kyle and the others to return. He found the eerie silence of the building to be disturbing. He was starting to wish that he would have been watching where he was going. He had twisted his ankle three towns back, chasing after some rebels. *If they would just learn their place, then we wouldn't have to chase them down*, Sam thought to himself. He was trying to concentrate on something else, hoping to alleviate the terror that the darkness brought. It seemed to surround him, waiting to swallow him whole.

His new life wasn't as glamorous as Kyle had promised, but it was better than living in filth with those rebels. His wife and children could not realize that the war was over. The Trepidation had already won. It had been some time since he had seen them, not that it mattered now. They were traitors to the cause, hanging onto the dreams of the past. *It's foolish. We're living under a new hope now. The Trepidation is watching over us.*

Sam stood there, staring out into the distance when a loud buzzing pulled him from his trance. The alarm on Sam's watch went off. He shook his head as he reached down to turn it off. "I'm sorry, kid," Sam said. "I hate to do this, but rules are rules." Sam pumped the shotgun, chambering a shell in the barrel. He started to raise the gun when something fell in the back of the store. The barrel pointed in the direction of the disturbance, but nothing could be seen. He turned on a flashlight as an eerie noise came from his right. Turning in the direction of the noise, the only thing he saw was a white head and a mouth full of razor-sharp teeth. They closed around him. From outside, there was nothing but silence.

Toben disposed of the body, keeping it out of Warren's sight. Toby and Naven had come to an agreement that they would not make their friends carry any of their burdens. If Warren would have seen the mess that they had made, he would have been worried.

Standing just outside the kitchen freezer, Toben heard footsteps coming up behind him. The snakelike eyes darted toward their origin. A well-built man was approaching with sunglasses and a designer jacket. Toben snarled at him.

"Hello, Mr. Raven," the man said. "Or should I say Mr. Ravens?"

Toben squeezed his eyes shut, turning his head away and grunting. Turning back around, his face was exhausted and twisted with only the left eye open. His eye was orange, swirling with a grayish blue color, in the normal shape of a human eye.

"Tobias Raven," the man said. "You don't look as well as I thought you would have."

"You have no right to call me by that name, devil." Toby's voice rang out independently, not fused with Naven's.

"So you've figured out how to suppress your friend in there? That is impressive."

"What do you want?" Toby asked, turning to completely face him. He crouched down ready to pounce if needed.

"You sound like we are no longer friends," the devil said. "I helped you back in your own world and when you got to the Outland too. I made you who you are today. I gave you a friend who would not forsake you. You owe me."

Toby scoffed at him. "Things don't always work out the way you want. I can no longer help with you. I lost that fight."

Satan smiled in return. "You did not lose the fight, you gave up. But that is fine. I will not need you in the end. A friend of yours has been taken by a powerful foe. Leave here and head for the subway. I will provide a way for you to return to normal and a way for you to find your missing friend."

"Why should I trust you?" Toby asked.

"I still need you," the devil replied. "I may not need you in the end, but you are still an important asset to me. Surely you can allow me to help for now. After all, you are smart enough to know how to use the devil's talents for good. I'll leave it up to you when you stop using me."

Movement came from the front door. As soon as Toby took his focus off Satan, he vanished. With a snarl, Toby opened his right eye, letting both consciousnesses flow back together. Confusion swirled Toben's head, but he quickly regained his composure. Toby worked hard to suppress the conversation with the devil.

Warren's eyes slowly opened. He stretched out his arms and yawned, fully energized and ready to take on the day. Getting to his feet, he looked out the window of the store. It was almost morning.

"Morning," Toben said. "Feeling well?"

"I feel great," Warren answered. "I haven't had such a good night's sleep for a year now."

"That's good," Toben said. "We need to get moving before something else happens."

"What happened?"

"William and Lee were kidnapped, but they said that we should meet them at the Empire State building."

"Where's that?" Warren asked, unsure where anything was in this world.

"It's in New York," Toben said. "We might meet up with them before that, but we need to get going now."

"Right," Warren said, picking up his satchel. As he picked the bag up off the floor, he noticed a sawed-off shotgun on the ground. "What's this?" Warren asked, picking the gun up.

Toben silently sneered at the gun. He quickly recovered, acting as if nothing had happened. "One of the men left it behind," Toben said. "He's probably losing his head over it right now."

"Well, it's only going to slow us down," Warren said, pumping it, letting the shells fall to the floor. Once the gun was empty,

Warren reached down and collected the shells. "I might be able to use these again."

"Great," Toben said, following Warren outside. "Here." Toben handed Warren a map of the United States. "I found it inside. You'll need it."

"Thanks," Warren said, taking the map. "I'm sure—" Warren paused as he heard something clambering up the road.

"What is that?" Toben asked, stepping forward to get a better look at it. "It sounds like there are a lot of them." Slithering up the street, a lizard appeared under one of the street lights. It looked like an odd komodo dragon crossed with another type of lizard. "Is it a chimera?"

"No, it's a spine lizard," Warren said, pulling out one of his pistols. "It's a dangerous Outland animal." The lizard took a couple steps forward and opened its mouth. The creature's back arched as a tongue stretched out of its mouth. It slithered through the air like a snake. At the tip of the tongue was a small oval shaped ball with a dozen thistles on it. "They're poisonous," Warren said, aiming for the tongue.

"What are you waiting for?" Toben asked, taking a step back.

"Wait." Warren kept his gun focused on the tongue.

"We've got trouble!" Toben yelled.

"What?" Warren asked. There were several spine lizards coming down from the tops of the surrounding buildings. They were crawling down to meet the two of them.

"Over there!" Toben shouted as he ran for a staircase that led down to the subway.

Toben and Warren sprinted down the staircase as fast as they could. Once they hit the bottom, Warren spun around ready to start shooting, but the lizards just stood at the top watching them and waiting. "What are they doing?" Warren asked.

"How should I know?" Toben answered. Warren rolled his eyes. "Why don't they come after us?"

"Maybe they're afraid to?" Warren said. Warren stood there for a moment watching the lizards. Then he heard footsteps behind him. Warren spun around with his gun ready to fire. Two little kids screamed as the gun came in their direction. Warren quickly lowered the weapon.

The children standing in front of them were cold and scared. They looked as if they had been wondering alone in the dark for some time. The tallest one was a boy, about eight years old. He was covering a girl, who was about six, protecting her from the evils that might want to harm them. They were dirty, and their clothes were poor and full of holes. It seemed that they had been down in the subway for some time. Warren looked back to the staircase to see how the lizards were reacting to the children, but they were already gone.

"Are you two okay?" Toben asked, bending down to get a better look at them.

"Y...yes," the little boy said, stuttering in fear.

"It's okay," Warren said. "We won't hurt you."

"Who are you?" Toben asked.

"I'm Abe and this is my sister, Nell."

"I'm Toben, and this is Warren."

"You're cute," Nell said to Toben, less afraid than her brother. "Are you a Raptor?"

"Raptor/Dogen mix," Toben replied, lowering his head even more so she could pet him.

"Are you guys down here all alone?" Warren asked.

"Yes," Abe answered. "We were waiting on our brother."

"Well, it's not safe here anymore," Warren said. "Let's get going."

"Can I ride on Toben's back?" Nell cried to her brother, pulling on his ruined shirt.

"You have to ask him," Abe said, giving her a heedful glare.

"Sure," Toben replied. "I don't mind." Warren helped Nell onto Toben's back. The four of them hopped off the platform and onto the tracks. The tunnel was pitch-black. No light seemed to be able to escape its clutches. Warren led the way through the dark tunnel, holding onto Abe's hand as Toben followed behind.

Warren could feel Abe's hand shaking in the blackness, afraid of the things that lurked in the dark. "It'll be okay," Warren reassured him. "Nothing's going to happen to you." Warren could see him nod his head in the dark. It was a useful trait, being able to see in the dark.

The four of them remained silent as they traveled through the tunnel. It wasn't that they didn't have much to say, but the moment had seized them. The eerie dark played with their minds, keeping their attentions on more important matters. In this world, the darkness seemed to come alive, chasing after people.

The first subway station that they passed had no lighting whatsoever. Warren was about to mention that they might try to get back to the surface when Abe squeezed his hand. Warren decided it was for the best to wait until they found a better place. The next station was rundown. A massive battle had taken place there. Bullet holes rattled the walls, and several chunks of tiles had been blown off. The flickering lights helped add to the scene.

They continued on through the subway till they came to the Maple Avenue subway station. "Let's stop here," Warren said. "We should rest." It was a much better location. The lights were all fully functional, and there were minimal damages to the structure.

Toben jumped up onto the platform and then helped Nell off his back. Warren lifted Abe up onto the platform before climbing up himself.

"Now what do we do?" Toben asked.

"Decisions, decisions," a voice said from one of the benches. "You never can tell what you're supposed to do next, I do believe." A tall man sat there, reading a newspaper casually as if he was waiting on the train for work. "Do you know what I find fascinating?" the man asked.

"What?" Nell asked enthusiastically.

Warren stepped between them.

"The things people forget," the man answered. "Some of the most important information that people come in contact with just gets pushed away like it was nothing, as if they just didn't seem to care. It's a shame really. That it is."

"Who are you?" Warren asked.

"I am a messenger. My name is Cormon." The man lowered his paper. He was a handsome man in his late thirties, wearing a nice brown suit. Cormon stood to his feet as the faint sounds of a train approaching came racing down the tunnel. "And this is *our* ride, I do believe." A train stopped at the platform, and the doors opened. The train was deserted, and after a quick inspection to make sure there were no traps, Warren and the others boarded it. Under normal circumstances, Warren would probably have suggested another way, but his mind was cloudy at the moment, and Cormon seemed like the type of person to have some answers.

In the back of the car was a desk where Cormon took a seat. Once Cormon was seated, the doors closed and the train started moving again. He looked down at the two little siblings. "Are they with you?" he asked Warren.

"Yes," Warren said defiantly. He felt overly protective of the two children as if they were family. He could not come to trust this man yet, however, they were now inside of one of the gates, and their minds were compromised by the dreamlike state.

"Good." Cormon began to address the two children, "Have you made your decision yet?" Abe looked down at his sister who returned the look. Then they both nodded. "Good. Do you know when you'll proceed?" The two children shook their heads. "That's fine as long as you understand the consequences of your actions and what will happen once you start." Cormon nodded, turning his attention to Toby. "Toby Raven, I'll get to you in a moment." His head swiftly turned to Warren. "Warren of Weremore, do you have any questions?"

"Yeah, what's going on?" Warren asked. "What are you doing here, and why are there Outlanders appearing here in the Inland?"

"I suppose you are referring to Sal?" Cormon asked, referring to his own statement as a rhetorical question. "Sal is a construct of the spirit, using an image from the mind to materialize it here. You saw the intoxicated horde roaming the land as dead men and so, Sal just took the image of one who controlled them in the Outland. It was from your minds that he chose that image. You will come to realize that you have a direct connection with the Temps and an even greater connection with the power they wield." Cormon sidestepped the entire question, trying to make them assume their own answers. He took a moment to look at Toben. "I bet it's tight in there. I do believe."

"As a matter of fact, it is," Toben said with a disrespectful tone.

"I guess I deserve that," Cormon said. "I shouldn't pick on those in pain. That I shouldn't."

"But why are the Outlanders here?" Warren said, interrupting. "I thought Outlanders couldn't cross over to the other side."

"In most cases, you're right. The only way to cross over is to breach the gate that contains the power. The only way to do that is by anchoring a towline between worlds. Of course you need substantial amount of material on the other side to keep the form."

"How? How did the Trepidation breach the gate?" Toben asked.

"That part isn't important," Cormon said. "You need to understand that this is not the stopping point for any of you. You need to concentrate on getting out of here, and for that, you need to face the Trepidation. Once you overcome him, you can leave."

"So how are we supposed to defeat him?" Warren asked.

Cormon stood to his feet as he walked around his desk. "To defeat him, you must defeat the fear within yourself. That you must."

"Are we strong enough to beat him?" Warren asked.

"You don't have to be strong to defeat him, just have enough faith in yourselves to overcome him. Once you understand that, the Trepidation cannot face you. Toby, come here," Cormon said, stretching out his hand. When Toben stood in front of him, Cormon placed his right hand on Toben's chest and his left hand on the back of his neck. "Stay calm. This will feel…funny."

"Funny?" Toben asked, concerned with Cormon's choice of words. "I don't know if I like funny." Warren gasped, catching Toben's attention. "What?" Toben's voice sounded even more distorted than normal. A lump started to form on his chest where Cormon's hand was, and it seemed as if his body began to blur. "I don't feel..." Toben paused, and his face began to sink. "Funny?" Toben looked as if he wanted to throw up. "I don't feel so hot." By now the lump in his chest was the size of a baby and the color in Naven's coat started to come through.

"I feel sick." Naven's voice rang out clear. The room seemed as if it were spinning around him. Toben's eyes began to roll into the back of his head. "No!" Naven shouted.

"Almost there," Cormon said as the lump fell loose into Cormon's hand.

The train came to a stop at the next platform, and Toben ran to the door. "I'm going to be sick!" Toben yelled, running out as the doors opened. Warren chased after him onto the platform.

"What's happening?" Warren shouted.

Cormon pulled him back by the shoulder. "You'll want to step back. Without the catalyst, this might get messy. That it will."

"Messy!" Warren said enraged.

Toby screamed while Naven's roar accompanied it. Toben hit the floor with a commotion. In a small flash of light, Toby and Naven flew apart in opposite directions. Both of them landed twenty feet from their original position, landing with a bounce. Toby and Naven lay on the ground for a moment, not moving.

Naven's coat had faded from a rich red to a dull, rust-colored orange. It no longer held the same glory that it did in the Outland. Even Toby's clothes were tattered and torn severely, along with the pair of goggles he had from the city of Granite.

"Please stop the ride. I'm done," Toby whined as he rolled over to vomit.

"That was terrible," Naven said, getting to his feet. "It feels like that time we ate those pancakes you made."

"I didn't know those berries were poisonous," Toby said, climbing to his knees. "And if you thought that was bad, I should take you to an amusement park!"

Warren raced to Toby's aid, comforting him for a moment, before lifting him to his feet.

Cormon looked down at the catalyst that held them together. It was the Jelly Mold that was given to Toby in Kendor. It had been fed part of Cecil's body while still in the Outland. The little form was slowly transforming into the body that Cecil had taken. His little stumps wiggled with enthusiasm. Cecil's mouth and nose had grown out in the form of a muzzle. He also started a tail along with two small bumps on his shoulder blades.

"You're much cuter in this form," Cormon said sarcastically, flicking his nose.

"Where are we?" Warren asked.

"We're here," Cormon said, stretching his hand toward the stairs behind them. They led up out of the station. "This is the tunnel. This is the way. One of your friends is trapped here and that person needs your help to get back home. Be careful of the dangers that lurk around every corner."

Cormon walked over to Toby. "I have something for you," Cormon said, tying a leather bracelet around Toby's wrist. "This is yours and so is this." Cormon reached into his pocket and brought out a small ball of light. "This is a new weapon to fight against your enemies. You can call on it anytime you wish." Cormon handed the ball of light to Toby. Toby took the ball, and as he gripped it, the light transformed into a sword. It was a medium-sized, double-edged sword that weighed as much as a small stick.

"It feels like it's made from titanium," Toby said.

"Only it is lighter and stronger," Cormon said. "It'll cut through steel and flesh alike."

"Thank you," Toby said with enthusiasm. He glanced over at Warren with a bright smile, anticipating what he would get. "What about Warren?"

Cormon took Warren's hand and tapped on his bracelet. "With this you can transwarp at will. Do not use your powers for selfishness. You need to limit how often you transwarp. Your powers will eventually consume more than just your energy." Cormon knew that Warren would use his powers selfishly only to an extent. However, he knew that the nature of the flame inside of him would not allow him to stray too far. In this case, it was best he live an upstanding and semivirtuous life, confident in himself and his own power. After all, as long as he thought he was a good person and lived decently, he would not see a need for a savior and that was when the demons really won. It is not in the evil deed that gives them their power but in the rebellion against God.

The train whistle blew twice, alerting everyone that it was time to leave. Cormon swiftly walked back to the train and stood in the doorway. "Go find your friend. That person needs you now more than ever. When you're ready to go, come back and I'll take you home. Remember that you need to destroy the Temps if you ever want to get home." Those were his last words before the train slowly pulled away from the station.

The group gathered together on the platform. "Now what?" Toby asked, clinging to his sword.

"Find our friend," Warren answered, looking back toward the staircase.

Once Warren and Toby stepped out of sight, Cormon stepped back into view. He had actually remained in the shadows of the train station, not leaving on the train. He looked down at the now sleeping Jelly Mold who would become like Cecil. He sneered, tossing the little lump of flesh across the platform.

The sound of wings fluttered through the station as the little body was scooped up. Amos landed behind Cormon with the Jelly Mold, Cecil, in his arms. He had a stern look upon his face. "What do you think you're doing?"

Cormon smiled, his face twisted with a self-gratifying smirk. "Those two belong to me now, Amos. You honestly thought you could keep them merged together with that little Jelly Mold. Even with it being a part of General Cecil, I easily broke the seal. You should just watch out for the ones you've secured for yourself."

"Acting nice will only get you so far," Amos warned. "Though you were able to separate them, through the time they spent merged, they have grown a deeper bond that will not be broken. You cannot use them for your master's wickedness. They will catch on."

"They will walk willingly into his arms, and you know it." Cormon chuckled. "I've got a few surprises in store for them. They will taste power and long for it. And the day will come when that Little Cecil will cross swords with them."

Amos drew his sword, raising it against Cormon. Cormon fell back, cowering in fear. "You know better than that, Amos!" Cormon shouted. "We can't fight here. We're supposed to be watching them, guiding their hands from the shadows. Leave the fighting to Michael." Amos snarled at him, wanting to finish him off. "Hard, isn't it? Going from someone who once fought so valiantly now reduced to a babysitter."

"I will have my day with you," Amos said, "on the battlefield of the Black Heart."

"I'll wait for that day." Cormon brushed his hair out of his face.

Warren led the group down the abandoned street, overwhelmed with the sight of the vacant city. The world felt lost and empty. The sky was the color of rust with clouds floating close to the horizon. The air was cool and filled with the stagnant smell of decay. The wind did not blow, and the air itself stood still.

"Hey, Warren," Toby said. "Let's stop for some clothes. It's starting to get cold."

"Right," Warren said, pointing to a small store with a mannequin in the window. "There's one." It was a quaint little store, a real bargain hunter's find. The store looked like it belonged to a mom-and-pop outfit for gently used items. Toby had other ideas though. Warren had marched across the street to the front door before he turned around to see Toby walking toward another store with fancy writing in the window. Warren stopped, disappointed in his choice. "Where are you going?" Warren called after him.

"With unlimited credit, why shop at the bargain bin?" Toby said, opening the door. "Besides, I always wanted to shop here."

The store wasn't big, so Warren rested against the open door, keeping watch while the rest of them were inside playing and trying on the different clothes. Warren didn't like the smell of the city. It reminded him of an old city in the Outland, the city of Heric. That city was the home of a fierce battle hundreds of years before Warren was born. The battle had killed everyone on both sides. No one was left to claim victory in that town. Thousands of people had lost their lives. The city had lain in ruins for all of those years with no one to rebuild it. It had been some time since Warren had crossed through Heric and to that day it was still a pile of rubble. The city served as a constant reminder that there were battles that nobody won. However, not too many people knew the true story behind Heric because it had been turned into a legend by this time.

The only comfort this place gave Warren was the feeling of increased power. With that, he could defend those who he loved. Being here was like the dream that he had in the desert. There his power was increased tenfold. The unsettling sensation deep down was that this place did not feel real. He was waiting to wake up, somewhere more familiar.

Warren stood quietly at the door waiting on Toby to finish. He stood his ground in silence as something in one of the upper rooms across the street caught his attention. A face gazed down at him through the shadows though it was not trying to hide itself from him. It was an Imp. Warren didn't move and neither did it. It just sat there looking at him with its beady red eyes and a scary smirk spread across his face.

"Hey," Toby said, slapping Warren on the shoulder. Warren jumped, stretching out his hand at Toby. "Hey now, I didn't mean to give you a heart attack. How do I look?" Warren looked back up at the window, and the imp was gone. "Tell me the truth." Warren looked back at Toby, looking him over from head to toe and shook his head in disappointment. Toby was wearing a pair of tan khaki pants with a bright orange hooded sweater and a pair of Nike sneakers. To set off his personal style, he had a denim jacket with the sleeves cut off; it was buttoned halfway up. "Well, I'm sorry. Some people just can't pull off the whole Johnny Cash look." Toby's head slid back and forth, adding attitude to his statement.

"How effective do you think you'll be at blending in, wearing that?" Warren asked, looking around for any sign of the Imp.

"I might not be the best at deep recon, but I'll blend in with a crowd better than you." Toby replied, brushing off his coat.

"Look at us!" Nell shouted as she came out of the store with her brother. Naven followed them. Both of the children were wearing new clothes and jackets.

"You look good," Warren said not paying attention to them.

"I told you he wouldn't like them," Abe said. "He's more of a necessity-only kind of guy."

"We've got to move!" Warren said, spotting the Imp through one of the ground floor windows.

Toby and Naven took the lead with Abe and Nell following after. Warren stood his ground for a moment waiting for the Imp to make its move. Warren locked eyes with the foul creature ready for a fight. After a short moment, Warren realized that it wasn't going to make its move, not while he was watching, so he decided to follow the others.

"What's going on?" Toby shouted not turning back.

"Trouble," Warren answered. "We've got Imps on our trail."

"What?" Toby shouted, stopping midstride and spinning around. "We can take 'em."

Standing in the middle of the street was a man dressed in a dark blue cloak. He had a think white beard with soft blue eyes. The look in his eyes seemed to ask why the boys were running through the streets.

"Where's the fire?" the man had a thick British accent.

Warren and the others regrouped around Toby once they realized that the Imp was not following. They did not recognize the man, and it did not seem like he belonged here either. Was this the person they were looking for? No one asked, waiting for him to offer up the information first. There was no need for them to tip their hand just yet.

"Who are you?" Toby asked. "Why are you here?"

"I'm just watching the time pass by in this world," the man offered. "And you?"

"We're looking for a friend of ours," Warren said, still looking around for the Imp.

"Don't worry about those Imps." The man waved them forward, trying to get them to relax. "They're a part of this world." He spoke as he moved for a bench that was sitting on the sidewalk.

"What do you mean?" Warren asked.

"The purpose of the Imps is to keep people from lingering around in the gate." The man sat down on the bench as if he was getting ready to tell a long story. "You see, it is unnatural for people to linger here, so they keep this place clean. This is the way between worlds. It would be disastrous if people could just wonder in and out. You see, this place corrodes a person's psyche, causing them to see it as if it were a dream. Spend too much time here, and you will go mad. You should feel a great power come to you in this place, and you feel like you could be run over with a truck and remain unhurt, but this is only a dream world."

"Are you trying to tell us that those Imps are our friends?" Toby could not ask the question with a straight face. He found the idea ridiculous.

"No more than spiders are your friends because they get rid of flies." The man shrugged off the question no different than if he had just been asked the time of the day.

Warren found Toby's attitude disturbing. He was becoming accustomed with talking to this man and in this environment of all places. Warren could see the Imps, scurrying about their business, most not even giving them a second glance. However, Toby and this man were talking casually about philosophy and the usefulness of spiders and Imps. It was as if neither of them actually understood the danger they were in.

Interrupting their conversation, Warren stepped between them to ask, "Why don't they attack? Their job is to keep us from staying too long, right?"

"It seems that there is another person out there, causing problems for them," the man explained. "I would say that they are letting things even out just to see what happens."

Toby's eyes brightened, asking, "We're looking for a friend of ours, could that be who is causing trouble?"

"No, I doubt it," the man said. "I think the person you're looking for is being pursued by him."

"Pursued?" Toby asked, stepping forward. "Are you saying our friend is being chased by someone?" He reached his hand out, looking to grasp something; the gate obviously affecting his personality more than the others. "We got to save them!"

"Hold on," Warren said, wanting to gain control of the situation. "Who is this troublemaker? What does he have to do with our friend?"

"You'd better hurry," the man said, standing to his feet. He turned, heading the opposite direction. "They're down by the coast, tearing up the warehouse district. Keep heading down this street, and you'll run right into them."

"What about you?" Toby hollered after him. He was concerned about the man, worried if he'd make it all right by himself.

"I'll be fine, but you'd better hurry." The man just waved them on as he walked by.

Turning sharply to Toby, Warren slapped his shoulder, breaking his attention off the man. "What are you doing?" Warren whispered. Anger was buried in his voice, upset with how easily Toby seemed to be distracted.

"What, he might be in danger if Imps are running around. I thought he might have wanted to tag along."

Shaking his head in contempt, Warren jabbed his finger in the air, pointing at Toby as he spoke. "You know nothing about him. He could be our enemy!"

Toby shrugged. "He doesn't seem like an enemy. I thought he was nice."

"You just met him. You know nothing about him." Warren was adamant about his point.

Toby stole a quick glance at the children, making his own point.

"That's different!" Warren demanded even though there was little difference between either of their actions. "Are you even awake?"

"I think it's this place," Naven interrupted. His demeanor was different, more confident and outspoken. This caught both Toby's and Warren's attention though they did not say anything.

"He may be right," Warren admitted, lowering his head in submission. "This world definitely feels different. Maybe it is affecting our judgment too."

"Then let's find our friend and get out of here." Toby placed his hand on Warren's shoulder, letting him know that he was still there for him.

Warren smiled back, comforted by the words. He never really had a substantial friendship with anyone before. As a Warrian, several people looked up to him, but no one he would actually consider a friend. For the first time, this boy here actually seemed like he could be one.

Taking a step in the direction that they were told to go, Warren felt a crunch under his foot. Everyone moved in to see what it was. A crude-looking knife was broken into three pieces by Warren's boot heel. It was made entirely out of bone.

"What's that?" Toby asked, knowing what it was but actually wondering where it had come from.

"I think it's from our friend," Warren said, looking up in the direction they were heading. "Maybe we should hurry."

Toby and Naven nodded in unison.

The building was cold and damp. The salt water from the ocean ate holes through the steel sheathing used to cover the walls, turning what remained to a dark red. Barrels of oil towered over wooden crates and slats of other materials. A girl, just over fourteen, shivered in the corner of a warehouse—hungry, cold, and scared. Curled up behind a stack of rusty old barrels, she rocked herself back and forth. Her once beautiful dress was now ripped and ragged. It had been several days since she first started running from the mysterious man. She had never seen him before, but for some reason, he had kidnapped her and now was toying with her. Two days earlier she had lost her shoes, and now her feet had cuts and blisters. Closing her eyes, she desperately hoped for a few minutes of sleep. Her body was exhausted, her feet ached, and the wounds that she carried bled. The girl forced her eyelids closed while she faintly struggled to stay alert. She slowly drifted off into the comforting blackness when a loud bang woke her. There stood the man that had been chasing her. It was the same man that William and Lee had met in the bar though of course she did not know this. He had knocked over several of the barrels that the girl took refuge behind, and the scattered barrels were now blocking her escape.

"Sorry, girl," Alex said with a cold face. The sport was no longer any fun. The prey was all out of fight. "Game's over." He pulled out a bone knife from under his coat and raised it, ready to strike. The girl covered her face, lost in hopelessness. Without warning, the man spun to the side and jumped over one of the barrels he had knocked over. He barely missed Warren's Mission's Level claws from ripping into his side. Before Warren landed on the ground, a bright flash of light came over him, transwarping back into his human form. The transformation took a matter of seconds. As he landed on the ground, he extended his arm out, creating a long flame in the shape of a whip.

"A fire former?" Alex said. "That's impressive."

"As if I'd be interested in impressing you," Warren said, standing his ground. "It's time for you to go," Warren said to the girl without taking his eyes off this new foe. Pointing to Alex, he asked, "Who are you?"

"My name is Alex. I am of a race known as the Multaroe. We are few and far between." Alex looked over at the entrance where he saw Toby with Abe motioning for the girl to join them. "He was right. She would bring you out of the woodwork."

"If you're looking for a fight, you just found one," Warren said, swinging his fire whip through the air. A strand of flame flew through the air directed at Alex who did his best to dodge it, but in the end, a tip of the flame snagged his arm, burning him. "Kale's brother or not, you won't touch them." Warren had heard the legends of the Multaroe from Kale and knew this was his brother. He had also witnessed their *power* and knew how strong they were.

Alex growled through the pain and charged. Warren tried to get another swing, but Alex grabbed his arm in time to stop him. Warren dropped his whip, and as it fell, it simply burned away into nothingness. Alex kneed Warren in the stomach, dropping him to his knees, but Warren didn't give up. He rolled out of the way and hopped to his feet. Alex spun, trying to connect a spin kick with Warren, but a wall of fire protected him from the blow. Warren jumped back while Alex was distracted, trying to extinguish the flames that clung to his clothes.

"Be that way!" Alex yelled, raising his hand in the air. A fierce trembling came from the ground as Alex used his power. Warren placed his hands in front of him, creating a sword from flames in a similar manner as he did his whip. Suddenly, a tower of water, in the form of a dragon, rose from out of the ground with a violent burst of energy. Warren stood his ground, ready for anything. Alex pointed toward Warren. Without mercy, the dragon lunged forward, its mouth wide open. Warren raised his sword preparing for the impact to come. Surprisingly, the heat from the sword was enough to cut through the dragon as it attacked, splitting it in two. As soon as the dragon started to fail, it collapsed in on itself. The water flooded over Warren in its wake, crashing through the rear of the building. The waves were massive and powerful, and the current was more than enough to sweep Warren out of the hole. Pleased with his accomplishment, Alex looked around the warehouse and realized he was all alone. Comprehending that they had all gotten away, frustration overcame him. He lowered his head looking for a trail. Once he had realized that he water had washed away all traces of the group, he stormed out of the building.

DESPERATION

The road had been long and rough on William and Lee. They had tried to head back for Warren and Toben, but they were not at the store. It was starting to feel like old times again, and William didn't like it. The last time Lee had been taken from the group, kidnapped by the royalty of Ram. Now Warren and Toben were missing. *At least Warren has someone familiar with this world*, William thought to himself. He could not help but feel that something was trying to separate them, forcing them to jump through hoops for its amusement.

William pulled his motorcycle into a gas station just outside of Oklahoma City. It was a charming little station with a built-in garage out back. Lee climbed off the back of the bike to stretch his legs.

"I don't know why you didn't just grab a bike of your own," William said, pulling the nozzle from the pump.

"I don't know how to ride a motorcycle," Lee said, rolling his eyes. He was exhausted and irritable. "Besides, maybe we can find a car around here."

"Good luck," William said sarcastically, slapping the gas pump out of anger. "Great, it doesn't work."

"Hold on," Lee said, waving at him to wait. "I'll look for the pump switch."

"Maybe that isn't a good idea," William said, calling after him, but Lee didn't look back. *Why does he have to be so stubborn?* William thought. *He's so undisciplined. Why can't he just listen?*

Lee had been riding with William too long. He was starting to tire of listening to him take charge of every situation. Walking away was the best thing for him to do at the moment. They needed to stay focused, and getting into a fight was the last thing that Lee wanted to do.

Entering the convenience store, Lee noticed that all the lights were out. After a quick survey of the store, he found the register located just right of the door. He hopped over the counter and found a row of light switches marked "pumps." Flipping the switches, a soft hum filled the air. The pumps and lights turned on.

Lee gave William a thumbs-up, letting him know that everything was ready to go. William dropped the nozzle and grabbed his gun. He took off for the front door, running as fast as he could. Curious, Lee turned around to see what the commotion was all about. A woman stood in front of the counter. She had long black hair that covered most of her face and clothes that looked as if she just escaped from a mental hospital. The blank expression on her face sent chills up Lee's spine.

"Are you okay?" Lee said nervously.

William burst through the door ready for a fight. The woman stood there without moving. "Get over here, Lee. We have to go."

"How would you like me to do that?" Lee asked, agitated at his predicament. He remained frozen, trying not to even move his lips as he spoke. "She's blocking all of my exits."

"I said get over here!" William demanded. *How did she sneak up on him?* William thought. *Lee has better hearing than Warren.* Fear crept up inside him. This person had to have some kind of special powers, and William didn't want to take a chance.

Lee stood up straight, challenging the woman. "Move now!" Lee pointed to the back corner of the store. "Out of my way."

The woman looked up at him.

"Lee, what are you doing?" William said. "Get out of there!"

"I am desperate. I am lost, and it was my husband who betrayed me to the darkness of my own Trepidation."

"Who are you?" Lee asked.

"Don't make conversation!" William ordered. "We have to attack."

"He gave me this ring and told me that we would be together forever. This ring is my Sin. It gives me power, and without it, I will die." The woman raised her hand to reveal two rings on her hand. On her index finger she had a beautiful ring made from gold. The ring housed several stones in it—ruby, emerald, and others that Lee couldn't identify. It appeared to be eating away her flesh, rotting around where the ring touched. The finger was turning black around the band with open wounds. On her ring finger was an old rusty ring with a single diamond on it. It was an engagement ring, ruined by age. The ring itself looked like it would be a health hazard. "He tricked our children and destroyed their bodies, and I did nothing to stop him. For that I am ashamed and will die cold and alone as I should. I'm so tired of running." She slipped the expensive ring off her finger, gripping it tightly. "Do not stay and fight. That is what they want you to do. We were made in the image of people so that you might get used to attacking."

"What do you mean?" Lee asked. Deep down he knew something was wrong, but why was this enemy helping them? William lowered his weapon only by a few inches, interested in what she had to say. Both boys could sense strings being pulled from behind a curtain, but they had no idea who it was pulling them.

"They want you to get used to fighting with people who look human. That way, when you actually get home, you'll be desensitized to killing and attacking people. You've got to stop fighting. Just stop! Run away!"

William and Lee stole a glance at each other, wondering what this woman was babbling on about. They contemplated leaving, but Lee wanted to get to the bottom of her original statement.

"And that's why they want us to attack you?" Lee asked, stepping forward. He wasn't buying it. There was something else.

The woman looked at Lee as if he knew nothing. "They'll start you out small, and over time, they gradually progress you to something deeper until they finally having you attacking God himself." The woman was about in tears. She threw the ring across the counter, almost hitting Lee with it. As she turned into a pillar of dust, Lee could see that it was a painful process. "You're just too immature to understand it now," she said through the tears. "But remember my words, violence and fighting will only lead to rebellion."

"What were you thinking?" William said, walking over to the counter. "She could have killed you!" William pushed the pillar of dust, knocking it to the floor.

"What are you doing?" Lee shouted. He reached out for the woman even though he knew he'd never reach her.

"She's an enemy, and now she's dead," William said.

"She was a person!" Lee demanded. "She helped us."

"I don't care. You're jeopardizing both of our lives and our mission. You're taking too many risks."

"Oh, please! I haven't taken as many risks as you. Besides, I don't care what you think because you weren't standing here in my shoes."

"I'm an experienced warrior," William demanded, trying to justify himself. "I am a Guardian."

"You were only in the Outland for six more months than I was, and you got hurt just as many times as I did!" Lee shouted.

Suddenly, William stopped and gave a blank stare out the window. "Oh no," he murmured. Outside, standing by the road, was a deranged-looking man in a loosened straightjacket. He had a twisted smile on his face as if it had frozen during a laughing spell. In one hand, he held a cleaver and in the other he held a lit road flare. Lee looked over at the bike. Lying down on the ground, the nozzle was still pumping gasoline.

"You left the pump running?" Lee asked, backing away from the window.

"I was in a hurry," William said, backing up as well.

With a chuckle, the man threw the flare toward the bike. Lee and William ran for the back door of the building. William jumped into the door, knocking it down. The door tore off its hinges, hitting the ground. As the two ran for their lives, the explosion shattered the little building into splinters, burying the two Guardians in the debris.

Once he regained consciousness, William sat up, pushing the scattered boards off his body. "Lee?" he called out. Lee quickly sat up and yelped. "You're alive!" William exclaimed, getting to his feet to help him. Lee grabbed his shoulder, which had a piece of wood sticking out of it. Lee groaned as he pulled it out, releasing a wave of blood with it. "Hey, man," William said. "That doesn't look too good."

"Stand back," Lee said. He stood to his feet with his head lowered for a moment. The white light of a transwarp tunnel covered his body as he changed his form to that of a Kalymor. Lee's feet were elongated, made to support all of his weight on balls of his feet, lifting the heels in the air. His ears were like that of an elf, stretching along the side of his head. Lee's clothes changed too. He was wearing a white shimmering shirt with gold embroidering around the trim, along with a matching pair of pants. Lee rotated his shoulder, which was now healed through the power of the transwarp tunnel.

"Are you feeling better?" William asked.

"I'll feel better if we get that loser. What was wrong with him?" Lee asked.

"He was a loon," William said. "What normal person walks around in a straightjacket with a meat cleaver in his hand?"

"Good point," Lee said, chuckling.

William tapped Lee on the shoulder and pointed behind him with a smile on his face. "Can you drive that?"

The building was ripped open from the blast, revealing a gently used jeep sitting where the garage once stood. "How far is it to New York?"

"Maybe two days if we drive straight through," William said, not even sure.

"We'll have to find another gas station." Lee chuckled.

The two of them ran for the jeep, excitement filling them. Turning the keys that were left in the ignition, Lee quickly determined that the tank was empty. Their excitement quickly turned to despair. Their hope was crushed.

"How far is the next station?" William asked.

Lee looked down the highway. He could see a city on the horizon. "Well, we can walk to the city, hoping to find a car, or push this thing down there, hoping for a gas station."

William groaned at the thought.

Warren watched the street from an upper window, not too far from where he was attacked by Alex. Warren was following Alex, doing his best to move silently in the shadows. He needed to either stop him before he found Toby and the others or find the others and escape. There was no doubt that Alex was strong, but he was not sure when the best time would be to make his move.

Warren moved with the shadows, stalking his prey. He felt like an animal again. His instincts took over. Darkness veiled him and he became one with it. The one thing that was still haunting Warren was the fact that Alex was a hunter too. They both shared a connection with their surroundings. Warren was sure that Alex could sense him moving.

Alex stepped into one of the buildings across the street. Warren stopped, frozen with anticipation. *Is that where Toby is?* he thought to himself. The boards behind Warren creaked. Warren leapt forward, throwing two shurikens behind him. Warren landed in the light, facing his opponent. Alex was standing behind him. The two shurikens stuck into a shield made of bone. As the shield retracted back into his arm, the two shurikens fell to the ground. *The Silamon blood trait.* Warren kicked himself as he realized what happened. *They can teleport in the darkness.*

"What's the matter, Warren?" Alex asked. "You don't want to play?"

"You want to play?" Warren asked. Flames engulfed Warren's fist as the anger burned from within. Warren ran after him, head-on. Alex used a wind blast to push himself back. The blast, likewise, pushed Warren back too. Alex disappeared into the shadows, appearing behind Warren. He spun, deflecting Alex's attack, countering with a wall of fire. The flame rushed toward Alex, forcing him in the opposite direction.

Alex slammed into the warehouse wall. It was proof that there was a solid element behind Warren's flame. He brushed himself off, ready for round two, as he made a mental note about the fire that Warren held. This was no ordinary fire former. He'd have to be careful. Even if the flame didn't do much damage to him, the physical element could.

Alex rushed for Warren, dodging two fireballs that he threw at him. Alex punched Warren in the gut, followed by a kick, slamming him into the floor. Warren rolled to the side, transwarped into his Trail's Level form, disappearing into the shadows. This was a difficult place to fight a Trial's Level Warrian. Trial's level Warrians can move swiftly in any environment. Their catlike bodies are able to squeeze in and out of tight places easily. Alex felt the lionlike claws rip into his back. Alex spun around, looking for the assailant, but Warren was gone just as fast. He used his Silamon powers to heal the scratches, trying to calm himself to listen to the sounds around him. For the size that Warren was, in his trial's form, Alex could hear the air being pushed past his body. He waited until Warren was attacking before he made his move.

Alex ducked past the attack, countering it with a kick of his own. Alex's foot landed across Warren's jaw, tossing him to the side. Warren momentarily lost consciousness, causing him to transwarp back into his human form. He bounced across the floor, sliding to a stop.

"You should have been killed from the beginning," Alex said as he approached. Warren regained consciousness, shaking his head just before looking up at him. "Amos and his cronies just couldn't stomach it, weaklings, all of them," Alex spat, pointing at him as though he were the enemy. "You don't celebrate when the enemy comes into your land, you destroy them." Alex was referring to the Warriors entering the Outland. "Any last words?" Alex asked, amused with himself.

"Geronimo!" Toby screamed. Alex spun around just in time to see Toby come down on his arm with his sword. Toby sliced sideways, trying to dig deep into Alex's ribs. Alex jumped back, dodging Toby's sword. Toby jumped over Warren's body, his sword raised to defend against Alex's attacks. Alex wasted no time on reforming his arm using his Silamon powers. "It's over for you," Toby said, charging while swinging his sword horizontally. He aimed at Alex's rib cage again. Alex jumped over the sword, kicking Toby in the face with the heel of his boot. Toby tumbled backwards, giving Warren room to hit him with his fire whip. Alex winced at the crack, rebounding in time for Toby to knock his feet out from under him. Alex didn't give them much time before jumping back to his feet. Once he gained a solid footing, Alex hit them both with a blast of wind, blasting the back wall out with the mighty gust.

Splinters rained from the ceiling as Toby struggled to climb to his feet. Warren moved to aid his friend. Alex escaped out the hole he had made, leaving them alone for the time being. He had other things to do.

"What was that about?" Toby asked, gaining his breath.

"I don't think he's that interested in us," Warren answered, taking in his surroundings. The blast of wind ripped through the upper level, tearing at the ceiling and compromising the integrity of the structure.

"Why is he attacking us?" Toby asked, stretching out his back.

"We're getting in his way," Warren answered. "He's hunting down that girl, but I don't know what he's trying to achieve."

"I just can't believe a Multaroe could be that strong," Toby said, rubbing his arms. "I took his arm off, and he just grew a new one back."

"All of the powers in the Outland," Warren said, slightly irritated with Toby's inability to stay focused.

"Do you think he has the powers of a zombie?" Toby asked.

"What?"

"You know, the zombies in Daniel. Do you think he has their powers?"

Warren shook his head at the bizarre question. "Zombies don't have powers," Warren insisted. "And besides, zombies, and Lymures for that matter, were made as a product of the Black King's corruption. They're not legitimate species in the Outland."

"Wow," Toby said, staring into space for a moment. "What kind of powers do Lymures have?" Warren shook his head walking away. "What?" Toby ran to catch up with him.

"Are our friends safe?" Warren asked.

"Yeah, they're bunkered down away from here. Naven's on top of it," Toby reassured. "We probably shouldn't go back there right now."

"I know," Warren agreed. "Alex is probably watching us. But we need to get back to the train station. Get the others to safety."

It was the height of the afternoon, and the sun was beating down upon the earth with all of its fury. William sat in the driver's seat, steering the jeep, while Lee was pushing. William was surprised at how fast Lee was able to push the vehicle. For a scrawny person, Lee had some muscle and stamina. They had gone for almost five miles now with Lee pushing the whole way. The city was still twelve miles away, but William felt they were making excellent progress.

"I'm done," Lee said, leaning on the jeep as it slowly came to a stop. "I can't keep it up."

Once the car had stopped, William hopped out of the driver's seat, tossing Lee a bottle of water. William and Lee were able to scrounge up some supplies from the ruins of the gas station.

"Time for you to take a break. I'll take up the next shift." William braced himself against the back of the jeep.

Lee shuffled his way to the driver's seat to steer as William gave his shot at pushing the jeep. Lee growled slightly as he turned the wheel to the right. Lee was too tired to have seen the gas station up to the right. He would have finished out the push if he had seen it.

The jeep pulled up to one of the pumps. "Don't leave the jeep this time," Lee said, getting out. He walked toward the store to turn on the pumps. "I'm not pushing the next one."

"Just keep your eyes open," William shot back. "I don't want to have to save your butt again." Lee was able to just laugh off the insult. He was far too exhausted to be concerned with words.

Lee entered the store with his eyes and ears alert. William was right. He didn't want something to get the drop on him again. This store was maintained much better than the last one. The shelves were stocked. The glass coolers were still clean with the exception of a little dust that had accumulated over time. Lee hopped over the counter, quickly flipping on the pumps. He spun back around, looking to see if anyone was trying to sneak up on him. No one was there. Lee hopped back over the counter and joined back up with William.

"The place is well stocked," Lee said. "Is there anything that we need?"

"I think we're stocked up," William announced. "It wouldn't hurt to have some more water for the trip."

"Just what we need," Lee decided. "We won't take any more. There may be others who need it too."

William nodded, pulling out his shotgun. "Do you think anyone's in there?" William wasn't malicious in his thinking, just cautious.

"No, I doubt it. But I thought the last place was empty too." Lee looked back to the entrance of the store. "You concerned about the crazy man?"

"Who knows where he ran off to," William stated. "I just want to keep an eye out for him. I don't want him getting the drop on us again."

The pump snapped off. The tank was full, and they were ready to get going. William replaced the nozzle in the pump and closed the gas cap. Footsteps rushed him from the side. The crazy man with the cleaver tackled him, trying to cut him with it. William was able to block the knife with his shotgun, pushing him back.

Lee came in from behind, struggling to pull the crazy man off his friend. The man pushed Lee away with an incredible force, knocking him to the ground. The man stopped struggling with William, just leaning forward and applying pressure. He grabbed the shotgun with one hand, raising the knife with the other. With a twisted smirk on his face, he dropped the cleaver. William winced, waiting for the impact to tear into his flesh.

In a flash, Lee was able to catch the cleaver, swinging it at the crazy man. The man ducked under the swing, rolling off William and away from the fight. Lee stopped, his face twisting in pain. Something about this knife made his blood burn from within. The veins in his forehead began to rise out of his skin. He felt an intense pressure pushing out from his skull. He could feel the madness calling him. It was the same madness that called to him in Mear, thirsting for blood. Lee swung the cleaver again, ripping into the side panel of the jeep. Madness twisted in his mind, curling onto his lips. Lee rushed past William, aiming for the crazed man. He swung again, digging deep into the gas pump. The madness screamed in his ears, begging him to swing again, calling, pleading for blood. Lee used the resistance from the pump to pull his hand away, collapsing to the ground. He laid there in fear. He knew that the madness had overtaken him. It had control of his body, pulling him along like a puppet. Lee's body quaked, trying to get back on his feet, knowing that the fight was still being fought.

William jumped over Lee's body, grabbing the cleaver from its resting place. William wasn't a fan of knives, but he hoped that it would give him some sort of advantage. He swung the cleaver, trying to dig the blade into the crazy man's flesh. William's veins began to surface on his forehead. His movement started to loosen, no longer sharp and precise. William became infuriated. He wanted to tear away the man's flesh. Madness had engulfed him. He became obsessed with killing. A scream tore away from his lips as he delved into the madness. He quickly felt frustrated, unable to land a single blow with the cleaver. Infuriated, William threw the cleaver away. He raised his shotgun, wanting, yearning to see the man explode. William stopped. His mind was starting to clear. He became conscious of what he was thinking; appalled by his own thoughts. It was unbelievable what had come over him. Suddenly the words of the woman, back at the other gas station, filled his mind about violence and killing.

The man pounced on William as he stood there contemplating his own actions. William was once again on the ground with the man on top of him. He refused to allow the thought of killing this man to enter into his mind, not now. All he could do was keep the shotgun between them, hoping that the crazy man did not get in a good blow.

Lee was up off the ground by now, watching the madman trying to bite William's face. He was still shaky, but he knew that he needed to do something. Lee tackled the man, pulling him off William. Now the problem shifted to Lee who had the crazy man pinned to the ground, kicking and screaming.

"I can't hold him for long!" Lee screamed.

William hobbled over to the jeep, starting it up. "I'm coming," William hollered back. "Get ready to get into the jeep!"

William unhooked the gas pump, pulling the hose over to where the cleaver was lying. *I hope this works*, William thought. "Hey!" William shouted, getting the madman's attention. William squeezed the pump handle. The man went into a fit as the gasoline poured onto the cleaver. William released the handle, but the man's frenzy didn't subside. *Perfect.* William dropped the handle, making sure the gasoline wasn't still pumping. *I don't need another incident like last time.* "Now!" William shouted.

Lee released the man as they ran for the jeep. Lee jumped into the driver's seat, stepping on the gas as the man picked up the cleaver. The crazy man cradled the knife for a moment and then took off after the two. Lee and William looked back to see how the man faired. He was running faster than most normal humans, but there was no way he could catch up to them.

"What was that thing?" Lee asked, exhausted.

"Who knows?" William started. "But he was intense."

"Was he a Temp?" Lee asked himself. "That cleaver he had, it controlled me, put crazy thoughts in my head."

"It made me want to kill him." William faded out. "No, it made me want to mutilate him."

"Should we go back?" Lee asked, afraid that William would want to.

William thought about it for a moment, afraid that Lee would want to. "I think we should leave well enough alone," William said, nodding excessively. "I think he's out of our league, and that one woman said that we shouldn't fight them." Her face flooded his mind, concerned about what she had said. Holding on to that cleaver made him question his resolve to finish this fight. He wasn't sure if he ever wanted to see something killed again.

PAST STORIES

Warren looked out of the second story window of a factory. He was about a mile from where the group was originally attacked by Alex. Warren had his coat draped over the girl whom Alex had attacked and left her lying on a table. She had been curled up there for nine hours now, sleeping restlessly, while mystery still surrounded her. Meanwhile, Toby was watching out another window, trying his best not to be seen. Naven was quietly playing with Nell and Abe in the middle of the factory floor.

"What's wrong with you?" Toby asked as Warren approached. "Is it the girl?"

"It's this whole situation," Warren answered. "Alex is too strong, and I don't have enough experience using my flame attacks yet." Warren looked down at his feet, taking in a deep breath of the damp air. "He can beat me."

"Don't say that," Toby said. "You are a good fighter, and together we'll take him down." Toby could tell that Warren was not comforted by the pep talk, so he took a seat next to the girl. Toby reached into his pocket, taking out the goggles that he wore in the Outland. Examining the holes and torn parts, he asked Warren, "Do you know why I used to wear these?"

"You lived in the mining town of Granite," Warren said, not sure where the conversation was going. "Human miners have to wear eye protection down in the mine." He took a seat next to Toby, thinking about what the question meant. That was when it came to him. "You weren't a miner. You were an inventor or handyman, weren't you?"

Toby nodded, continuing his story. "Inside Raptor villages, I was the Carmel. In other villages, I was just a boy from Granite, a commoner." Toby gripped the goggles tighter, letting the material fall apart in his hands. "I never wanted to be some kind of protector or even a warrior." Toby tossed the torn goggles across the floor. "But I cannot be that commoner anymore. We have responsibilities now, like to take care of this girl and figure out what's going on here. I am now ready to except the responsibilities of the Carmel. I will be a protector."

"Are you really Toby Raven?" the girl asked, sitting up on the table with Warren's coat still draped over her shoulders. "Are you really the last Carmel of the Raptors?"

"What do you mean last?" Toby stood up, turning to face her more directly. "Did something happen to them?"

She smiled at him, excited to see him. "You are a legend. I've heard all your stories."

"Who are you?" Warren asked, stepping in. "Why was that man after you?"

"My name is Lillian and I am…I was the queen of Ram," she said, looking away in disappointment.

"Lily!" Warren said surprised.

"Do I know you?" Lily asked, looking from Warren to Toby and back again.

"My name is Warren. I was a Warrian in the Outland."

"Warren?" Lily held her breathe, not sure what to make of it. "Is your namesake that of the famous Warrian—"

Warren didn't let her finish the sentence. "I am Warren of Weremore near the Eastern sea of Cam."

"You were the one who saved me from Dr. Emmit?" It was obvious that she did not believe it.

"But you were only eight years old back then," Warren said. "How can this be?"

"That was six years ago," Lily replied. "Everyone thought you had perished when the Black Castle fell into the canyon at the End of the World."

"The castle did collapse?" Warren asked, remembering the sensation of the building toppling though he had thought it was a dream.

Lily nodded, looking at Toby. "I heard that you were there too, but I only remember seeing you once. I thought it was a dream. It was while I was sick right after Emmit experimented on me. I wasn't sure if it was real."

"It was," Toby assured her. "But you said that I was the last Carmel. Why didn't the Raptors elect another one? What happened to them?"

"After you reunited the Raptors and the Dogens, after the attack on Logan, they felt that there was no one else who could replace you. You are the greatest hero of the Calkcaus Empire."

"The Calkcaus what?" Toby asked, surprised by this unfamiliar phrase.

"The Calkcaus Empire." Confusion riddled her face as she explained. "After the fall of the Black King, everything changed though I guess you weren't there for that." She looked away sheepishly for not thinking of that sooner. "The nations and tribes came together in an effort to celebrate peace. We formed a governing body to mediate between the nations and became a single empire. Peace reigns throughout the region, and hope is bright for the future.

"In honor of your part in bringing that peace, the Raptors have built three statues. The one in Mezue depicts you with a sword on the final battlefield, which they've renamed *Combonetue* also in your honor. It means 'no turning back.' Then there's one in Logan that holds the image of you and Naven joined together in the form of a dragon. It was the last form the people ever saw you in. My favorite one is sitting in New Granite. It depicts you both sitting in a field. It's a serene sculpture."

"So everything is okay back there?" Toby sat back down, letting out a sigh of relief.

"Okay as one would expect," Lily explained. "It's not like the world is without its problems, but we are not fighting over our petty differences anymore."

Toby smiled. He was glad to hear the news.

"But what happened to you?" Lily pulled the jacket on as she sat up all the way. "The Carmel looks the same as the day he left, and I am sure you are no different, Warren." Lily turned her attention to the boy who claimed to be the famous Warrian. Her mind was still in conflict with his claim, but she did see him transwarp in front of her.

"Time does not seem to add up," Warren started to explain. "Too much time seems to have passed here too. More time than leaving would have allowed."

"Maybe it has something to do with how we got here," Toby said. "I saw this movie once that—"

Warren raised his hand, not wanting to hear the explanation. "The problem is, we now have two people who we need back to the Outland, and we still need to get you back home."

"Finally," Alex said, entering the room. "I have you all in one place." The group was caught completely off guard. They had become complacent and never even heard him coming.

"Naven, run!" Toby shouted as he stepped between Alex and the group. Alex ran straight at him. Toby reached his hand out, and his sword appeared in his grip. Alex jumped, landing on his chest, knocking him to the floor.

Pushing off Toby's chest, Alex preformed an impressive forward flip landing in front of Abe. With a bone dagger in his hand, Alex cut off Abe's ear, starting his transformation into dust. Alex punched Abe in the stomach, scattering the dust that had already started to form into the air. By the time his body would have landed, Abe was already gone.

The air was so thick with the fine dust that Alex didn't see Warren snatch up the earring that Abe left behind or the sucker punch that followed into his gut. Warren's fists were engulfed with his flame. He was burning hotter than it had ever been before. After several hits, Warren saw his opportunity. He wrapped his arms around Alex, pushing them both out of the second story window. They hit the ground hard, but Warren was able to get up, landing on top of his opponent. He stepped back about twenty feet as Alex's body began to move. Enraged, Warren watched as Alex used the powers of the Silamon to repair the damage from the fall. With the power to create and recreate bone and flesh, Alex was certainly a hard rival to beat, but Warren wasn't about to lose that easily.

Alex stood boldly in front of his target. He was ready to finish this fight. By now, Naven had enough time to escape with Lily and Nell. Toby met up with Warren downstairs and charged Alex, swinging his sword aimlessly hoping to land a blow, but Alex maneuvered around them with ease. Alex clearly had the advantage of a Kalymor's agility. With a final swing downward, Alex gave Toby a sharp jab in his gut and pushed him back. Toby landed face up, gasping for air. Alex placed his hand on the ground and vines shot up, tangling Toby in their web.

A sizzling wave of fire raced for Alex as the sound of Warren's whip snapped. However, Alex was able to roll out of the way before it made an impact. Placing his hand against the ground once more, a large wave of dirt and stone rushed toward Warren. Warren easily dodged the wave, but when he took comfort in his safety, the wave had turned and was on its way back around. The pile of dirt knocked him to the ground.

While Warren was smashed into the ground, two fireballs engulfed the vines that held Toby down. Toby frantically patted at the fire on him as the vines gave way. Naven spit out a third fireball at Alex, but he extended his hand letting it hit his palm. "Now, now," Alex said. "I'm immune to fire. There is no power or ability that any Outlander holds that can overcome me. The Multaroe rules the Outland."

Not to be detoured from protecting his friends, Naven rushed toward Alex. By now Toby was free and had his sword in hand. This time Toby held more control over his swings. Naven lunged at Alex trying to sink his teeth into him. Once Alex dodged Naven's attack, Toby came close to making contact with his sword. Waiting for Toby's sword to clear, Naven took a step back and then jumped at Alex, hoping to dig his claws into him, but once again Alex was able to avoid Naven's razor-sharp claws. It was a like a dance, everyone moving in sync. As Naven was airborne, Alex kicked him out of the way, knocking him back a good distance. Furious, Toby brought his sword straight down hoping for a fatal blow. Instead, Alex caught it by the handle and pushed Toby down again.

Alex was able to pull the sword away from Toby and was now standing over him with his own sword pointing down at his chest. "It's your turn to die," Alex said, raising the sword. Suddenly, a bolt of lightning flashed down from out of the clouds striking the sword. Alex stood there for a moment before he fell, sprawled out on the ground. Toby got to his feet and reached out for his sword. In a flash of sparkling dust, the sword disappeared from Alex's hand, reappearing in his own. Toby waited until Naven got back on his feet before tossing the sword to the side, letting it disappear back to the place it called home.

Toby bent over, helping Warren to his feet. "I think he's dead," Toby said. "Lightning struck him."

"I doubt he is," Warren said, rubbing his neck. "Snogs have the ability to use electricity. They're known as lightning formers. He's just knocked out."

"Well, I'd say we should go ahead and scram before he wakes up," Toby offered.

Warren and Toby followed Naven to the building that he left the girls in. As they entered, Warren saw Lily comforting Nell who was crying profusely. Warren felt bad for her, but there were questions that had to be answered. "Are you hurt?" Warren asked.

Lily shook her head no.

"Why didn't you tell us you were Temps?" Toby asked.

"We didn't want you to hate us," Nell cried. "All we wanted was to be friends."

"Did we show you anything but that?" Warren asked, kneeling down beside her. Nell wrapped her arms around Warren and held on tight. "We are your friends."

After a few moments, she looked up at him with her eyes filled with tears. "Is it true?" she asked. "Is my brother really dead?"

Warren tightened his grip on the little girl. "It'll be okay," Warren said.

Nell started to breath normally. "His name was Abuse. His burden was forced upon him by our father. I am Neglect who was forgotten by our mother."

"But not by me," Warren said. "Never by us." Fear rushed over him as he raised his hand. Blood was seeping from her back. She was wounded.

Nell smiled as a warm feeling rushed over her body. "It was our fate to die here, for you to watch us die."

"What?" Toby asked, confused by the sudden statement. No one noticed him or his comments. He was like an outside observer.

Nell placed her small hand on Warren's face, tears still filling her eye as she asked, "You will stop the king of the Highland from destroying our brother, won't you? We need Vengeance. He's part of our family. You're part of our family."

"Stay with me," Warren pleaded.

Nell's face became serious as she said, "He only needs to kill you or the girl to fulfill his mission. That will ruin everything for us. We'll all be doomed then."

"What about us?" Toby asked about Naven and himself. "What is our part?"

Nell smiled, dropping her charm bracelet onto the ground.

Warren looked down in desperation to see Nell's body turning to a pillar of dust. "No." His words came out as whispers. "No. Fight it!" Both of her hands brushed up against Warren's face as her tears flowed down her dusty cheeks.

"We'll never forget you," Warren assured her. "We would have never left you."

Warren sat there in frustration for a moment. His thoughts haunted him as he held what was left of her. Rage, pity, and dozens of other emotions flooded him as he sat there. Not only did a little girl die in his arms, but there was nothing he could have done about it. Yet the most troubling thing that entered his mind was that if he moved, her little body would be destroyed. Warren squeezed a little harder, letting Nell slip through his fingers. Tears overwhelmed him as he grieved over the remains of the little girl. He screamed in rage, infuriated with what had happened.

"What happened?" Lily asked, ready to burst into tears. "What *just* happened here?"

"She was the Temp of Neglect," Toby said sternly. "Her whole life she felt abandoned and alone with no one but her brother to comfort her. She chose to die her way. After all, she was on the enemy's side. She probably couldn't bear it anymore." Toby made it sound so simple. He turned to the side, speaking to himself, under his breath. "But what was that about her brother? What was she talking about? Warren needing to watch her be killed?"

"She was released," Warren demanded, pounding the ground. "As a Temp, she was being used. Now she is free." Warren almost couldn't finish. He reached down and picked up the charm bracelet off the ground. That was when he realized that the Sins that gave them their power must have been a piece of jewelry just like Abe's earring that he had picked up. With an exasperated sigh, he got to his feet and wiped away the tears. "We have to go."

"No!" Lily yelled. "That little girl just turned to dust and all you can say is 'We have to go.' No, I can't! We have to do something. We need to avenge her somehow." Lily shouted as she took off out of the building.

Toby was ready to chase after her until he noticed that Warren wasn't going to follow. "What are you doing?" Toby asked, pointing after Lily.

"Maybe she's right," Warren said, pulling one of his pistols out of its holster. "Maybe I'm not—"

Toby punched Warren in the nose, knocking him against the wall. The gun slipped onto the ground.

"Don't you ever think about doing that!" Toby demanded, pointing his finger at Warren. "Never again! I won't stand for it."

Warren looked up at Toby with a fierce expression as he pulled Abe's earring from out of his gun holster. "Are you an idiot?" Warren asked. "What were you thinking? I would never commit suicide."

Blushing, Toby took a step back. "Sorry. It was kind of an awkward moment."

Warren shrugged off the punch, picking his gun up. "Let's go find her," Warren said bumping into Toby's shoulder. "That was a good punch."

"Really?" Toby said. "'Cause you know, I was holding back."

Lily walked through the warehouse district, thinking to herself, *I shouldn't have run away.* She was starting to kick herself for how she reacted. It wasn't what happened to the girl that made her upset, and she didn't put any blame on Warren. It was how Toby could just explain it away. *What gave him the right to just explain it away like that?* she asked herself. *How could he have no emotion about it? Saying that she was just a Temp. Did he have a heart at all?* She stopped for a moment. "I need to go back." As she turned, Alex was standing behind her.

"Sorry, girl, but you're not going anywhere." Alex's voice wasn't calm and collective like normal. Now it was rough and uneasy.

"Let her go!" Warren yelled. "I won't ask you again."

"I'm done with our little skirmishes," Alex said. "You die now!"

Rage filled Warren's heart as he swung his arm out, unleashing his fire whip. "Let's dance." The flame was a darker red than normal, no longer a bright orange.

"Vengeance?" Alex asked.

"That's right," Warren answered. "This is about vengeance. You should have never involved her or the children."

With a smile on Alex's face, he raised two fingers toward Warren. A streak of lightning shot out from Alex's hand. Warren raised his free hand, creating a massive wall of fire. The wall of fire rose from the ground and the lightning passed through as if it wasn't even there. The bolt struck Warren in the forehead. The electricity trailed around his head like a halo leaving a black mark in the center. Warren collapsed to the ground, the flames around him burned out.

"No!" Lily screamed, breaking away from Alex and running up to Warren's lifeless body. "No, don't go," Lily cried, shaking his body. "Come on, please!"

"It's no use," Alex said slowly approaching her. "He underestimated my power of electricity."

"No, he can't be dead," Lily pleaded.

"Sorry, darling, but he isn't sleeping," Alex said with a cynical smile on his face. Crying, Lily turned and ran away from him. He continued the chase, determined to finish the job.

OLD FRIENDS

Lee was asleep in the passenger seat as William drove up the interstate. The lonely darkness crept around him, chilling him to the marrow of his bones. William turned the heater up as he was playing with the radio. He was trying to get a news report, a clue to what was going on in the world. Tired of his endless pursuit of audible entertainment, he stopped on the only station that was available. It was a station playing a type of polka music. William figured it was better than nothing. Once the song was over, an announcer came on over the airwaves. "Gentle citizens of this great land give thanks for the blessing of the Trepidation and all that he has brought us."

"Oh please," William mumbled to himself.

"Remember a curfew is in effect till nine o'clock tomorrow morning and starts again at seven o'clock the following day. Also, as a special announcement, the city of Indianapolis has been closed permanently due to unexplained reasons. All violators will be executed on sight. And now we bring you more polka action."

It was at that point that William turned the radio off. "Indianapolis?" he said with curiosity. They were already heading in that direction, so he didn't have to alter his course. He set his focus on this forbidden zone in hopes that they might stumble across a clue to the mystery that seemed to shroud their situation.

The warm sun shone down on Lee's face as the purr of the engine slowly called him from his sleep. Lee kept his eyes closed for a moment. He was still in his Kalymor form and his hearing was far more acute than his eyes. He listened for William to see if he should break his cover or not. He was not entirely ready to start driving again. Unable to hear William breathing, his eyes shot open, and he sat up in his seat trying to find his bearings. The jeep had stopped, and the driver door was wide open. Unbuckling his safety belt, Lee stepped out of the vehicle. They were parked behind a three-foot wall where it seemed that an earthquake had caused a section of the road to collapse. Lee yawned while scratching his head. He didn't hear anything out of place so he didn't start to panic, but where had William gone, and why did he leave the car running? After taking a few steps forward, something caught his attention. It was the sound of crackling plastic. Lee knew it was William helping himself to one of the candy bars from the last convenience store they had stopped at for gas. Lee hopped over the wall and made a left turn where the noise was coming from. Sitting on a pile of rubble that was once a building, William looked out into the city with a set of binoculars.

"Are you sure it's safe to be sitting there?" Lee asked, scratching his head again. "This building probably collapsed for a reason."

William smiled as he lowered the binoculars. "Maybe," he said.

"Where are we?"

"Indianapolis. It's been closed off. Intruding is punishable by death."

Lee scoffed at the news. "Most of the people we've seen outside of the hospital can't even think for themselves."

William handed the binoculars over to Lee. "Straight out in front."

Lee looked through the binoculars in amazement. "There must be hundreds of them," Lee said.

"Thousands at least," William corrected. Lee stood there, staring at a massive army of humans marching across the city. Their numbers alone made them look like a swarm of black ants. "They're ready for war. Between them and the chimeras that they've unleashed upon the country, I don't think we have a good chance on getting through this thing."

"Starting to wish we could have stayed in the Outland?" Lee asked.

"They would have gone back there eventually. We're just getting a jump on them now."

"Good," Lee said with a large grin on his face. "Now where do we go from here?"

With a deep sigh, William said, "We meet up with Warren. He might not have being a human down yet, but with his phoenix fire, he does have power."

"I think we need to move on the Trepidation," Lee said. "Cut off the head and kill the snake."

"Good plan," William said. "Do you happen to know where in the world he is?"

"No," Lee said with a disappointed look. Suddenly, the sound of glass breaking caught their attention. "What was that? Do you think it was looters?"

"Well, I don't feel like waiting around to find out," William said.

Ignoring William's words, Lee ran in the direction of the breaking glass. He leaned up against the wall that was parallel to the street. He could hear the sound of glass under someone's feet. "Okay, jump down," a deep and powerful voice said.

"Don't you people know how to be quiet?" Lee said, trying to mask the joy that filled his voice. Lee stepped around the corner and leaned against the wall, standing about fifty feet away was his old friend Andre. Andre was a Kalymor from the city of Lymar. He had no shirt on, and his pants were tattered.

"It's good to see you, my friend," Andre called back, looking back into the display window he had just jumped out of. He stuck out his hands, waving someone to come out. "Okay." A female Kalymor jumped out of the window into his arms.

"Kyla?" Lee said shocked.

"Lee!" the girl shouted, jumping out of Andre's arms and running for him. Kyla almost knocked him over, running into him. "I thought I would never see you again," she said, squeezing him tight. Lee was happy to have found his two traveling companions from the Outland. He did not even think to ask how they had gotten there; he was just glad to be reunited with them.

"Sorry to break up the party," William said coming up behind them. "We should be going."

Without warning, two creatures flew out of another set of department store display windows. One of the creatures looked like a cross between a werewolf and a gorilla while the other looked like a prehistoric Raptor. The werewolf was using one foot to keep the Raptor's feet up in the air and used its hands to keep the Raptor's mouth from closing around his head.

"Tomas!" Andre shouted as he started to run to his aid.

Tomas was of a race of creatures known as Lymures. Lymures were large werewolf-like creatures. They had a similar makeup of a werewolf but with a few differences. They had a large muscular upper body with arms a bit longer than normal, giving them a gorilla-wolf hybrid look.

Tomas knocked the Raptor over and jumped to his feet. Before the Raptor had a chance to get up, he had him by the neck. Tomas picked the Raptor up and tossed him across the street into the opposite building. Just then a second Raptor leapt out of the same broken window and was heading for him. The Raptor stopped when he felt a sharp pain pierce its neck. It slowly turned its head to see Lee standing beside him with his knives drawn. In its rush, the Raptor didn't see Lee rush up on his right side. Lee had leapt over the Raptor, cutting into the back of his neck, landing on the other side. All of this took place without the Raptor realizing it. It fell limp, dying on the road in front of Lee.

"Good to have you back," Tomas said in his native tongue. Tomas was cursed to only be able to speak in the Lymurian language even though he understood other languages. Lee was the only person who understood him. "It's so boring having no one to talk to."

"It's good to see you too, old friend," Lee said, giving him a hug.

"So now what?" Andre asked.

"We have to go to New York. We're meeting Warren and Toben there," William said.

"They're alive?" Andre sounded relieved.

"It'll be good to see the silly little ones again," Tomas said.

"First, I think we should get these two some new clothes," Lee said, pointing at Andre and Kyla.

With a sigh, William nodded. "I'd have to agree."

The hour seemed to drag on as the two scavenged the stores for something to wear. William sat on the hood of the jeep while Lee and Tomas wrestled in the middle of the street. It seemed like the best way for them to spend their time while waiting for Andre and Kyla to finish with their shopping. William was exhausted just watching Lee get pulverized by Tomas. It was almost embarrassing.

"You're done," Tomas said with Lee pinned underneath him. "The only chance you have is if you actually wanted to kill me."

"Don't push your luck," Lee said, flailing around with one arm free.

Or what?" Tomas said, squeezing him. Lee closed his eyes in order to concentrate. The transwarp tunnel opened around Lee, tossing Tomas off. Once the light faded, Lee jumped to his feet in his human form. "That makes no difference," Tomas said. "You're even weaker in that form."

Lee wiped his nose while entering a fighting stance. "We'll see."

"That's so cute," Kyla said, emerging from one of the stores. "It's so nice to see you two getting along." Kyla was wearing a light green shirt with a pair of tan pants and a purple towel hanging in the front like a sash.

"What is that?" Lee asked.

"It's customary for female warriors to wear a sash around their belts. It's to symbolize—" Lee raised his hand to stop Kyla from talking.

"In my country, women don't wear towels," Lee said, taking the towel. "It looks ridiculous. But that's a nice jacket though." Lee turned and started to walk back toward the jeep.

Kyla looked down at the slick black leather jacket which was similar to Lee's. "Are you being honest?" Kyla said with a more than serious tone.

Lee stopped and looked back at her. "Yes, it's a nice look on you."

"Thank you," Kyla said with a happy tone, heading toward the jeep. Kyla stopped in front of Lee and brushed some dirt off his shirt. "You looked better as a Kalymor," she teased.

"She's right," Tomas said passing by.

Lee rolled his eyes, dropping the towel on the ground. "I prefer the body God gave me, thank you."

"Technically, God gave you both," William started before Lee glared at him. William chuckled. "What? Am I wrong?"

"Ready?" Andre asked, slapping Lee on the back. Lee stood there for a moment looking at Andre in irritation. He was wearing a black tank top with a pair of black jeans and sunglasses. "What?"

"Is that what you're planning on wearing?" Lee asked with a disappointed tone. Andre smiled, handing Lee a pair of sunglasses that were identical. Lee shook his head while taking the glasses. "Let's roll out."

Lee's bonds with his three old friends were so deep that his team now felt complete. Selfishly, he did not even think about Warren and Toben anymore. These were the people he counted on to stay by his side, and a new sense of confidence was built up in him.

Thunder shook the lonely hotel as it towered over Central Park. There was nothing out of the ordinary about the hotel other than the lack of customers. The Trepidation made very few changes to the face of the hotel, adding only trapdoors, secret passages, and other hidden surprises for any intruders.

In the highest room of the hotel, the Trepidation sat on his throne. His loft overlooked the dying flora of the park; the night giving an especially dark hue to the brown plants. The Trepidation wore armor that was as black as coal, flat and lifeless. A red trim danced along the seams of the metal plates, whipping in a wild and unique pattern. His eyes burned red like a fire through the sockets of his helmet. The room itself was expansive. The wall overlooking the park was torn out, replaced with roman style pillars, supporting archways that led out to the balcony. Dark silk drapes covered what they could of the opening.

The Trepidation rested in his seat as he received a report from one of the Temps. She was giving him the integral details on the oppression of the people in South America. She was overall droll in her explanations. The Trepidation found himself easily bored with the entire ordeal.

"Rebellion is up by three and a half percent while conversion is still holding at ten percent. The facilities in the desert are still operational. As for the Warriors, they are growing stronger as we speak. They show extraordinarily strong reflexes and will be able to manifest shortly. Once they grow into suitable hosts, they will serve our purposes well."

The Trepidation's exhausted breath echoed from under his helmet. "I'm not interested in the failed attempts of the forest facility or how the manifestation period is progressing. What I want to know is how long will it take for the Warriors to get here? All collateral damage is tolerable."

Just then, a soldier came into the room. "She's here, sire."

The Trepidation sat up in his seat, eager to get to new business. "This can wait. Bring her in."

The Temp turned to the door with disgust at the girl who stole the spotlight. She was a wretched little thing, maybe in her twenties. Dirt covered most of her facial features, and the hideous rags that she had around her hid the best parts of her figure. Her clothes were plain with a dirty tan cloak wrapped around her. Holes revealed more than one layer. She looked like a vagabond, an obvious waste for the Trepidation's time.

"Brittany of Vencore." The Trepidation stood to his feet as she entered the room. "I heard you were looking for me." The

Trepidation's joy could be heard as he spoke; he was excited to see her.

"I heard you were the one who destroyed my world." Brittany matched glares with the Temp, who was still kneeling on the floor, as she spoke with the Trepidation.

"I had nothing to do with its destruction. However, I am the one in charge of keeping it this way."

"Then I've come for your head," Brittany replied.

"All I ask for is two hours." The Trepidation stepped down from his throne. "If you have not been recruited to my side by then, you may take my head and anything else you'd like." He motioned to the guard. "Give her your sword."

"Sire," the guard acknowledged, handing over his sword.

"Come with me." The Trepidation motioned for Brittany to follow. The Temp and the guards remained still, watching the two disappear into the back room.

Brittany was skeptical of the armored man but was curious as to what his goal was. Besides, she had the upper hand now, right?

The Trepidation spoke as they followed a long hallway. All of the lights were dark, only the lighting from the storm outside lit their way. However, that did not matter as they walked through the blackness. The Trepidation seemed to know where he was going. "I knew your friends would not have shown up by now. They are obviously waiting, trying to weaken my stance in the world's flow of power. However, by doing this, they are foolish."

"How so?" Brittany asked, not pleased with him talking down about her friends.

"The more they wait, the stronger I become, and the more fear builds in their hearts. I am in control of all the powerful beings out there so that must mean that I am even more powerful yet. They could have easily overtaken me if they had simply came here first."

"Fear is a strong motivator," she offered.

"Indeed, and what I am about to show you will confirm your rationalization." The Trepidation stopped, opening a door for Brittany. She stepped in. The room was lit by a single source of light, shining out of a cement birdbath. The light swam across the walls, emanating from under the bath's water. It was far from a plain room, decorated in a Roman fashion with no windows or openings. The one door was the only way out.

The Trepidation took off his helmet, placing it on the rim of the fountain. His face seemed attractive enough, nothing that would strike her as ugly, but it did not stand out as gorgeous either. Certainly far from what she had expected from the ruler of the world.

"Who are you? What do you want?" Brittany asked.

"The people I am associated with don't have any wants. We are a group that was fashioned for one purpose, to keep balance and order in the world. We do not have feelings or emotions associated with mankind. We were born to function as laws to govern. Nothing more."

"You were made?" Brittany was taken aback by this development. "Then why are you doing this? Who is your maker?"

"My maker is the same as your maker. The purpose as to why I am here is the same reason why you have come."

Brittany was confused by the statement.

"You are here to learn why I am here." The Trepidation touched the bath. "The laws were designed for balance. To make the earth spin, to make the animals herd together and roam. Given the design and meaning of the earth, we are needed to make things work."

"Then what law are you?"

"Fear."

"Fear?" Brittany chuckled, unconvinced.

"What does trepidation mean?" he asked.

"That's not it," Brittany tried to clarify. "What type of law is fear?"

"Fear governs the world more tightly than you realize." He gave her a stern look. "Fear gives people sense and reasonability. Keeps people from injuring themselves or even killing one another. You have no idea what chaos would befall the world if there was no fear. What would nature do without fear to motivate it?"

"Doesn't the Bible say that fear is our enemy? 'Be not afraid' and all?" Brittany thought she had him.

"Have you read the Bible?"

Brittany shrugged. "But doesn't—"

"You are mistaken. Do not be confused with the fear that can lead to sin. I am neither a temptation nor an actual sin. I am a tool used by both friend and foe in order to sway the hearts of man. We are not your enemy nor are we a friend. Laws are born to have no bias. Neither Fear, nor Death, nor Gravity can be bartered with to join a side. And once this world is over with, Death and even some of us laws will perish in the fires of Hell."

"Then what are you doing here?" Brittany asked.

"I am to make ready the Warriors."

"Who are the Warriors?"

Fear smiled but the expression was lifeless. "They are the ones who are supposed to stop the apocalypse."

Brittany's face sank. "The what?"

"The Warriors are supposed to stop the apocalypse." Fear pointed at the water in the bath. "This is the Wellspring of Foresight. Touch the water, and it will show you the future. It will tell you how things will unfold. Think of how you can react differently and it will correct the line for you. Play with it for a little while but realize that this is not meant to be used as a fortune-telling device. It takes a much wiser and knowledgeable being to foretell the actions of people."

Brittany reached out hesitantly and touched the water. An image of William appeared; he was standing at an altar. The fountain was like a television. A wedding march played. "Who?" Brittany gasped as she saw the bride. "I'm supposed to marry him?" Brittany looked up with shock. "I know there was a *little* thing between us but I—how could it lead to this?" Brittany stepped away shaking her head almost as if she denied that it would ever happen.

"Why not?" Fear asked. "Do you think he will be a bad husband?"

"Well, no, but that's not my point. Why are you showing this to me?"

"Because I need your help." Fear stretched out his hand, opening it toward Brittany. Resting inside of his palm was a small reddish flame. "Only when the Warriors can defeat you with this can they leave this place. They need to be that strong to survive the trials that await them in the real world. If they ever hope to stop the apocalypse, they need to grow at least that strong. This is the phoenix fire."

"Like Warren's fire?" Brittany asked, reaching for it. She stopped halfway, wondering what the price would be for such an item. She pulled back.

"The flame that Warren has is not the Phoenix Fire. His flame is stronger and more temperamental about its users. That flame will consume him one day, and it will be out of his own selfishness."

Fear touched the fountain. It showed Warren in a human form with fiery wings on his back, fighting high above a city. He held a red-flamed sword, fighting off a bright orange flame. The flame was relentless, attacking him with no mercy. It had no owner, fighting him on its own, and Warren was losing the battle. He could hold it at bay for a little while, but he would ultimately get knocked back.

Warren's sword was knocked from his hand, and the flame cut into his wings. The red wings burned themselves out, letting Warren fall to the roof of a nearby building. He climbed to his knees just before an orange fiery spear slammed through his back, pinning him to the roof. Warren coughed blood just before his entire body was caught up in flames.

"Warren!" Brittany cried. "What is Warren doing in the form of a human?"

"I told you, this fountain shows you the future. This is the path he is on right now. His flame will consume him, and he will fail."

"He will fail?" Brittany looked down at the fountain again, touching the water, changing the image.

"You need to know where to start." Fear picked up his helmet, heading for the door. "Experiment with it. Think of it as a whiteboard. Mark out your path and then try and make it come true."

The Trepidation returned to the throne room once again. Everything remained unchanged. The Temp kneeling on the floor glared at the Trepidation.

"Should you really be helping her?" she asked. "My master will not be pleased."

"I do not answer to your master's whims," the Trepidation answered. "I follow a different path that has been paved for me. He has the Warriors at his disposal. The rest is up to him."

"My master didn't even want those others here in the first place. Why those fools were allowed to enter this place is beyond me."

"All of this is beyond you!" the Trepidation shouted. "You are even less of a being than I am. I will be burnt in the fires of the Everlasting Flame. But you, you do not even exist. You will fade into nothingness as their hearts turn you away!" The Trepidation sat in his throne, watching the woman squirm under the weight of reality. "Leave me now before I dispatch you."

HOPE

Lily tripped, falling into the dry dirt that covered the back alley. Her knees screamed out in pain as tears ran down her face. She could taste the iron-soaked dirt in her mouth as she struggled to get to her feet. Warren's jacket slipped off her shoulders as she turned to see where her attacker was. She was out of breath and low on energy. The air burned her throat. Her arms didn't want to work, and the pain in her legs was almost too much for her to bear. She knew that now was the time to stand and fight or else she would surely die.

"There's no point," Alex said, closing in. "Your boyfriend is dead. Quite a shame too. He was a strong Warrior. If only he had chosen a different side." Alex was still a good fifty feet away. Lily turned sideways and threw a punch. Three daggers, made of bone, flew out of her fist. He raised his arm without stopping. A shield of bone formed around his forearm where the daggers ultimately landed. "Don't be foolish. I have the same powers as you do. You're wasting your time."

Lily turned and ran for another warehouse. "It's nothing personal, you know?" Alex said, entering the warehouse with no one in sight. "You're just the last loose end. My job is to ensure that the end of the world goes smoothly. I wouldn't have had to kill Warren if you would have just died quietly. You don't have a chance of making it out of here alive." Alex stopped. "I could always just leave. Then the Imps can do my dirty work for me. They'll rip you to shreds and feed—"Three daggers landed in his chest. Alex grunted through the pain.

Lily landed twenty feet in front of Alex. She had elongated her feet, like that of a Kalymor, balancing her weight on the balls of her feet to increase her agility. She had longer fingernails to be used as weapons and two bat-like wings on her back to increase her jumping ability.

"If you want me dead, just try and do it yourself." Lily lunged at Alex. Her rage was her fuel now, powering every muscle in her body. Alex dodged the first attack but wasn't so lucky with the second. Lily shredded Alex's shirt and cut some of his flesh. Alex went for a punch, but Lily followed through with a kick to his the face. As soon as her foot touched the ground, Alex rushed her, knocking her to the ground. Following through with his attack, he swung his arm, launching four daggers out of his forearm, but Lily rolled out of the way before they were able to make impact. She rushed at him, cutting into his chest with a kick. Her desperation was the turning point of the fight.

Toby had been wandering the streets looking for Lily and Warren for some time with Naven following him. Toby stopped at an intersection. "Where is that boy?" Toby rhetorically asked, sitting down on a bench.

"I don't know," Naven said.

Toby sighed, trying to keep a smile on his face. "Well, let's go back. Maybe we'll be able to back track his location."

"Sounds like a good plan," Naven said, looking around. Naven pointed north, up one of the streets. "That way?"

Toby didn't get up right away. His thoughts lingered on more depressing matters. "Maybe we should have stayed in the Outland," Toby was thinking to himself but in Naven's direction.

"We didn't have a choice," Naven said. "We were brought here for a reason. Now we have to help our friends." Naven's answers were aimed inwardly too.

"I know that, but it's starting to get old. I'm tired of all of this running around. I didn't like it when we had to do it back home." The conversation shifted. Toby was now speaking to Naven. "That's why we settled in Granite. I didn't want us to live as nomads, traveling from land to land."

"We live the lives we are given. Besides, you threw away your goggles, didn't you?" Naven said. Toby did not know that Naven had seen him do that. It caught him off guard a bit. "That means you've given up on that last bit of Granite, the thing that was holding you back from becoming the Carmel you were meant to be. You lasted longer than I did though."

"What do you mean?" Toby sat forward, wanting an explanation.

"My bear." Naven reached for the bear that once hung around his neck. He had given it up back at Kendor to save Toby's life. "I realized that you are the person I want to become. I want to be just like you. I tried to build up a naive persona before, living in fear of being responsible. But you have shown me that ignorance is no excuse. I have to accept my past mistakes, repent of them, and take responsibility. I'm glad I had the chance to meet you."

Toby smiled, looking away. He had no idea what Naven was talking about, but this seemed like a mature conversation, and they did not have too many of those. "I never regretted coming to the Outland. I hope we can continue to travel together." Toby may have never regretted going to the Outland, but he never wanted to go home either. His memories of home had softly faded away over the two years in the Outland. He didn't miss his family, and he couldn't remember any of his friends. He had no reason to go home, and Naven was the only thing he had left. Deep down, he knew that people in his world would want to take Naven away to kill him and to study him. The people that were in his world would be afraid of Naven. They'd never give him a chance to show them that he was a real person just because he wasn't human.

After sitting there for a while, Toby and Naven began their journey up the street. They walked, loosely searching for their lost comrades. After walking the length of a football field, a ray of hope emerged. They saw a body lying in the middle of the road. Around the body there were three imps slowly circling. A single little flame on the ground seemed to be keeping them back. Every time one of them got closer to the body, the little flame would leap at them chasing them back. Naven fired a few shots at the imps, making them scamper off like the lowly scavengers they were. Toby approached apprehensively as the little flame climbed up onto Warren's chest. It waited patiently until Toby was close enough to kneel down beside Warren's body. Once Toby knelt down, it slowly burnt away.

"Warren?" Toby said softly, shaking him. "It's time to wake up. You have a job to do." Toby shook him a little harder. "Come on. You can't do this. You're stronger than any of us, come on."

"Oh, I have a killer headache!" Warren said, sitting up.

"Warren!" Toby yelled, wrapping his arms around him knocking him over again. "I thought you were dead!"

"Good for you," Warren said, starting to choke as he pushed himself back up off the ground. "Let's go."

Toby released Warren and backed away. "I'm sorry. I was just worried."

Warren started to rub the side of his head. "That lunatic zapped me with an electrical charge. I wasn't thinking clearly. Fire can't stop electricity."

"Well, at least you're alive," Toby said.

"Yeah, I shouldn't be," Warren said, getting to his feet. "Can you find her trail?" Warren asked Naven.

"No, I lost her trail," Naven replied, sad that he had failed.

"She still has my jacket," Warren said, brushing himself off with one hand. "I put a bottle of perfume in one of the pockets. Follow the scent of the flowers."

Naven sniffed the air frantically trying to capture the scent. "Why do you have perfume in your pockets?" Toby asked. Warren rolled his eyes.

"Lavender!" Naven said excited. "I've found her!"

Lily hit the ground hard. She could taste blood in her mouth where Alex had broken a few of her teeth. She fought through the pain. She didn't have time to fix it now. Alex was still full of energy, and her second wind was already gone. One of her wings was broken and the other had been cut completely off. She struggled to her feet as her body slowly reverted back to normal. Using the last bit of energy, she made a knife. "Haven't you learned yet?" Alex asked. "Your bone can't hurt me."

"How about fire!" Toby yelled from the large doors of the warehouse. Toby had his sword in one hand and pointed at Alex with the other. "Now!"

Naven began spitting fireballs at him. Alex placed his hand out, letting the balls of fire dissipate on his hand. "It looks like that hand has to go!" Toby said, charging at him with his sword drawn back.

"Ignorant worm!" Alex said. "I was supposed to let you live." Toby stopped, throwing his sword at Alex. Learning from his last mistake, Alex lifted his hand up. A piece of metal shot up from out of the ground, shielding him. Before the sword hit the barrier, Toby called it back to his hand. Alex stood there for a moment wondering what he was up to and then he heard it. The sound of a crackling fire moving fast through the air. Alex had just enough time to turn around when two streams of fire from Warren's whip burned into his flesh. The streams of fire moved with a strong force, knocking Alex back into the metal shield. Warren stretched out his hand toward Alex and formed a fist. The flames that were attached to Alex's body exploded with a violent energy. Toby covered Lily from the blast as it rocked the warehouse.

Once the smoke had cleared, Toby and Warren moved in to see what damage Alex had sustained. Alex laid there on the ground, his eyes wide open and his clothes severely torn to pieces. His body was twitching as he laid there on the dirt floor. Steam rolled off his body even though there were no burn marks on him.

"Do you think he's dead?" Toby asked.

"No, I doubt it," Warren answered with joyful confidence as he dusted off his reclaimed jacket. "He's immune to fire attacks. I think he'll be up and about in a couple of days, but I plan on being long gone by then."

"If he's not affected by fire attacks, how could you hurt him with yours?" Toby asked.

"Because his fire isn't like any other," Lily said slowly approaching. "He has a fire that seems like it's alive."

"The phoenix fire," Warren said.

"No, it's something else," Lily said. She had heard the stories of the Phoenix Fire, and Warren's was different—moving with a mind of its own and stronger than ordinary fire.

"Well who cares?" Toby said, walking away. Suddenly he stopped, turning back toward Alex. "Shouldn't we go ahead and finish him off?"

Warren shook his head, pulling Toby along. "Let the imps deal him from here on out. Besides, he would probably just regenerate. You know Snogs have the ability to regenerate their heads once they've been cut off."

"Really?" Toby was shocked and grossed out. "Well then, let's ditch this popsicle stand. I'm hungry."

"Oh, me too!" Naven said with enthusiasm.

Warren laughed. "Okay, guys." Warren stopped to address Lily in a serious tone. "I'm sorry I wasn't there for you. I'm sorry you had to face him alone." Warren looked down at his feet. "I'm..."

Lily wrapped her arms around Warren, hugging him tight. "It's okay. I'm sorry too."

The group decided to take shelter for the night in one of the apartment buildings near the harbor area. The imps seemed to leave them alone, staying a far distance away. Even in these bleak times, it was a time for celebration. In the morning they were planning on returning to the subway where Cormon had left them.

Once they were settled in the apartment, Toby headed straight for the kitchen. Lily, Warren, and Naven gathered at the table.

"So what happened?" Toby asked from the kitchen. "What happened after the battle?"

Warren turned his full attention to Lily.

"We thought you all had died," Lily answered. "After the Black King was destroyed, the castle's foundation fell into the canyon. It swallowed the entire castle. It was known as the battle that united all the tribes and kingdoms."

Warren had a soft warm smile on his face. "We did it."

"Why are you here?" Toby asked. "How did you get here?"

"After my training with the Silamons, I went back to Ram to take my rightful place on the throne. That was less than a year ago. I recently started to teach the children of the people who work in the palace the history of Ram. I hope that they will learn from our lessons and not be doomed to repeat them. It was during one of these lessons that Alex showed up. I was able to distract him long enough so the children could escape, but in the end, he caught me. He was able to open some kind of portal, dragging me here, to this horrible place. He's been hunting me down ever since."

Toby shook his head, coming up with ideas as to what was going on.

"What? What is it?" Lily asked. She was afraid that they didn't believe her.

"Wormholes," Toby said.

"What?" Warren asked.

"Wormholes, openings in time and space," Toby said, pondering the great mystery. "That would explain the gaps in years when we jumped."

"It's okay," Warren said, turning back to Lily. "We just have to concentrate on this moment. We'll figure out how to get home later."

In the morning, the group followed the harbor on their way back to the subway station; the morning sun was shining down on them. The cool, salty air filled their lungs with a calming effect. They could tell that it was going to be a good day. Naven and Toby were in the lead while Warren and Lily were a few feet behind them. Toby and Naven were laughing and joking as if everything were back to normal. Warren watched them with humorous curiosity. It never ceased to amaze him the bond that the two shared. How could they act like nothing wrong had happened when the world was falling apart around them?

A familiar voice called out to them, breaking Warren's concentration. "Hello!" Cormon yelled from offshore. He was steering a large-sized fishing boat close to shore. "You guys are late. I've been waiting here forever."

Cormon brought his boat into the docks, inviting the group aboard and down to the galley for something to eat. Naven and Toby jumped on his invitation, taking off to find the galley.

"Who is this?" Lily asked, stepping onto the boat with Warren close behind.

"This is the conductor of the train I told you about," Warren said.

"And you must be Queen Lily from Ram." Cormon reached out to help her aboard.

Lily extended her hand with caution. This man seemed odd to her. His demeanor was sly and snaky, holding a dark presence behind him.

Down in the galley, Naven and Toby were already helping themselves to a homemade pizza when the others arrived. "I don't like pizza," Naven said disappointed.

"Hey now, I apologized about that!" Toby said taking a slice. "It's hard to make pizza in the Outland. I'm sorry that it turned out so bad."

"I hear Lee did a good job," Warren said, taking a slice too. "He got one of the king's honors for it."

Toby had an irritated look on his face. Warren's words had hit a soft spot. Naven took a bite in hesitation. "You're right," Naven said, eating the rest of the slice. "You don't know how to cook at all. This is good."

"I'm surrounded by traitors." Toby said, pretending to be hurt.

"Don't be so hard," Cormon said. "You made it out of there just fine."

"Not so much," Warren said, laying down his pizza.

"Yes, well, I am sorry for the loss of the little ones. However you will be surprised at what their sacrifice will mean to you later in your journey."

"What do you mean by that?" Toby asked, offended by the comment. Despite his lax attitude, he had been paying attention.

He remembered Nell's and Alex's words. A feeling grew up from within. He knew Cormon was up to something.

"You'll see soon enough," Cormon said with a smile. "Go ahead and get some rest. You'll need it for later." Cormon took his leave, heading back up top.

"I need to know where they are!" Harper shouted. He was standing in the field command center. Seven men sat at computer terminals, typing away at the keyboards, trying to locate their targets. "I need results people!" Harper was pacing, thinking about strategies to fulfill their mission.

One of the operators announced, "Location found at Gate Junction ninety-two."

"Where is the junction heading?" Harper barked.

"South America, Amazon district."

"Can we redirect the tunnel?" Harper was starting to get nervous.

"We can only redirect a Gate's path to a common field," the operator replied.

"We need to abort the current trajectory."

"We have a trajectory plane," another operator blurted out. "Toby and Warren are both experiencing a nightmare and so are William and Tomas."

"Do we have anything else other than nightmares? We need a reliable field." Harper knew that this would work, but he did not want to join the group there.

The operator blushed. "Two of the females and one of the males are sharing a common field, but I wouldn't recommend it."

Harper swallowed his comment, knowing what he had to do. "Do it. We need to force the rest of them asleep and merge their locations."

"Opening Gate one fifty-six," an operator announced.

"Amos will be most displeased." Harper leaned against the back of his chair, frustrated with the progress.

"How's everything going?" Jonas asked, entering into the tent.

Harper waved for him to exit, following him out. "Is everything complete on your end?"

"Almost," Jonas assured him. "I just stopped in to make sure everything was going smoothly. Has there been any change in our enemy's movement?"

Harper shook his head. "We're just holding on at this point, waiting for those boys to make their decisions."

"What was going on in there?"

Harper shook his head, knowing that he was about to be criticized for his actions. "We've been waiting for them to fall asleep so that we could merge their paths together. The only problem is that the only common ground they share is a nightmare."

"Nightmares are unreliable," Jonas instructed.

"I know," Harper said. It was a textbook answer.

"They could end up separated again."

Harper nodded. "I realize this. I'm sending word to Amos to see if he can redirect their paths if that happens. Cecil's out, working on counter preparations and speaking with His Majesty on our progress." Harper raised his hand, pointing behind Jonas. "Do me a favor and drop him off. Amos picked him up a little while ago, and I think he'll be useful."

Jonas turned, seeing a Mission's Level Warrian standing behind him. "Are you kidding me?"

"Nope," Harper replied.

"Is that the Jelly Mold we used to bind Toby with that Raptor hybrid?"

"Yep." Harper patted Jonas on the back. "He's copied most of Cecil's attributes, but he is far from the original. I'm hoping he can at least aid the Raven Clan in their journey."

Jonas was not happy about this. The Jelly Mold was less than a copy of their commander. He was restricted to a Warrian body and might as well be a second class creature from the Outland. However, orders were orders, and Jonas was not interested in disobeying his commanding officer's wishes. This could make things more interesting, but Jonas was betting that things would not end quite as well.

NIGHTMARES

William was floating down a river, which lay deep in the mountains of a far away kingdom. The river flowed far out in the wilderness, far beyond the reaches of any man. The cold water engulfed his body, causing his limbs to go numb. It felt like a thousand needles were piercing his skin, and even though he desperately wanted to get out of the icy water, his body wouldn't move. Even though he could no longer feel his limbs, the icy water did nothing to sooth the gaping wound in his chest and stomach. *I can't believe I'm going to die*, William thought. *Is it really the end?* His eyes felt weak and heavy. Everything started to turn dark. Slowly he felt himself slipping deeper into sleep. Fear started to seep into his heart, afraid that he would never wake up again. *I have so much I wanted to do*, William thought to himself. *One more day, a week would have been enough.* His mind started to go numb. *I don't want to go into the dark abyss!* The cold had taken its toll on him. Consciousness started to leave. Then a warm feeling came over him. It started small at first, spreading from his back and behind the knees. Once his vision started to come back, he noticed a man had pulled him out of the river. William's eyes fluttered more clearly. He saw a man with white hair holding him.

"Are you ready?" the man said in a warm and comforting voice. "It won't be easy, but I will always be there beside you."

It was late at night when a curious howl rang out. The howl startled William, waking him from his sleep. The lone cry of a creature, out in the wilderness, lurked some distance away from their location. William sleepily looked around, studying his surroundings. Feeling comfortable again, he resumed his position, resting against Tomas's warm fur. William pressed firmly into the soft hair as if the large creature were his favorite teddy bear. William was sitting in the backseat of the jeep with Tomas. Kyla was sleeping in the storage space behind William with one of her legs hanging out of the vehicle. Andre was sitting in the passenger side with Lee behind the wheel. Suddenly something caught William's attention. They had stopped. William sat up again looking up at Lee. Lee was sitting behind the wheel, sleeping. The jeep sat dead in the middle of the road. The night crept over them with no sign of cover. William slapped Lee on the back of the head. "What are you doing?" William said, getting out of the jeep. "I can't believe you fell asleep." Once William was out of the jeep, he walked to the front of the vehicle and slammed his fist on the hood. Tomas woke with a commotion, standing up in the jeep in the excitement. "Oh, stop it you big baby," William shouted at Tomas.

"What happened?" Lee asked getting out. "I don't remember anything." The street was bare, surrounded only by woods. The smell of pine rolled over them.

"How much *do* you remember?" William asked, not particularly interested in the explanation. Fury was building up within him.

"I remember driving out of Indianapolis but after that..."

"You fell asleep and the jeep died here," William said aggravated. "Well at least you didn't take us off the road," he continued, looking the jeep over. It was still in good condition, and there was no sign that Lee had hit anything. "If you were tired, you should have pulled over and switched drivers."

"I wasn't tired," Lee insisted. He wasn't interested in explaining himself, but he was concerned as to why he fell asleep. "If I simply fell asleep, don't you think the jeep would have gone off the road?"

"Where are we?" Kyla said, stretching beside the jeep. Andre yawned, joining Tomas by William's side.

"Who knows?" William scoffed. "Does the jeep run?"

Lee hopped back into the jeep, turning the key. The key turned but nothing happened. No clicks, nothing turned over, it was all silent. "The battery is dead," Lee announced.

William raised his hands and shrugged in frustration. "I guess we walk." William turned, heading up the road.

"What's his problem?" Lee asked under his breath.

The street was practically the same for the next mile. Trees stretched as far as the eye could see. The street seemed to be the only thing that civilization had touched in the area. The light of the moon was the only light that illuminated the path. The group seemed to walk blindly down the road, not exactly following a plan.

"It can't be," Lee said, walking ahead of the group. Everyone stopped, watching him. His face was riddled with confusion and concern.

"What?" William asked.

"How long do you think we were asleep?" Lee asked, looking directly at William.

"I don't know, maybe a few hours," he answered.

"We're only a few blocks away from my house." Lee took off down the street to make sure he was correct. "We're in Pennsylvania."

"That's not possible!" William said in disbelief. "We had at least another day."

"Trust me," Lee shouted. The rest of the group followed, catching up with him. Lee had slowed down to a brisk walk, continually rambling off random facts about his family. "My family comes from a wealthy lineage. My parents were actually the first professing Christians in my family for generations. My father owns the Tri-Technical Industries here in New York."

"So you guys are loaded, eh?" William said.

"You could say that," Lee answered.

The group entered a cul-de-sac, which had a large bus sitting on the left side of the road. The cul-de-sac had five houses sitting around the street with a large white house at the end. There were four streetlights, evenly spaced. "This isn't right," Lee said, pointing at the white house in the center. "That's my house, but we don't have any neighbors. Not for at least a mile in the other direction."

"I know," William said, shocked. "That's my apartment building." William pointed at one of the buildings to the left. "This can't be happening."

"This can't be our home," Lee said. "Where are we?"

Lily slowly opened her eyes, finding herself on Cormon's boat. Her head rested gently on Warren's chest. The group was resting peacefully on the floor after they had filled their bellies. She felt warm and safe knowing that Warren was there to protect her. It felt like nothing could harm her. She listened closely to the rhythmic sound of his breathing. Warren opened his eyes, noticing that she had moved her head.

"Thank you," Lily compassionately thanked him, "for saving me and all."

"I'm glad we found you," Warren confided in her. "It would have killed me if something were to happen to you."

She looked away. "No one has ever come to my rescue before."

"You've never needed it," Warren assured her. "You're strong and brave. No one can touch you. Hey, you know I'll always be there for you?"

"I know."

"I'd be lost without you. I wouldn't know what to do with myself."

Deep in her complacency, she closed her eyes to drift back to sleep, but she only got a chance to close them when someone shook her awake. She had dreamt the whole thing.

Warren stood over her with a confused look on his face. "Time to wake up," he said, watching her desperately cling to her pillow.

Drool clung to the side of her face. "We've got problems." Lily covered her face and groaned realizing that she had only been dreaming.

"Come on, sleeping beauty," Toby said, walking behind Warren. "Nap time's over."

Lily sat up and looked around. They weren't on the boat. "Where are we?" Lily asked. She stood to her feet, grabbing the coat she had been sleeping on.

"We're on a bus," Toby said, moving toward the front. "It's complicated."

Naven waited for Lily to move, so he could follow behind her.

"You talk in your sleep," Naven said with a straight face.

Lily blushed. "Why did I say?"

"Mushy stuff." Naven's face was like stone, not revealing anything.

Lily turned away, face flushed with embarrassment. *What if he heard me?* she thought.

The group shuffled to the front of the bus. Warren and Toby stepped out into the middle of the street finding their friends only a little ways off.

Tomas turned around, spotting them. "It looks like the Carmel has brought guests," he said.

Lee turned. "Warren!" Lee forgot about the predicament that he was in, lost in the excitement of the moment. He ran down the street to greet them with a hug. "Glad to see you guys alive."

"You too," Toby said, returning the hug.

"Who's your friend?" Lee asked, looking at Lily.

"It's me," she said timidly. "Lily."

"Lily?" Lee said amazed. "How?"

"There's no time for that," William said. "We're in the middle of a dilemma."

"Hey, that's my house," Toby said, looking at a deformed house sitting on the right side of the cul-de-sac. "Or at least it might be." Half of the house looked like Toby's but the other half looked like it was ripped apart by green vines and leaves. "What happened to it?"

"We don't know," Lee said. "None of these houses should be here."

"Wormholes?" Naven asked.

"I don't think so," Toby said.

"Does anybody hear that?" Warren asked, his words going unheard by the group.

"What about wormholes?" Lee asked, pointing at Naven.

"I think that's how we've been transported between worlds," Toby answered. "I did some calculating last night, and I can't seem to get it right."

"What are you, a child prodigy?" Lee asked.

"Somewhat," Toby answered, beaming with arrogance. "I've been told that I could have graduated early from high school if I wanted to. I just think it would be a waste of my talent."

"Sounds to me like you're overconfident," Lee said with a smirk.

Warren's attention was elsewhere. He moved his focus to a small trailer to their left; there was a rumbling coming from it. The trailer gave Warren an odd feeling of anxiety. There were no lights around it or even coming from it. Darkness had engulfed the little home. Warren's hands shook as the rumbling grew louder.

"It's coming," Tomas said in a state of fear. "He'll destroy us all" Warren turned to him in a state of shock. Warren actually understood every word that came out of his mouth, but Lee was supposed to be the only one who understood him. Warren moved toward him wanting to ask how he understood him, but he was interrupted by a crackling noise coming from the trailer.

In a horrific display of violence, the trailer was ripped apart. Thousands of pieces littered the air. Everyone's attention turned toward the trailer where a troll stood in the remains. It towered over them, roaring.

The troll stepped forward as it attacked the group with a large wooden club. William and Lee hit the ground as Warren covered Lily, pulling her down with him. The troll swung its club at the group. Andre and Kyla jumped over the club as it hit Tomas, sending him flying into one of the houses across the street. Everyone jumped to their feet, except Lily, who remained curled in a ball on the ground. Lee transwarped into his Kalymor form, and Warren pulled out his dual pistols and began firing on the large brute. Toby stretched out his hand, calling for his sword, as Naven spat fireballs at the monster.

William pulled up his shotgun, pumping a few rounds at the creature. After a few shots, the shotgun was empty. Quickly, he reached into his bag for more shells. During his search, he stopped long enough to see Andre and Kyla soaring across the street in the same direction as Tomas had been thrown. Unfortunately, that was William's biggest mistake. As he turned back around, the troll hit him with his club, tossing William's body up into the air. William flew backwards, landing through his apartment window.

"No you don't!" Toby yelled, stabbing the troll in the leg with his sword. In a fit of anger, the troll grabbed Toby, snarling at him.

"No!" Naven yelled, hurling fireballs at the creature. With the same hand that held Toby, the troll snagged up Naven. They were thrown into the building, which resembled Toby's home.

"Just us!" Lee said standing by Warren. Warren was breathing heavy, and Lee had hurt his ribs during the same attack that the troll made on Andre and Kyla.

"Let's take him," Warren said, stretching out his hand at the creature, unleashing a fireball. As it hit the creature, the troll wailed, lowering its club. Lee saw his opportunity. He jumped on the club using it as a bridge to the troll's head. Lee ran up the large log, but before he had a chance to attack, the troll was able to catch him. Infuriated, it pitched him across the cul-de-sac and through one of the windows of his own home. The troll looked back at Warren who had his whip in hand.

The troll stood straight up in defiance. Warren snapped his whip. A trail of fire raced up the troll's chest. It didn't blink an eye as the flames that stuck to him charred and blistered its flesh. Warren flung his whip at the creature again. The troll reached out and caught the whip with his empty hand and pulled it away from Warren. The flame burned up as the troll raised its club. It swung down for Warren. He performed a side flip, avoiding the catastrophic blow. Somehow, in this place, he could feel greater control over his body. Here in this place, what he imagined actually happened. Side flips would almost be impossible for him in any other world.

The troll swung its club sideways trying to connect again, but he missed as Warren executed another side flip in the other direction. He rolled on the ground, hopping to his feet as soon as the club had cleared. He continued to fire his weapons until he was out of ammunition. Once he was out, he had to resort to his flame whip again. Warren dashed for the troll's feet. While Warren was this close, the troll's club was useless. However, the creature's feet were still a problem. The troll stomped as Warren easily ran between its legs to the other side. As the troll turned to face Warren, three daggers pierced his back. It turned its head back around to see Lily standing with more daggers in her hand.

Blood dripped from above her eye where she had hit the ground during the fight. She was out of commission for a few minutes, but she was back on her feet now.

Warren raised his whip again, striking the creature several times in a combination of slashes. It shrieked in agony as it dropped to its knees, landing facedown as it died.

Warren was shocked. *Was that all it took?* he thought to himself. *After everything we threw at it? How did we not win sooner?*

"Warren?" Lily called out. Warren stretched out his hand for her. She ran to him and grabbed him, holding on to him tight. "I'm sorry I passed out on you like that."

"Don't worry about it." Warren seemed unaffected by the sudden show of affection toward him. However, a gentle smile indicated that he was not opposed to it. "We need to look for the others." Lily nodded.

Warren turned, heading for the broken trailer, feeling that was the way they needed to go. It was not a voice calling to him, but the presence of an old friend pulling him along, telling him that his friends were in that direction. After spending so much time in this place, where dreams become real, it ate away at the mind. Both of them were much more susceptible to spiritual influences and manipulation.

"Where are you going?" Lily asked. "The others went into those buildings over there."

"But *we* need to go over here," Warren said, following his instincts. "There's a gate over here." Lily gave Warren a curious look as she followed his lead.

"What are we doing?" she asked as they climbed down a set of stairs. The steps led into a cellar. "I don't understand."

"We're not in the real world anymore." Warren said. "Can't you feel the increase in your power? We're still in the tunnel, or way, or whatever they want to call it."

"But how?" Lily asked as Warren opened a door at the bottom of the stairs. She gasped as it swung opened. The door led to the middle of a forest. "That's impossible."

"Cormon only moved us," Warren said. "Time and matter doesn't exist here in the tunnel." Warren and Lily walked through the gate into the forest. They walked for only a little way before they stopped. Standing before them was Nell.

"I thought I heard you calling," Warren said with a look of distrust upon his face. The feeling that directed him before came from this boy who was supposed to be dead. Lily became frozen behind him, listening intently to everything that was said.

"And you came. Thank you," Nell said with a smile. Her voice was as calming and pleasant as ever.

"What's going on?" Warren asked as he circled her.

"Do you know who you are?" Nell asked. "Because I know the truth of your past, pup." Nell's words were composed and sturdy as she spoke. "Lee wasn't the only member of the Raven's Clan who was forced to drink from the fountain."

Warren's face froze. "What?"

"You don't remember the night that your mother left you in the city of Weremore, do you? Of course, back then it went by the name of Bronze Heart."

"What do you know?" Warren demanded. "Tell me!"

"That is how you gained the power of transfiguration. It was from the fountain that your father tried to drown you in. Your mother took you after he had failed, and then she dropped you off in Weremore so that they could watch over you."

"No," Warren said softly in denial. "How can that be?"

"I am the fruit of your mother's neglect. I am the product of her failure to notice your pain. I bring you understanding of the *true world*."

Warren looked at her in confusion. "And I am fruit of your father's abuse," Abe said, coming forward from Warren's left. Abe's voice seemed stale and absent of all emotion. "I am the product of his hurt and his ignorance. I bring you strength."

"I don't understand!" Warren yelled. "What are you talking about? If I was a human from the beginning, and was in fact transformed by the water, then why did I transform back? Lee had to find the Pedestal of Truth in order to regain his body."

"And he did, and he was judged," Abe said in a monotone voice.

"But you are special. You don't need the things that Lee needs. You're stronger than that," Nell said in step.

"This is too much for me," Warren said, grabbing his forehead.

"It was through your suffering that gave us meaning," Abe said.

"It was your suffering that gave us life," Nell followed.

"It was through your father's abuse and your mother's neglect that brought you to the Outland. You were brought here to escape from your father," Abe said.

"It was your father's wrath that tried to drown you in a Fountain of Truth," Nell followed.

"And it was in desperation that you were taken to Bronze Heart where you were watched over. Through desperation you stayed in the Outland."

"You need to fight off the Temps."

"You need to get stronger so that we will not die."

"Get strong enough so that you never need to rely on anyone again."

"Save yourself from pain, despair, and even death."

Lee climbed to his feet, brushing the broken glass from his body. He stopped once he realized that he was standing on a rooftop in the middle of a city. There were no signs of where he once was. The window that he had flown through was gone with only the glass on the ground to prove that he wasn't crazy. He picked the glass out of the fur on his hands as he looked about his surroundings. He was hoping to get an idea of where he was when a cold chill raced up his spine. The sound of footsteps had stopped just behind him. His heart skipped a beat as he turned.

"Amos, it's you! It's good to see you." Lee straightened up, taking a few steps forward, happy to see him.

"As it is to see you," Amos replied. Amos was wearing a blue shirt and a matching pair of pants. A black overcoat was draped over him. It looked old fashioned and handmade; similar to the outfit he wore in the Outland. "I see you've kept your *fuzzy* look," Amos referred to Lee's Kalymor form.

"It's been crazy," Lee said full of excitement, waving his arms in the air. Lee stopped suddenly and his face turned serious as he remembered something. He took a single step back. "But I don't need to tell you. You are actually some kind of angel, aren't you?" Lee almost sounded angry.

"What's the matter?" Amos asked. "Have I done something wrong?"

"How about getting all of us involved in your war then not even showing up to help in the end?" Lee said.

"I was there," Amos said. "Or don't you remember?"

"Of course I remember!" Lee cried. "Why didn't you help us? We needed you, and you weren't anywhere to be found. My friends almost died, and I nearly did too."

"That wasn't my fight and neither is this one."

"What? You're the one who took me there!"

"I did get you involved in this mess. And as you obviously know by now, this is not your real home either. You were brought here to be a light to these people, that you might spread the gospel and help show them what they really are, sinners in need of Jesus."

"What are you talking about?" Lee was dumbfounded. How was he supposed to evangelize in a place like this? Was this even a time for that?

"The enemy is using this place to try and get you all to fight. The more you fight here, the more you become the Warriors that they need for the final days. They need you to grow stronger and more aggressive."

"And you want us to stop them?" Lee still did not understand what it was he should be doing.

Amos shook his head, placing his hands on Lee's shoulders. "Not in the manner that you are thinking. I want you to pray and then talk to William and the others about Jesus and the sacrifice that He made for you all."

"What do you mean, William?" Lee asked, brushing Amos's hands from his shoulders. "William and Warren were both given armor, like mine, to fight against the Black King. I prayed with Toby and Naven. They're all saved already." Lee shook his head, trying to understand what Amos meant. "You mean Kyla and Andre, right? And Tomas too? The others have already accepted Christ!"

Amos shook his head. "You are still the only saved person among your friends."

"No!" Lee insisted. "That can't be true."

"William was given armor to help you defeat the Black King and bridge the gap. Warren was given armor too but not by us. As for Toby and Naven, you never told them the gospel or how to be truly saved."

"What do you mean?" Lee urged. "I know I told them! They're fighting for good, aren't they?"

"Do you even remember how to be saved? What it takes?" Amos challenged him.

"Of course!" Lee spat back.

"Then explain it to me. Why did He die on the cross?"

"So we can get to heaven," Lee answered.

"No," Amos said. "Why can't you get to heaven? What's stopping you from getting there on your own?"

Lee thought about it, calming down as his brain worked. "Because we're sinners." His voice was still heated.

"Because, all have sinned and fall short of the glory of God,"[1] Amos replied. "And the wages of sin is death, but the gift of God is eternal life in Christ Jesus."[2]

Lee stepped back, thinking back to Amos's original question. What it took to be saved. "Repent, then, and turn to God so that your sins may be wiped out, that times of refreshing may come from the Lord.[3]

Jesus died on the cross so that our sins could be washed away."

Amos smiled, glad to see that he finally understood. "God demonstrates his own love for you in this: While you were still a sinner, Christ died for you."[4]

"His love is unconditional, loving us enough to die for us even before we knew him." Lee couldn't look up at Amos. He had raised his voice for no good reason. "God was trying to save us long before we ever did anything to deserve it."

Amos nodded again, adding, "And He's still waiting to save people."

"I stand at the door and knock. If anyone hears my voice and opens the door, I will come in and eat with him, and he with me.[5]

It's an opportunity that we have to accept and interact with."

"And you are sure that this is what you told Toby and Naven? You told Warren and William too?" Amos stared down at him, waiting for his answer.

Lee hesitated. Deep down he had convinced himself that he had presented the Gospel fully, and the two of them just ran through that together, so Lee was sure that he had. "Yes."

"Liar!" Amos shouted. The word cut straight through Lee as if it pierced all the way down to his soul. An angel of God just called him a liar. How could he argue with him? "I've heard you tell your companions that all you need to do is believe in Jesus, and they will be saved."

"No," Lee started, thinking back to all the conversations he had ever had about God with his friends. He searched diligently for an explanation, something that would justify him; anything that the angel might have missed.

"It is good that they believe Jesus is the son of God, but even the demons believe that—and shudder.[6] They need to understand that they are sinners and accept the free gift that has been offered to them. As the old saying goes, 'You can lead a horse to water, but you cannot make them drink.' The same goes for people. They can believe that the water is there, but unless they willingly drink, they will eventually die."

Lee dropped to his knees, realizing that Amos was right. He had watered down the truth, failing his friends and his Lord. Whether it was because he was afraid of ridicule or he was afraid the group would make fun of him, he restricted the truth from them. Using big "churchy" words, he offered something that sounded like truth without actually explaining it.

"How can I face them now?" Lee asked himself. "I already told them that they were saved. Admitting my mistake might push them further away."

"But you need to tell them. Stand by the truth and admit when you are wrong. Repent of your false teaching and never return to it." Amos reached down, helping Lee to his feet.

Lee nodded, building up his resolve. "I will. I want to see my friends saved."

Amos returned the nod. "Now, I know you will find it necessary to fight here. The devil has this place crawling with the same Temptations that are currently lurking inside of each of your hearts, powered by the sins that control your lives. Though you can occasionally fight temptation through the physical means, the blood of Christ is the only way to deal with sin directly, so physically fighting with these Temps serves you little to no purpose. Although I personally would not like to watch you fight at all, it will be impossible for you to make it out of here without some conflict." Amos placed a knife in Lee's hand. "So I will give you the power to call upon knives or even a sword whenever you need them. Toby has a similar power, but do not confuse its source with that of your own. Like the armor, in your last battle in the Outland, the enemy will disguise their efforts to look like ours. After all, Satan himself masquerades as an angel of light."[7]

"How will I be able to tell the difference between you and the enemy?" Lee asked, earnestly wanting to learn if for nothing more than to defend his friends better.

"Listen to what they say. Demons will try and demote Christ, devalue God, and deify man if for nothing more than to watch them fall. Know that anyone who perverts the Gospel of Christ is working for the enemy."

"Okay," Lee acknowledged.

"One more thing," Amos said, motioning for Lee to follow him to the ledge of the building. "Watch out for William. It was so hard to get you to cross over I had to recruit another boy who was close to the Outland but not a part of them. He's not saved, and he may end up hurting a lot of people if he has his way. You'll be the only one he can turn to, so watch out for him. Be an enduring light here in a prevailing darkness that wants to swallow you all."

Lee looked out into the middle of the street where he saw William surrounded by Imps. Amos could sense him holding his breath. "Relax," Amos said, placing his hand on Lee's shoulder. "There's nothing to fear."

"Is that—" Lee started to ask, watching another man approach.

"The King of the Highland. Prince of Syma. The Christ," Amos answered. "He came to save mankind, died, and paid the penalty for all."

William slowly made his way through a darkened alley; the smell of musk and mold surrounded him. Even with the sun resting above him and the birds chirping as if it were spring, it felt like the depths of night. The tall buildings around him seemed to dampen the glories of the sun. William was halfway to the end of the alley when two Imps landed behind him.

"We are the guardians of the way," one said.

In a panic, William ran for the freedom of the street, not even waiting for them to finish their lines. The creatures just laughed as they made their pursuit. William bounced off a dumpster in the alley, trying to escape them. Once he hit the street, he blindly ran from the two fiends. It was hopeless. Hundreds of Imps littered the road, blocking his path. With nowhere left to go, William slowly came to stop. Every exit was blocked, and he had no weapon. However that didn't mean he was going down without a fight.

"Don't," a man's voice said. The voice was refreshing and calm yet loud and clear. The Imps stopped in their tracks, snarling at William. He searched the layout of the land for the owner of the voice, but the man was nowhere to be found. It was upon his second turn around when he finally saw the man standing in the middle of the Imps. The Imps moved away from him as if they were afraid.

Fear overwhelmed William as he recognized the man. Taking a step back, he tripped over his feet, landing on the ground.

Startled by the sudden movement, three Imps leapt at William. "No," the man said without raising his voice. The three Imps instantly exploded into dust, falling to the ground harmlessly. The group around the man opened their mouths to hiss and snarl. The moment they did, the entire lot of Imps burst into clouds of dust.

Once the dust settled, the man calmly walked over to William. His clothes resembled that of Lee's in his Kalymor form, only these were whiter. So much more that they almost seemed to glow. The man bent down to get a good look at William. He had white hair with soft eyes, but even though he had a calming presence, William seemed terrified before him.

William would not look him directly in the eye as if he were guilty. He felt as if he were nothing more than a stain on the bottom of this man's shoe. This person was so holy that he wished the man would just pass by without giving him a second glance.

"Are you okay?" the man asked in a calm and gentle voice. "What's wrong, don't you remember me? It wasn't that long ago."

"It's you," William said, remembering the time he was floating in a river. "You were the one who saved me from death."

During the battle at the End of the World in the Outland, William had broken away from the main group, heading south to aid a small group that had forced away from the battle. They were being overwhelmed, and William led a small battalion in their direction, hoping to save them from their attackers.

Having a flashback of that time in the Outland, William remembered the feeling of riding on horseback into the field of battle. He was overcome with a sense of excitement. This was the moment he had been waiting for his whole life, his chance to prove his worth in battle. All of his training had come back to him; it was as if no one could touch him.

Calling out from his immediate left, Captain Donald Hazer approached. He rode up beside him, shouting over the fighting and clanging of armor. "William, a group of my men has been pushed south to the edge of the Forest of Zoar."

"What are they doing all the way over there?" William shouted. That was a mile outside of where all the fighting was supposed to be taking place.

"They were overwhelmed," Hazer explained, embarrassed that his troops would allow themselves to be pushed back that far. "Can I send a group of men with you to give them support and to bring them back?" Looking over Hazer's shoulder, in the direction of the group in trouble, William consented to leading the team out to support them.

The separated group was quite a distance away, almost out of sight from the rest of the battle. Their cries went unheard, drowned out by the thunderous rage that took place on the main field. William and his team rode as fast as they could trying to reach the stranded soldiers, but as they rode, the little group was pushed back even further until they had disappeared into the forest.

William and the others grumbled as they entered the forest after them. A few of them thought that they were too far from the main battle to get relief while others thought that if the battle ended soon, then they would not be able to go to the victory celebration, people thinking that they had abandoned their posts. William sided with the ones complaining that they were not given more of an opportunity to fight in the main battle. At first he did not mind because they were still out in the open. Now they were in the woods, looking for their lost friends. The main battle could still be heard, throwing off their perceptions as the sounds of war echoed off the trees.

Suddenly enemies ambushed from the right. They had been hiding in the forest, waiting to strike whoever came chasing in. William felt his horse buckle, twisting to the side. It had been hit, and the horse tossed him on his back.

Rolling backwards, William used the momentum to hop to his feet, swords in hand. The troops that Hazer had given to him were holding their own, keeping most of the enemy at bay. William charged the ones making their way into their defensive perimeter, striking down as many as he could.

Hearing the sound of a fellow soldier hitting the ground drew William's attention away, allowing an opening. A flash of light brought him back to his senses just in time to block a sword from striking him down. As he blocked it, he rolled to the side. His new opponent was a brute; a muscle-bound goblin, large for his kind. William ignored the size of the beast, focusing only on the obstacle.

William swung his sword, letting the goblin block it while he impaled him with his other sword. William was shocked. He had made plans for two more moves before cutting into his enemy. The fight ended so soon or so he thought. The goblin grabbed the handle of the sword, along with William's hand, pulling him in closer, driving the blade deeper into his belly.

As William swung his other sword down, hoping to get the beast to release him, the goblin grabbed on to his forearm. It stared at him for a moment, squeezing his arm until it eventually broke. William screamed in pain, dropping his sword. His cry was quickly silenced by a sharp pain to his stomach. He couldn't look down or to the side, just forward. Shock had taken over.

It was far from logical, but as William fell backwards, he landed in a river. He knew there were no rivers in that vicinity, but there he was. He concluded that it must have been all an elaborate dream, caused by the shock. Of course, it never entered his mind that he was already dead before he hit the ground. He was deep in the mountains, floating down this icy river, far from the reaches of man. Even though the water froze his skin, it did nothing to help soothe the open wound in his belly or his broken arm. He wanted out. His limbs slowly went numb, and his skin felt like it was being pricked with a thousand needles. *I don't want to die*, he thought. *Is this really the end?*

His eyes started to get heavy. Everything turned dark. He was starting to fade away, deeper into a dark place. Fear seeped into his heart, and he was afraid that he would never wake up again. At this point, even his mind started to feel numb. That was when a warm feeling came over him. At first it started from behind his knees and his back and slowly grew to his whole body. Once his vision returned, he was able to make out the figure of the King of the Highland. He was holding him, up out of the water, like a child in their parent's arms. Somehow, he was able to transport them from the Outland to wherever they were now.

"I was dead," William said, petrified.

"I know, but I've come to bring you back. It is not your time to go." The King's smile warmed William's soul, helping him gain strength. "Are you ready to go back?"

"But I died." William was afraid to die again.

"Call out to me, and I will come to your aid. Lean on me for power and strength. As proof of my power, I will give you armor."

Back in the gate where William was speaking with the King of the Highland, the king helped William to his feet. "You have to trust me. The road won't be easy, but it will be worth it. The best thing for you to do is measure the cost of following me. Then decide if the path is one you want."

"This place is so painful," William said still trembling. "Everything that I thought that I wanted is worthless. Before I went to the Outland, all I ever wanted was to prove my worth in battle, but now I don't want to fight anymore. I'm afraid to face death again. I have so much to lose. Can't you make it go away?" William was flustered and angry, not wanting to face the pain again.

"If I told you that more than one life would be spared, if you finish this out to the end, would it be worth it?"

"Yes," William said without hesitation, not thinking about the consequences.

"You have made your decision then, and there is no convincing you otherwise." The king pulled out a sword that was tied to his belt. "Take *my* sword with you. Whenever you need it, all you have to do is just call for it. Just imagine that it is in your hands, and I will send it to you." The king then placed a ball of light in William's hand. "These are the prayers of all the people throughout the world who are praying for you to make it home safely. Hopefully, they can be a comfort to you. And do not be impatient, answers will come in time."

The king placed one hand on William's chest where his heart rested and his other hand on his shoulder. "I'll be with you all the way. Do not fear." The King gently pushed him back. William started to fall. He desperately reached out to grab the king. *Trust in me. I won't let you down*, the king told William as he fell. William fell back toward the ground, and it seemed as if he had fallen into a hole. As the king faded into the distance, a light broke through the darkness. William landed on a soft pile of grass in the middle of a forest. No one was around. Though he did not understand fully what the gate was or that the angels were using the gates to move them around in the training ground, he realized that what he experienced must have been a dream or vision. Only now did he understand how crazy the dream was or that it was not real. The hit he received from the troll should have certainly killed him. William laid there for a moment before sitting up. "Go to the Trepidation and remove him from the land."

William sat up looking around searching for the king who was speaking to him, but he couldn't see him. "Okay," William said, getting to his feet. "I'm goin'."

"Not without me," Warren said, leaning against a tree behind him.

"Warren? Boy am I glad to see you!" William said.

"What are you two waiting for?" Lee asked, approaching them in his human form. "We've got work to do."

"Right!" William said. "How about the others?"

"They have their own paths to travel right now," Lee said.

After their initial split out of the tunnel, Amos had succeeded in bringing three of them back together with the help of his master. They had lost Warren and Lily for a moment after they were abducted by the enemy, but they were able to steal them back with minimal effort. After the master sent word to Jonas about the situation, he sent the copy of Cecil to go and just watch over the other clan members. The demons were starting to make their play for the group and the fight was on.

UNLIKELY ENEMIES

Toby sat up rubbing his head after just being thrown by the large troll. "Man that was one crazy ride!"

Naven coughed on the thick dust that was beginning to settle in the room. "You can say that again," Naven said, pulling himself to his feet. Dust gently floated around the room, reflecting off the fluorescent lights hanging down from the ceiling. "I can't believe that we're still alive."

Toby got to his feet and dusted his clothes off while thinking about what Naven had said. "You're right," Toby said in a serious tone. "We probably should be dead after a toss like that. I wonder what happened." Toby pressed against the window that stood in front of him. The pane of glass wasn't broken. The moon was low on the horizon, big and yellow. Toby stared out of the window as the surrounding area became clear to him. They were three stories up and in the middle of a large city.

"Who knows? Where are the others?" Naven asked.

"We should go find them," Toby suggested. Suddenly a crash came from a neighboring room. Toby and Naven ran out of the door to investigate the commotion when a creature burst through the wall, entering the room that they were just in. The two of them stopped to see what it was. A Lymure was standing in the middle of the room, searching for something. It looked like Tomas, only covered in gray dust from the plaster in the wall. The Lymure took a moment to take in his surroundings.

"Is that Tomas?" Naven whispered into Toby's ear.

"No," Toby whispered back. Toby could see that this Lymure had a light gray coat under the layer of dust, not a dark coat like Tomas. The Lymure turned his head toward the two and growled. "I think he heard us!" Toby said, pushing Naven to leave. The two ran down the hall with the Lymure chasing after them. A window sat at the end of the hallway, facing the street. Directly in front of the window was a staircase pointing down in the opposite direction. Naven took the opportunity that the window provided, leaping out of the pane of glass.

Toby knew that a human wouldn't be able to survive the jump from that height. Instead, Toby jumped over the railing of the staircase with the Lymure close behind. As Toby hit the stairs, he took one step and jumped over the next railing. Just as he made it over the second railing, the Lymure crashed through the top railing of the staircase. Toby hit the steps off balance, falling to the landing. Rolling to his feet, Toby could hear the Lymure coming down the stairs. Toby didn't bother stopping to take a peek. He darted down the next flight of stairs, hopping over the next railing with the Lymure's claws coming within inches off his arm. Without taking another step, he leaped over the last railing. He hit the stairs and flipped forward, managing to land on one knee. Surprised, he took a moment to quietly celebrate his achievement. It was something that he thought even Lee would be proud of. However, once he heard the Lymure hit the last landing, he bolted for the door leading out of the building.

Closing his eyes, Toby hit the doors, pushing them open. He only got a few steps out of the building before he tripped over his own feet, falling to the ground. The Lymure was already in the air, preparing to pounce on him. As the Lymure was in its descent toward Toby's back, Tomas tackled it. The two of them landed hard against the ground. Tomas was the first to his feet. He grabbed the other Lymure by the feet and tossed it down the street.

"Are you okay?" Tomas asked, not taking his eyes off the other Lymure.

"Tom! You're okay!" Toby said. "I can't believe it. Thanks."

"Be careful you foolish little boy," Tomas said.

"No problem. I'm glad to help," Toby said, not able to understand a word that Tomas was saying.

Tomas rolled his eyes. "What do you want with us?" Tomas called out to the other Lymure. "Did the Trepidation send you?"

"Do you have any idea how many people don't want him to continue his journey?" the Lymure said. "He's a liability. Do you want to be destroyed by delivering him?"

"He's my friend," Tomas said. "I'll protect him until my death!" Tomas rushed the Lymure with a fierce roar. While Tomas was busy fighting with the Lymure, a second roar came from behind Toby. Toby spun around to see a Warrian rushing toward him.

"No!" Toby said, falling back. Without warning Naven ran up to and bit down on the Warrian's neck, flinging it to the side, leaving it lifeless on the ground. Toby was frozen in fear as he sat on the ground.

"Leave him alone!" Naven demanded.

"What are you going to do to stop me?" another Warrian asked. This one was a female Warrian with pink feathers under her wings. She came from the shadows, standing on Naven's left.

"I'll kill you if you try to hurt him," Naven shouted. "I'll kill anyone who tries." The serious intent was evident in his voice, matched by the intensity of his eyes. It almost did not sound like Naven anymore. Seeing his forceful nature, Toby finally gained the courage to get to his feet and join Naven's side.

"What do you want?" Toby asked. "Why are you attacking?"

"I'm here because I have orders to bring him in," the Warrian said.

"Warrians are supposed to be for peace," Toby insisted. "They're supposed to protect people from the evil in the world, not join it."

"Oh, please!" the Warrian said. "That's a fairy tale for stupid little pups that can't face the hardships of reality. It's a cruel world."

"It's not true!" Toby yelled, shaking his fist. "Warrians are kind and selfless creatures."

"That's right," she said. "You are the great Carmel of the Raptor's pride, aren't you? You poor pathetic thing."

"Shut up!" Toby said, stretching out his hand for his sword but nothing happened.

"You have to concentrate harder," Naven said as the Warrian darted for them. Naven jumped, scratching at the Warrian. The two of them landed and began to bite and scratch at each other while Toby focused on calling his sword. Once he had his sword in hand, he stepped up to help his friend, but he never had the chance to.

A Mission's Level Warrian jumped on the female's back, digging his claws and teeth into her. As soon as he was able to pull her away from Naven, the two split, jumping apart to assess the situation.

"You have won this round," the female Warrian said. "My name is Mica. You will do well to remember it."

Toby, Naven, and the other Mission's Level Warrian remained ready to fight as the female Warrian tipped her head back and began to sing a beautiful melody. As the soft melody rang out, a stone wall started to form between them.

"No way!" Toby said under his breath as he looked at the wall. "It's got to be twenty feet tall."

"Wow," Naven said, joining with Toby. "How'd she do that?"

"She's a harmonizing multiformer," the male Warrian said. "She uses harmonic tones in her voice to organize particles of matter into solid objects. It's a rare gift."

Toby and Naven stared down at him, not sure what to make of his presence. "How do you know that?" Toby asked.

"Because when a Jelly Mold is fed a Warrian's feather, they retain that creature's memories," he said.

"Cecil?" Toby said shocked. "Is it you?" He could see the resemblance but was not sure if it was possible. His original intent was to bring Cecil back, but he never actually thought it would happen.

"How could you give me stolen memories?" Cecil asked.

"I don't understand," Naven said. "Didn't the chief at Kendor tell us that you would *become* the one that you consumed?"

"If so, then he was wrong. Jelly Molds take the form and the memories of the thing that they consume," Cecil said. "I was lucky that Cecil was trained with knowledge of Jelly Molds and their unique properties."

"I always thought that you liked us," Toby said, shrinking back from the scolding.

Cecil sighed. "I do like you guys. Besides you saved me from the Kendorians."

"Saved you?" Naven asked.

"Yeah, do you happen to know what the delicacy is in Kendor?" Cecil said, walking away.

"Ewww," Naven and Toby said in unison.

Suddenly, Toby's attention was stolen away. "Where's Tomas?" Toby turned and realized that he was on the other side of the wall. "Tomas!" Toby yelled running to the wall. "Tomas!" Toby yelled as he pounding on the wall. "Is he okay?" Toby asked with worry straining out of his voice.

"Are you worried about me?" Tomas said, sitting on the top of the wall. "I showed them a thing or two."

"Tom, you're alive!" Toby hollered.

"You gave us a scare," Cecil said.

Tomas jumped from the wall onto the ground. "That one was a multiformer," Tomas said, pulling thorns out of his fur. "She's skilled too."

"I'm sure you are," Toby said with a smile. "We'll get you something to eat here soon."

"You don't have any idea of what he's saying, do you?" Cecil shook his head, already knowing the answer.

"Not a clue," Toby said enthusiastically. "Do you?"

"Very few can actually speak the tongue of the Lymure," Cecil said.

"You've been spending too much time with William," Tomas said. "That idiot tries too hard to rip my words apart."

"I know you love us," Toby said with a grin.

Tomas rolled his eyes as thoughts of choking Toby came into his mind. He shook his head and realized Naven was standing beside him with saddened eyes. "What?"

Naven leaned in and gave Tomas a big hug. "I love you too," Naven said, holding on tight. Tomas started to push him away, but with a discouraged look on his face, he decided not to.

"Where to now?" Cecil asked.

"I don't know," Toby answered. "I've been winging it till now. You have Cecil's memories, why don't you lead us?"

"Warren always led the pack," Cecil said, offering an excuse so he did not take the lead.

"Well I guess we should find the others," Toby said.

"Great. Where should we start?" Naven said, joining the group with Tomas.

"How about under our noses?" Tomas said.

"What?" Toby asked.

Tomas pointed toward one of the buildings as the glass door shattered. Andre emerged from the building, brushing himself off as Kyla and Lily joined him. "Andre!" Toby shouted.

"Hey," Andre said, approaching them. "What happened to the troll?"

"He knocked us into next week," Toby said. Andre looked at Toby with a serious expression. "I was joking. I don't know what happened."

"Wormholes!" Naven proudly announced. "He knocked us through a wormhole."

"I shouldn't have said anything—" Toby started when Andre cut into his sentence.

"No, wait. He's right. We've cut from one world, back to the other," Andre said.

"What are you talking about?" Toby asked. "How?"

"I don't know how, but I felt more power and sharper reflexes back at those houses than I do here."

Toby thought about it for a minute. "I did have to concentrate harder to call my sword here."

"Is that what is tearing up this world?" Andre asked.

"It might be," Toby said. "Too much activity between the Outland and the Inland could be overexposing us to the Outland's energy, causing all of these changes."

"Well, what's our next move?" Andre asked Kyla.

"I guess we wait on Lee and the others," Kyla said.

"They're not coming," Lily said. "They have more pressing matters to attend to."

"Then I guess we should find the Trepidation,"Toby suggested.

"All right," Cecil said, looking up at Toby. "You know this land better than any of us. You lead the way."

"Go for it!" Naven said, cheering along.

"You're actually letting the most irresponsible one in the group lead us? He listens to the childish orange one,"Tomas said. "We're all doomed."

Once their journey in the gate was over, William, Lee, and Warren found themselves in a small town on the edge of a desert. They really did not understand how they got there but neither William nor Warren seemed too concerned. They were more focused on the task at hand. Even though their entire visit to this world was illogical, they did not seem to question it at all. Only one goal seemed to keep them pressing on: to win the fight against the Trepidation.

The fine sand was carried into the town on the wind, adding to the decay of the already crumbling city. For a town that was big enough to hold several thousand people, there were only about a thousand people living there. The people of the city acted more like indentured servants than citizens. With the exception of a few individuals, most of the people there claimed to be happy, glad that the Temps provided for their needs, as long as they were obedient.

Out all of the people in the town, William and Lee were only able to find a few who were willing to speak about the town and what was happening there. The rest were too scared to talk openly about their opinions. Oppression was clearly evident.

There were two Temps that ruled over the area, Envy and Lust. They would often send their guards out to arrest groups of people at a time, taking them to the palace, never to be seen again. That was the determining factor for people's loyalty. They were not sure what happened to their friends, but it was a fate that nobody wanted to share.

After their legwork in the city, Lee and William met up with Warren in an abandoned building about half a mile away from the palace. It was located in an abandoned part of the town, with only a few guards patrolling the area for stragglers. The building was crumbling in decay after the Temps picked the neighborhood apart.

Surveying the land, William and Lee peered out of a hole in the wall, taking note of the guard's movements and the palace. Warren sat against the wall, not bothering to take a second glance. He had been watching the movements while the other two were talking with the locals. He was confident that he knew all there was to know about the area.

"So what do we have down there?" Warren asked.

"From what the people have told us, there are two Temps," William replied. "Envy and Lust."

"I don't think we should be doing this, guys," Lee said. "We should be going after the Trepidation instead. Remember the original plan? Cut off the head of the snake?"

"We need to knock these Temps out first," William countered. "They're in our way. Besides, we were dropped off here, remember? We might as well get rid of them so they can't interfere later."

Lee shook his head, not wanting to make waves.

"I think I should take Lust," William said.

"I doubt it," Lee argued. "Given her name, she obviously has some sort of charm over men. I think I should face her. I have a stronger will against temptation than you."

"Oh please, you've fallen for every girl you've come in contact with," William said. "I think she'd have a field day with you."

"I have not!" Lee demanded. "There was just the one, and she went psycho and came after me."

"What makes you two think it's a girl?" Warren asked, not trying to argue with them.

The two boys sat there with a dumbfounded look on their faces. "Trust me, it's a girl," William said.

Warren rolled his eyes. "Then I should face her," Warren said, getting to his feet.

"Why you?" William asked.

"Because even though I have this new shell, I am still a Warrian at heart," Warren explained. "Her charms won't work on me."

"Well, whether they take longer to work or won't work at all," Lee started, "either way he does have a better chance than us."

"Maybe you're right." William sounded disappointed. "Then while you take care of her, we'll find Envy."

"Sounds like a plan to me," Lee said. "So how are we going to get in?"

"Well I don't know about you two." Warren said closing his eyes, concentrating on forming his fire. Two fiery wings sprouted from his back in a burning glory. "I'll be flying in." Warren moved to the hole in the wall, leaping out and taking off into the air.

"Well, that was nice," William said, watching Warren fly away.

"Hey," Lee said, placing his hand on William's shoulder. "You know, I never really got a chance to explain to you about God's plan for salvation."

"Not now," William whined, rolling his eyes as he got up.

"This is important," Lee tried to explain.

"I know it is," William said. "But this is important too. We have some pretty big problems to deal with here first. I tell you what, after we get done with this here, we can talk about your churchy stuff."

"Are you sure we'll have time later?"

William shook his head, exiting the room. He was not in the mood to talk about religion or any other things of that nature.

He wanted to be focused on getting into the palace and dealing with the Temps.

While William and Lee were making their way through the town, avoiding guards and sneaking up to the entrance, Warren made good use of his ability to fly and landed calmly on the roof of the palace. Once he had landed, his fiery wings burned away. Warren stretched his arms out to relieve the pressure building in his shoulders. He had already forgotten what it felt like to fly. The physical aspect of his flame strained his muscles as if the fire wings were actually mounted to his back.

Before long, Warren was able to find an entrance on the roof, sneaking his way in. As he sneaked through the building, he saw an uncomfortable resemblance to the palace at Ram. Though the structure and floor plans had changed, the design was still the same—from the carpets in the halls to the tapestries on the walls. He had never thought about it before, but he was starting to recognize how the two worlds were unnaturally similar, merging in a sense. The thought quickly passed as he focused on the mission at hand. He could not spend any more time on this matter, or more accurately, he did not want to.

Excitement rushed over Warren as he delved back into the creature he once was. He was a stalker, a predator in the night. Slipping in and out of shadows while hunting down his prey, it made him feel alive. His adrenaline pumping, the anticipation of the strike overtook him; this was the environment that he wanted.

It did not take long to search the top two floors, finding nothing of importance. Warren was ready to give up on his search when he found a group of prisoners being led back upstairs to the south side of the palace. He did not remember seeing anything back in that direction, but he decided to follow them just to see what was going on. Up to the next floor, he watched as they pulled a lever that moved a large statue away from a secret door. It was no wonder that he had missed it on his first pass. It was obvious that the Temps had many elaborate passages in this place.

Warren made his way to the edge of the doorway, spying in on the prison. The cells themselves were plain with a large open window on the outside each cell. The odd part was that there were no bars on the windows. It was almost like an invitation for the prisoners to jump out given that the cells were several stories high. With the exception of sand and dust covering the floor, the cells were clean; the walls matched the color of the sand on the floor. Warren found himself disgusted with the depravity of these Temps.

"Beautiful isn't it, lover boy?" a female voice whispered in Warren's ear. Warren spun around the corner, moving away from the voice while turning to face her. It was a beautiful young woman wearing an elegant blue dress. She was Caucasian, radiant with an air of arrogance around her. Though she could have passed for some kind of actress or beauty queen, something dark and sinister loomed within her. Two blue stones hung from a pair of earrings that she wore. The color matched her tightly fitted dress tastefully. "It's so nice of you to come visit me. Won't you stay for dinner?" Two guards grabbed Warren by his shoulders and wrists, restraining him from running away. "What is a little child like you doing in a place like this?"

"You know why I'm here," Warren demanded. "Hand over your sin."

"Oh, you're cute," the woman said with an intrigued smile on her face. "Don't worry, this won't hurt a bit."

"I doubt that," Warren said, pushing away from her. Warren waited for the woman to come within reach and then he leapt forward. He planted one of his feet on her leg, kicking her in the chin with the other foot. The guards pulled him back down, but Warren unleashed his flames, letting them run up his arms. The men screamed in agony as the fire clung to them, but the flames were hard to extinguish.

Warren spun around the frantic guards, moving to a more open area. Once his movements were no longer restricted, he swung his arm back, unleashing his fire whip. Flinging it forward, he took one of the woman's earrings off. She yelped in pain.

“I’ve taken your Sin,” Warren said arrogantly, pleased with his accomplishment. His pride quickly dwindled as she glared at him. He expected her to turn to dust, but she straightened up with an equally arrogant expression on her face.

“You’ve only taken the one!” she said, obviously not pleased as blood dripped down the side of her face. She opened her palm toward Warren and an invisible force knocked him back into the air. Warren was able to use one of his hands to break his fall, rolling back onto his feet. “You’ll pay for that!” she exclaimed.

Warren released a fireball in her direction, followed by a strike of his whip. She dodged the first strike but caught his whip in her hand. She willingly took the damage from his flame in order to counter the strike. She raised her hand violently, unleashing another invisible attack. It was as if two invisible blades had risen out of the floor, barely connecting with Warren’s body. Fear struck him as two cuts formed in his jacket from the attack. Though he did not see anything, he certainly felt it brush against him. He also felt the blood dripping from his cheek. He wasn’t sure if she missed on purpose or if she just misjudged the distance, but he understood that she was a stronger opponent than he had first anticipated. Deciding that there wasn’t much more that he could do, Warren opened one of the cell doors and closed it behind him.

“Open that door!” she demanded as she inspected a tear in her dress. She was not interested in merely eliminating an intruder, but she was more interested in toying with him, like a cat with a mouse.

Warren raised two sets of keys for them to see. “Tell me something. Are you the dreaded Lust?” Warren tossed the keys out of the open window.

The woman walked over to the cell with a cool demeanor. “Who wants to know?” she asked in a seductive tone.

Warren chuckled, still convinced that he had the upper hand. “I’m Warren of Weremore, and I’ve come to destroy you.” Warren had a glowing smile.

Lust smirked at his attempts of humor. “You will die and—”

“Madam,” a soldier said, entering the room. “You’re needed in the court room.”

“I’m in the middle of something here!” Lust barked, displeased with the interruption.

“I’m sorry, but Miss Envy ordered me to bring you there immediately.”

Lust smiled graciously at Warren. “My apologies. It seems that I have an urgent matter that needs my attention. If you’ll excuse me, I’ll be back shortly.” Lust winked at Warren, turning to walk seductively away.

Warren waited until she took a few steps and unleashed his whip again, taking the other earring with his whip. “Got you!” Warren shouted with celebration, but his face sank as Lust turned back around.

“You can’t get rid of me that easily!” Lust demanded, grabbing the face of one of the guards. The man screamed and struggled as his body transformed into dust, exactly like a Temp who had lost their Sin. As she released the man, she gave a quick push, causing the body to join the rest of the sand that littered the prison floor. Lust straightened up, brushing herself off showing off her new figure. She looked five years younger with both ears reformed on her head. Even the wound on her hand was healed.

“How?” Warren asked. “You’re a—”

That’s when he realized what he was standing on. It was not merely sand, but her past victims. That is what she used the prison system for, to feed her obsession. He came to a new understanding of how deep her sadistic nature actually went.

“I believe here we call it a vampire,” Lust said, applying a fresh coat of lipstick. The idea was that she lived off of the energy that made up other people, reducing their bodies to the basic minerals that made them up. In essence, she was literally living off their life force. That was what made her unique among the Temps. She was able to place the payment of her sin upon other people rather than taking it upon herself. This was able to sustain her and even make her look younger and more beautiful. “Make sure he doesn’t leave that cell. He’s dinner.” She pointed to the soldier that came to retrieve her. "Come." She obviously did not know the extent of his powers or that he could fly, but Warren did not want to show his hand yet. This gave him an opportunity to consider what had just happened and time to come up with a new plan.

William and Lee hid behind a jeep that was parked next to the palace entrance. The palace guards were busy playing a game of cards on a wooden crate by the entrance. It was the only visible way into the building, and the guard's had decided to change their pattern at the last minute. William and Lee were stuck there for the moment until they came up with a new strategy.

"There isn't any other way in," Lee said, peeking around a jeep that was parked out front. "What do you think we should do?"

Looking into the jeep that they were hiding behind, William just happened to see a couple of guard uniforms sitting in the backseat. They had just been brought back from the dry cleaners and had not even been taken out of their wrappings yet.

"Here you go," William said, handing Lee the uniform.

With their disguises, they were able to make their way into the building. The guards did not bother taking a second glance. The two of them acted as if they were just moving about a normal day, it seemed, to work. They did not draw any unwanted attention and were able to blend in with the other guards that were patrolling the palace. They made sure not to open any doors that were not inviting or make any careless moves.

After making a few rounds, they finally stumbled upon the throne room. It was massive as if made for giants. Sections of the north and west walls were removed, the ceiling being held up with massive pillars. The room was elegant, to say the least. Everything was trimmed in gold with rubies and other precious stones ornamenting it. Three thrones sat in the center, the middle one far larger than the other two. The stone floor was waxed, polished, and shined every day. However, the room was empty without a soul in sight.

"I think we found it," William said.

Without a sound, a sharp point poked William and Lee in the back. They had been found out.

"Bind them," a voice shouted as something heavy was struck across the back of their necks.

When consciousness came back to William, he found himself on the floor with Lee, lying facedown in the middle of the room with spears at their back. The largest throne had a brute of a man sitting upon it with a woman sitting on his lap. She leaned into the man's chest. The woman seemed to be of Middle Eastern descent with darker skin and black hair. The man looked more like a Native American with a well-sculpted body. He had a dark tan with long black hair as well.

William remained calm, not moving but just looking around. He looked over at Lee, who had one eye open, already taking in the situation. "That must be Lust," William whispered, looking up at the woman.

"I don't think so," Lee said, looking up at her.

"Get up," a guard yelled, poking William. The guards forced William and Lee off their bellies and onto their knees.

"Want to bet?" William asked Lee as he got up off the floor. He wanted Lee's help to distract them, signaling him with his eyes to play along. By acting like they were goofs, they would be able to force them to lower their guard.

"Deal," Lee said.

"Silence!" the guard yelled, hitting William across the head. "Quiet that mumbling."

The woman on the throne raised her hand to the guards, signaling for them to leave. The two men stood to attention and then scampered out of the room.

"What is it that you want? You have wagered your very lives by coming here."

"Tell me, who is Lust?" William asked.

The two sitting on the throne looked at each other curiously. "I am Envy," the woman said.

"And I am Jealousy," the man added.

"Man!" William said.

"You lost that bet," Lee said, chuckling.

"Hey, he's not Lust either," William insisted.

"I told you that *she* wasn't Lust. You owe me," Lee said.

"Hey, hold on a minute," William said, pushing the game a little further. "Aren't jealousy and envy the same thing? How can there be two Temps of the same thing?"

The woman scoffed at him. "You two know nothing. It is true that the two are closely related, but the difference is that one wants what the other has while the other hates you for having it."

"So which one are you?" Lee asked. "What kind of talent landed you that Sin?"

She rolled her eyes, disgusted with their questions. "Each Sin does carry its own special power, sometimes mimicking the characteristics of the sin it is named after, but not always. Addiction's Sin allowed him to make and control the drug that infected countless people. Murder's Sin gives him an incredible amount of strength and a bloodlust incomparable to any other. But we are not our Sins." Envy pointed between Jealousy and herself adding, "My husband and I were chosen to carry these Sins, not because we acted a certain way, but because we are loyal to the cause. We're just ordinary people with special gifts."

"Jealousy, I believe you are needed down stairs," Lust said, coming into the room.

"Very well, Lust," Jealousy said, getting up. "Just don't kill them before I get back."

William didn't bother turning his head, but his eyes strained from side to side, looking for her to enter his vision. Lust slowly joined Envy at the thrones and took her seat.

"What should we do with them?" Envy asked.

"Let's eat them," Lust said. "I get the little one."

William and Lee looked at each other with a worried look on their faces. "Who's the little one?" Lee asked.

"I'm bulkier," William said. "It must be you."

"I'm taller than you," Lee said.

"Don't argue," Envy said. "You'll both have your chance to serve your kingdom."

While the two Temps were distracted with William and Lee, Warren flew into the room. Once he was on target, his flame wings faded, and he launched a fiery stream from his whip at the two women. They leapt off of their thrones, landing hard against the ground. Warren hit the ground and rolled onto his feet. Once Warren settled on his feet, two little fireballs shot out from his hand, engulfing the ropes that held his friends. Thanks to the nature of Warren's fire, like that of the fire of the Nova, his friends weren't harmed. Lee quickly transwarped into his Kalymor form while William called for his sword.

"What is the meaning of this?" Envy shouted, pulling herself up, only making it to her knees before Lee kicked her down, catching her necklace with his foot. Lee pulled it, snapping the chain from around her neck. The necklace flew to the floor. Envy's hands chased after the necklace like a beggar chasing after a few coins. Turning into a pillar of dust, she turned her head back toward Lee with one hand extended toward him and one still reaching after her Sin.

William charged after Lust, thrusting his sword toward her. She raised her hand, using the invisible blast to shoot him across the room. He landed facedown, and with one bounce, the sword disappeared in a flash of light. Lee's eyes followed William across the room, not seeing Lust crawling behind the throne where she slipped into another secret passage.

"Where's Lust!" Warren barked, looking around the room.

Lee ran to William's aid, answering, "I don't know. Weren't you watching her?"

"I was distracted by William." Warren was making excuses. He had hesitated during the battle, remembering his near defeat the last time he fought her. His flame was not strong enough, and her invisible power frightened him; and when William was tossed across the room, it broke everyone's concentration.

"Don't go blaming this on me," William said, checking himself for broken bones. "I didn't know she could do that."

"Let's get out of here," Lee suggested. "There are still two more out there, and by the looks of it, her husband will not be pleased." Lee was looking down at what was left of Envy.

"Let's see if they have a car we can take," William said. "I'm tired of walking."

Several hours later, after the three had left the palace, Jealousy marched back to the throne room enraged at the thought that he needed to babysit the troops downstairs. It did not take him very long, but he was upset that he missed time with his love. He returned to the courtroom to find Envy kneeling on the floor. Jealousy chuckled at the sight as he called out, "What are you doing?" He was often amused at some of the games she would play. When she didn't move, he began to feel uneasy. "What's wrong, dear?" he said, coming closer. Finally, he saw the damage done. He saw that she had been turned into a pillar of dust. "No!" Jealousy ran to her and fell to the ground in front of her. "How could this have happened?" he asked weeping. "What have I done? What have they done?" His grief turned to anger as the rage consumed him. "I'll hunt them down and kill them all!"

LIES

The afternoon sun was starting to fade away, yet the sky had not started to change color. Toby and the other members of the Raven Clan were left alone in a large city, wondering how William, Lee, and Warren were doing. It had been a couple of days since they had seen them, and there were no signs as to what city they had been dropped in. Using the sun to guide them, the group continued to make their way east, hoping to either find a map or the coast. Toby figured that they would be able to follow it north, finding New York after that. The last time they were separated, William said that they would meet up at the Empire State building. Toby assumed that was still the plan.

Slouching forward, Toby's head sank a little. He tucked his hands into his pockets, mulling over the depressing thoughts that rolled around in his mind. Deep down, he felt as if he could have done more to keep the whole group together. Guilt was starting to move in. He wanted to be stronger so that no one else had to get hurt. Abe and Nell, even Warren and Lily, all of them ended up being hurt by Alex, and there was nothing that the "great Carmel" could do. He felt weak and useless.

"I had no idea that this is what you were describing," Naven said, looking up at the buildings. "This place is wonderful." He made himself sound cheery, sensing his friend's depression. Nothing hurt him more than when Toby was sad.

"I know." Toby chuckled, masking his sorrow. "It's been some time since I've been to the city. At least three years now." Toby hadn't put much thought into it, but he had been away from home for a long time; though the dates and times in his head weren't exact, he knew it had been a while.

"Who built this place?" Andre asked. "Everything is shiny, like diamonds."

"I don't have a specific name," Toby said. "But ordinary people built the city. Engineers and other smart people made all of this possible."

"It's amazing," Kyla said.

"Hey, look at this," Lily said picking up a hunting bow that was lying on the ground. "Do you want to see something cool?"

"Yeah," Kyla encouraged as she approached with some of the others. Toby simply turned to watch, but Cecil stayed vigilant, keeping guard at the rear.

"Watch this," Lily said. A long thin shaft launched out of the palm of her hand, moving along her fingers. The shaft had three flaps on the back end. She had made an arrow completely out of her own bone and cartilage; the power to spontaneous generate bone was a convenient power for her to have, especially with a bow. "It was the first trick taught to me." Lily pulled back on the bow with the bone arrow in the firing position. She shot it through a window.

"Amazing!" Kyla said. "That is an incredible power."

"Cool," a man standing out in front of them said. He was a skinny man of an average height with a short haircut. An evil aura seemed to radiate from him. He seemed like the type of slimy person you would find pushing something illegal on a street corner. "Although I doubt it could be that effective in battle."

Toby turned with his hands still in his pockets. Something about this guy set him on edge. "Who are you? Are you with the military?" Toby noticed that he was wearing a pair of military issue pants with a tan T-shirt. He figured it would be something a soldier might wear, but that was not the sense he got from the man.

"No, those dogs couldn't match up to me," the man said.

Toby scoffed at him. "What do you want?"

"Your head," the man replied nonchalantly.

"You think you can take it, you reject?" Tension rose in Toby's voice.

"This coming from a Backstreet Boy knockoff?" the man mocked. "I am Lie. I am many and I am strong." He raised his fist, showing off a watch that had two red stones on both sides of the band.

Toby laughed at the taunt. "Why do you want to die?" The arrogant man just showed them his Sin, essentially showing them how to kill him. It was as if he was trying to goad them into a fight. "You must know who we are."

"I do, and that is why I will destroy you all." The man moved one leg behind him to form a fighting stance. Toby took one hand out of his pocket and formed his sword. A small light appeared from the man's watch, and two clones appeared beside of the man. Then two more spread out from them and so on till there were twenty of them.

Toby sighed. "Have it your way."

In unison, the man and his clones pointed at them and yelled, "Attack!" Toby quickly gripped his sword and charged them. The Raven Clan split, starting their counterattack.

Kyla took the left side of the group, using her agility and the walls of the buildings to help her. She bounced off the wall executing a spin kick downward, slicing one of the clones across the chest with the claws on her feet. By time she landed, the clone had already turned to dust, covering the ground. She slashed one of the other clones, executing a jump kick on another. With her athletic body structure, her nimble attacks were not only effective but quick as well. She could use every piece of the environment as a weapon and every surface as a battleground.

Meanwhile, Andre and Tomas were protecting Lily as she stood back using her bow to fire arrows at the clones. Tomas enjoyed picking up clones and using them as a clubs to beat the other clones with. They only lasted for about two swings before turning into dust as well, but Tomas found it to be enjoyable nonetheless. One of the clones jumped at Tomas in hopes of knocking him over, but his agility was no match. Tomas jumped in the air, grabbing the clone with his foot. Tomas was able to use his feet in battle just as effectively as he could use his hands.

Andre tossed clones to the side and slammed others into the ground. With every clone Andre tossed to the side, Lily was able to hit one with an arrow. Andre did his best to keep a close eye on Cecil who was in the middle of fighting a group on the other side of the battle.

Cecil never stopped moving as he fought. His little body didn't touch a surface for more than a fraction of a second. Cecil hopped from one clone to the next, not making enough damage to destroy them on the first hit, but it was enough to keep them occupied.

The street was filling with Lie's bodies. He would double his clones for every one clone that the Clan destroyed. The odds were slowly shifting in his favor. The Clan could easily hold their own against the weak clones, but their stamina couldn't last forever. They would eventually tire, and when they let their guard down for that moment, that is when they would lose.

The battle field was starting to become full. The overcrowding of Lies was becoming an issue. The Raven Clan couldn't avoid bumping into the enemy. Toby hit the ground as Naven pounced on the clone that knocked him down.

"There are too many," Toby said, getting up. He scanned the crowd of clones to find a unique one that could possibly be the original.

"What do we do?" Naven asked, looking back. One of the clones attempted to jump on Naven's back, but he ducked in time. As the clone got to his feet Naven closed his jaw around his head turning him to dust. "Eck," Naven said with his tongue hanging out of his mouth. "That's just eckfull."

"Naven!" Toby yelled as a group of clones jumped on Naven, knocking him to the ground. With a growl, Naven transwarped into his larger form. The blast knocked all of the clones back. That was when Toby noticed him, one of the men standing downfield. He just stood there, staring at Naven as he came out of the transwarp tunnel. Toby had a plan running through his head, but he would have to get closer to execute it. He dashed through the clones cutting as many as he could. He did his best not to run in a straight line hopping not to give away his plan. Toby stopped and spun, slicing into one of the clones. Once he stopped, he took his sword and threw it to his right. Toby's aim was true, digging into Lie's shoulder. All of the clones wailed as holes opened in their shoulders. "Got him!" Toby yelled. "Naven!" Toby shouted, pointing at the true Lie. "Get'm, buddy." Naven shot a fireball at the man. As the ball hit, the dust scattered in all directions, and all of the other clones fell to the earth. Toby laughed. "We got him." The team shouted in joy, standing victorious on the field of battle.

"Is everyone all right?" Andre asked.

"You bet," Toby said. "That was just what the doctor ordered." Toby was full of energy and began to punch at the air. His depression had been defeated. "Hey, you better revert," he told Naven.

"I thought we could cover more ground this way," Naven said. "Climb on and we can move along faster."

Toby smiled. "Okay, sounds like a plan to me."

As the words left Toby's mouth, several cans of gas flew out into the streets. "Ambush!" Andre shouted, running for cover. "Get out!"

"Toby!" Naven shouted as a dart pierced his skin. Naven roared in anger as he turned in the direction that the dart came from, but his roar quickly turned into a whimper. Naven passed out, falling into one of the buildings.

Toby stopped, turning in the direction of his fallen friend. "Naven!"

Andre grabbed him from around the waist. "You can't save him like that!" Andre lifted him, carrying him toward a nearby building.

"We've got to go back," Toby screamed. "I won't leave him." A dart hit Toby in the leg. "What is—" Toby fell limp in Andre's arms.

The group ran into one of the abandoned buildings, hiding from their pursuers. "I hate to admit it," Lily started. "But Toby's right. We need to go back for Naven. They could be killing him right now."

Andre shook his head. "I'm glad Toby isn't awake to hear that." Andre laid Toby on the hard tile floor, grabbing his own head. The room was slowly spinning in place. "I think that gas was poisoned." He collapsed to the floor, trying to hold himself up, but it was a losing battle.

"You breathed too much in," Kyla said, trying to keep him up. "Tomas—" Kyla turned, noticing that Tomas wasn't with them. "Where did Tomas go?"

"Did he follow?" Lily asked.

"I'll go check," Cecil offered.

Softly, Cecil navigated back out of the building. He wasn't surprised that the troops had followed them into the building, but they couldn't discern where the rest of the group was hiding. Making his way back to the ambush site, he saw several dozen men in white full-body suits. They were wrapping Naven in harnesses, getting ready to transport him. Tomas lay several feet away, knocked out from the gas. He was too proud as a warrior to run from battle. He ended up playing into their hands. *We all played into their hands*, Cecil thought to himself. *Lie was a diversion to pull our attention away from the ambush waiting for us.* Cecil took careful observation to notice that the men were Echoes. *Baccale!*

Snap. A piece of glass broke directly behind him. Cecil jumped out from the barrier that he was hiding behind. A tranquilizer grazed the ground behind his foot. He took a hard right, avoiding the next tranquilizer, ducking into a storm drain and vanishing from sight.

Baccale had sent a special group of Echoes after the Raven Clan to collect them so that he could finish the job of anchoring them to this world. Their plan was coming along according to schedule.

"What's going on over there?" Baccale called.

"A Warrian is running loose," one of the Echoes answered.

"A Warrian?" Baccale was confused. The only Warrian on the list was Warren, but he was being picked up by someone else.

There shouldn't have been a Warrian in this place. "Where is the Warrian that we recruited to hunt them down? The harmonizing multiformer, Mica?"

"She should be back at the laboratory, setting things up with that Lymure of hers."

"It must be that little Jelly Mold then," Baccale said under his breath. He remembered the reports about Cecil's clone following the group. "It'll be fine. That creature cannot interfere with us. If it tries, kill it."

Kyla and Lily managed to move to an outer window undetected. They could see Tomas being loaded into a van, strapped down tight to a metal board. Naven, meanwhile, was strapped into the harness, which was being tied down to the street. The men looked like they were preparing to do some sort of surgery on him. Machines were being wheeled up alongside his massive body.

"What are we going to do?" Lily asked, worried that their friends were going to be taken away.

"I'm not sure yet," Kyla answered, fear creeping up inside. "Lee and William do this stuff all the time. I'm sure we can do it too."

"Do they always go up against so many people?" Lily wasn't sure if they could. "Maybe if Toby and Andre were awake."

"We don't need them," Kyla replied. "We're just as good as any man is."

Lily looked out at the street. The situation was starting to get out of hand. She knew they were good, but were they *that* good? They held their own fine with the clones, and she was able to stand up to Alex, but there were a lot of troops out there. "What's our plan?"

"I don't know yet," Kyla answered. She was agitated that she had not thought of one already. "Okay, we have the element of surprise. We need to hit them where it hurts, cripple them, and make sure they can't get up to counterstrike."

"Great!" Lily exclaimed. "How do we do that?"

"Well..." Kyla thought about it for a moment. "That guy down there looks like he's in charge." Kyla pointed at Baccale. "If we take out the leader, then the rest of the troops should run."

“I don’t know about that,” Lily said. “It worked for Lie, but I don’t think that guy is a Temp. And besides, they have guns, like Lee and William. I can’t dodge one of those.”

Suddenly there was a commotion behind them. “Sir, I’ve found two more.” Silence. “A boy and some freaky mutant thing.” Another pause. “I don’t care what it’s called. They’re both knocked out.” The man waited for a reply. “I’ll bring them down now.”

The girls looked at each other. They were on their own now, and they were not going to let the boys do all of the fighting. They made up their minds, and they were going to beat the impossible odds. The plan was simple, take out the leader. Kyla insisted that she would make a break for him. Her speed and agility would prove to be critical in the operation. She needed to stay undetected as long as possible. Lily would wait until Kyla was spotted, then go for the van that the troops were keeping the boys in. Kyla hoped that this would make the troops think that it was their plan to rescue the boys. In part it was, but Kyla wanted this to give her the opportunity to get a strike in on the leader.

Lily’s part was bigger than just a distraction. She could form shields out of her bone, like Alex did, and that would prove vital when fortifying her position. Once she got to the van, she would need to wake the boys up and secure it for a getaway vehicle. Toby would never forgive them if they left Naven behind, so they had to make sure that they got him too.

Kyla waited in the shadows of the building for an opportunity to emerge. The leader was preparing to stick needles into Naven, hooking him up to the machines. Kyla had to make her move quickly. In a decisive moment, Kyla changed her plan. She ran out into the light of day, charging down the middle of the street for all to see her. The troops went into a temporary state of shock not knowing what to do.

Lily hesitated for a moment, waiting for a reaction from the troops. She wasn’t going to blow her cover until she saw that they were going to attack. Kyla was able to dodge the first shot, giving Lily her signal. Lily burst through an upper window, two stories up landing in a rolling position in front of the van. Two guards rushed her, getting a bit of a surprise. Lily kicked the first one in the chest, knocking him to the ground. As her foot landed, Lily moved into a leg sweep, knocking the legs out from under the second guard. As Lily flung the side door open on the van and a dart hit her in the stomach, a soldier was waiting for her, gun drawn and ready.

Kyla didn't know it, but she was now on her own. A group of soldiers lined up between her and the leader, ready to take her down. *Now or never*, she thought to herself. As the men raised their guns, Cecil crashed into one of their faces. The impact caused two of them to topple over, the rest stood in shock of what had happened. Kyla leapt over the line, thankful for Cecil's help. She landed in front of Baccale. "I've got you now!" she shouted, far too cocky for her own good. Baccale's face was unchanging as if she was nothing more than a noisy gong. His interest was no more piqued than when she hiding.

A single shot rang out. Kyla could feel a sharp pain dig into her neck. Fire ran through the muscles and down her spine. She opened her mouth, wanting to scream, but nothing came out. She landed face-first on the asphalt.

Baccale looked over at a sniper who was kneeling down at a broken window. He was on the third floor, pointing his rifle down at Kyla's body. "At least one of you is useful," Baccale said, laying a set of needles down on a tray. "Did you get the clone?"

"Sorry, sir," one of the Echoes pointed down the street. "He got away."

"He does not matter," Baccale said, slightly annoyed. "Pack up Raven's Clan. We need to get them back to the lab." He stuck two needles into Naven's neck, switching on the machine. "I still need to revert this one back to his smaller form."

The jeep that William, Lee, and Warren took from the desert palace ran out of gas just outside of a ruined city. Slabs of cement, stones, and other pieces from buildings littered the streets. It was as if a bulldozer had run the city over, decimating everything in its path. It was the earmark of war. Many of the cities that they had once visited were now unrecognizable. Everything had changed.

Warren took point, walking about fifty yards out front. William and Lee walked at a more casual pace, taking in the destruction of the city. It was a depressing sight for them. Seeing their world torn apart they way it was made them wish there was more that they could do.

A small rock was kicked in their direction, bouncing in front of Lee's feet. Standing on a mound of rubble was the demon's master. Even with his designer shades on, it was as if his gaze pierced through them.

"Who are you?" William asked, not understanding this man's intentions or power. "Are lost or something?"

"I'm just a fellow wanderer," the man said. "Roaming through the earth and going back and forth in it."[8]

Lee growled, knowing that line. It was how the devil answered God in Job, and this man seemed like he could be a devil. He remembered Amos warning him about the enemy disguising themselves like the good guys and to test them. "What is the gospel message?" Lee asked.

"What are you talking about?" William said, trying to stop Lee's churchy talk by pulling him back. He did not want to insult this new friend, especially since he looked to be a cool and important person.

"It's all right," the man said. "That Jesus came to earth, dying for your sins, allowing you to go to heaven," the devil said easily. "You're all basically good people, and God loves you all the way you are."

"And what do you need to do to get to heaven?" Lee drilled harder, already knowing that this was not sent from God.

"Nothing," the man replied. "You're already good enough. Just keep on being a good person, and you'll be fine."

"You're a demon!" Lee shouted. "That is not the Gospel. Christ died for us so that those who repent may be saved by grace through faith."[9]

"Stop!" William shouted.

Lee had enough. He formed his knives in his hands, throwing one at the man. The devil easily dodged it by slightly turning to the side. Lee threw the other one while reforming the first one back in his hand. The devil calmly walked down the mound of rubble, avoiding the next attack. Infuriated, Lee transwarped into his Kalymor form while calling back the second knife he threw. He charged, overconfident in his own skills, and the devil agitated the matter even more by chuckling at him. He never saw the devil draw his sword or even the devastating blows that flashed through his body. He only felt the burning pain and ribbons of blood pour from his wounds. He landed face-first, already passed out from the attack.

"Lee!" William shouted, forming his sword in his hand.

The devil was already on solid ground by time William made his sword. Warren was still on his way, but he would not make it in time. Satan turned, avoiding William's swing while plunging his sword into William's back. The blade moved in and out smoothly with the precision of a surgeon. William fell to the ground, still conscious, but unable to move. He grunted at his own humiliation. He had no idea who this man was, but in one blow, he was able to defeat him.

The devil waited for Warren to get closer, before swinging his sword in his direction. William's blood, still fresh on the blade, splattered against his face, triggering a deep rage. Red flames engulfed his fists as the devil antagonized him further by smelling the blood on his sword. Warren flung his fire whip forward, which the devil caught with his bare hand, pulling it away from him. Warren could not breathe. Not only did the man pull away one of his strongest weapons, but now he disappeared from his sight. Briefly looking down, he saw the man underneath him, swinging his fist upward. Three ribs broke with an audible crunch as the man made contact. His diaphragm was now paralyzed. The man rose, slamming his fist into Warren's back, driving him into the ground.

A clapping came from behind him. "Congratulations, sir," Morygon praised as he approached. "Was it a good workout?"

"Hardly," the devil said as he brushed himself off. "It was not even enough to be considered a warm-up." Morygon reached down to pick up William's sword when the devil called out to him. "Don't touch that!"

Morygon jumped back like a frightened child. "What's wrong?"

"That sword belongs to the King of the Highlands. Touching it could kill you."

"But that boy was wielding it. Why would you fight against him if he had such a dangerous weapon?"

The devil laughed as he approached Morygon. "Just because someone has a powerful weapon like that does not mean they know how to use it. Even though he is not a Christian, that boy has been given the power that all Christians have to call the king's sword. However, most of them cannot even unsheathe such a sword, let alone kill anything with it. If a more skilled technician had been wielding the sword, such as John Wesley, they might have lasted a few minutes but certainly longer than this weak little boy. He fell before me in one blow."

"What do we do with them now?" Morygon asked.

"Take them to Baccale's laboratory," the devil said. "Preparations need to be made."

"What about the Christian boy? Should we get rid of him?"

"No," Satan ordered. "If he were to disappear now, then the others would be distracted, running off to look for him. It is best if we just endure him for now."

Baccale stood over Toby, starting with his preparations of anchoring him to the world. It had been a long process, but Toby was the last one. Ripoll sat to the left of the operating table, watching Baccale work. Overall, Ripoll seemed captivated with the performance. It was a complicated yet fascinating procedure. All of the instruments for the procedure were laid out to

Baccale's left, sitting in front of Ripoll. Vials, clamps, and other instruments that were hard to describe were arranged in a semi-organized fashion. After so many operations, Baccale was less than organized with his equipment.

Taking a knife from the table, Baccale lifted Toby's shirt. He made an incision just above his belly, reaching inside to find what he was looking for. He then used a clamp to secure the location as he began to set up what he needed next in the operation. He took a vial from the table and secured it to a medical apparatus that had a metal loop on it.

"What is that?" Ripoll asked, pointing to the vial.

"That is a spirit," Baccale answered, continuing on with the procedure. "I call it Return. I mixed a bit of power with envy and discontentment into the vial, and this is what will pull them back, allowing their powers to draw forward. It's all a matter of pressure."

"So you made it?"

"No, our master gave it to me," Baccale answered. "I am not sure how he came about it, or if he isn't the one who made it, but I only added the compounds to make it more appealing, tempting them to use it more."

"Clever," Ripoll commended.

With a snap of his instrument, Baccale had finished setting the last anchor. He started to pull out his instruments, laying them back down on the table. As he started to sew up the incision he had made, Morygon burst through the doors with the last three remaining members of the Raven Clan. They were tossed onto a cart, being wheeled around as if they were produce.

"It's about time!" Baccale shouted, laying down his needle. "Finish this," he told Ripoll.

"We were halfway around the world," Morygon tried making an excuse, but in truth, he just wasted his time looking for the cart to carry them on.

"You should have just carried them." Baccale insisted. He picked them up one at a time, using one hand, laying them face-up on the next operating table. "What did you do? They're all torn up!" Picking at the holes in their clothing, he inspected the wounds.

"What's wrong?" Morygon asked. "It's not like they're going to die. Remember, this is just the training ground. It's like a dream. Unless that is you are starting to feel sorry for them."

"I'm the one who has to patch them up," Baccale huffed. "My hard work and my time. You always end up ruining any mission I send you on."

"Don't blame me for this. I did not lay a finger on them." Morygon rolled his eyes as he spoke. "Our master was the one who apprehended them."

Baccale could only shake his head. He would not argue with his master. Opening Warren's shirt, he just continued on with the operation.

"Would you like me to get started on this one?" Ripoll asked, reaching for Lee's body.

Baccale grabbed Ripoll's wrist, staring at Lee. "Not that one. Just sew up his wounds. Use this." Baccale gave him a tube that had some medical paste in it.

"I thought the master wanted us to anchor all of them," Ripoll said, confused by the order.

"Amos and the other angels have too much influence over him," Baccale explained. "Anchoring him will just work against us in the end. Besides, Amos cursed him. He cannot enter the Outland again."

"Cursed?" Ripoll asked.

"The Falling of Sorrows," Morygon clarified. He understood that Ripoll had not had too much experience dealing with the Outland, so he offered to explain. "Amos had the boy use the curse to clear the battlefield. Normally, this curse transforms the person into the living dead. It is the same thing that transformed the people in Daniel and those in the castle of Gama. The boy was just able to leave the Outland before he started to decay. Now that he has been cursed, he will not be able to go back."

"Is it possible to force him back?" Ripoll asked. "What would happen if you tried?"

"You'd probably just end up hurting yourself," Baccale scoffed. "Manipulating compounds and other materials, you might be able to pull him into another dimension though."

"I don't see why that would be necessary," Morygon said.

Baccale disagreed, saying, "Never underestimate the power of a crisis or a distraction."

"What do you mean?" Ripoll asked.

"What would happen if we were able to pull the Christian boy into another dimension?" Baccale asked. The two just stared blankly. "His people would surely pray for him, ignoring the world collapsing around them. If he were to disappear before their eyes, they would feel as if they had to stop praying for everything else. Humans have very little concept as to the power of prayer or how to use it. They would stop praying for their little matters, feeling selfish, ashamed, and petty."

"Is that when we manipulate what they see as little matters?" Ripoll asked, catching onto what Baccale was saying.

"Correct," Baccale affirmed. "We could be destroying the entire group from within, and they would let us. Their short-sightedness only allows them to see one thing at a time, making them easy prey."

"Speaking of prey," Morygon asked. "How are we going to reintroduce them back into the training ground?"

Baccale shrugged. "I don't care. Have them wake up here and just erase their memory of being defeated. Their brains are viewing this as if it were a dream anyway. They will not think anything of it."

Lee rubbed the back of his neck, pulling himself up off the cold concrete floor. His body was stiff and sore. It felt as if he had lost a battle, like his muscles had been ripped to shreds. The room was dark and musty; the smell of plastic filled the air. With a deep breath, he coughed up thick mucus. There was something wrong with this place.

"Hello?" William called out, picking himself up off the floor.

Toby was lying down on a wooden table, and with the sounds of people moving, he sat straight up. The members of the group had been placed on furniture with plastic drop sheets draped over them. The room where Baccale had been working on them had changed from a lab into a grungy mechanic shop.

"Eww," Lily cried, lying on a greasy sofa.

"Is everyone here?" Andre asked, helping Warren to his feet.

"Where were we?" Kyla asked, joining up with Lee, helping Tomas get up.

"Where are we now?" Warren asked.

After making sure that the entire group was back together, the Raven Clan made their way through the building and to the main entrance. The doors were boarded up; the wood was decayed and falling apart. Toby tackled the barrier, bursting through it as if it were made of paper. He landed hard against the ground, still unstable after waking up. The entire group felt unbalanced, shaky, and tired—side effects from Baccale's surgery.

"Be careful!" Naven shouted, running to his aid. "You're not fully recovered yet."

"I'm fine," Toby insisted, accepting Naven's assistance to help him up.

As Naven helped Toby to his feet, they were met by a group of gunmen. A small band of soldiers had been on patrol when Toby smashed through the door. The tension that rose up inside of the soldiers could be felt by everyone. They had not had any contact with Outlanders and could only compare them with the creatures that the enemy had created.

"Easy," William said, raising his hands, encouraging the others to follow along. "We mean you no harm. We're only passing through." He was not sure if they were fighting with the Trepidation; but considering how nervous they felt around the nonhuman members of the group, there was a good chance that they were fighting against him.

"My name is Max Chambers," the leader of the group said, lowering his weapon. "Understand our suspicions. The only chimeras that we've seen are the ones that the Trepidation controls."

"Chimeras!" Andre said, notably upset at the accusation.

"What did that insolent human call me?" Tomas declared.

"Calm down," Lee said, placing his hand on Tomas's arm. "This is not the time or the place."

"We're not chimeras," Warren said. "We come from a world known as the Outland, from a region called Calkcaus."

"Region, is that like your country?" Max asked, unsure if he could trust them.

"Yes," Warren replied.

"And what do you mean by 'we're'? You're one of them?" Max was skeptical as to Warren's relationship with the other, only seeing his human form.

"Several members of our group are native born to this land, but we have just recently arrived here from Calkcaus," Warren started to explain.

"We were kidnapped," Lee interjected, "taken there against our will. Now that we're back, our home has been destroyed."

"So you have no idea what's going on?" Max asked.

"We've filled in a few of the blanks," William stepped in, becoming more comfortable. "But we're still trying to figure out where the Trepidation is."

"Why?" another soldier asked.

"So we can defeat him," William answered.

"Let's go somewhere safer to talk." Max signaled his men to lower their guns. "I think we'll have an interesting conversation."

Max and his men started to walk away when Tomas approached Lee to speak. "I don't like this. It feels like a trap."

"I don't think we have much of a choice," Lee said. "Besides, if they can help lead us to the Trepidation, it might be worth it."

"Will you say the same thing if they kill you in your sleep?"

"They won't do that," Lee assured him.

"What makes you so sure?"

"Because you're there," Lee said.

Deep down, Tomas was proud of the compliment.

"Calm down, Fuzzy," William ordered, stepping between them.

"Since when did you become my better, you arrogant little meat sack?" Tomas barked even though he knew William could not understand him. "You are not my master."

"I think you need to check that attitude," William said with a cocky tone.

Tomas growled, ready to tear into him.

"Stop!" Lee shouted. "Don't you two dare start a fight!"

Tomas lowered his head and glared at William. "Look who's tamed now," William whispered.

"If it was not for him, saving your life, I would have already killed you.}Tomas smiled at William and chomped down on his teeth before walking away with Lee. "He is not my master or my better,"Tomas said. "I will not let him treat me as an insignificant servant. I am not his to command."

"I'm not asking you to be his servant," Lee pleaded. "I'm just asking you to ignore him, and don't kill him please."

"I will do that for you."

The soldiers that the Raven Clan had run into were part of a resistance group that was working toward a plan to overthrow the Trepidation. They were thrilled to hear that the Raven Clan was taking up arms against the Trepidation. Their base of operations was an abandoned military factory. The production line still had tanks sitting on them before they were shut down. Hallways were lined with bunk beds serving as sleeping quarters. There were hundreds of people living, hungry and cold, in the building. They were building up supplies for one last battle with the person who took their land.

People crawled out of their beds, stopped working, and gathered into a large group to stare at the strange things that Max had brought into the factory. It was the first time, for many of them, to see creatures like them. Their stares left the Outlanders uncomfortable.

Max took the group upstairs to the manager's office, which they were using as a war room. He wanted to hear their plan on how they would attack the Trepidation, hoping that he could implement it in his own.

"Would like some water?" Max asked, signaling one of the soldiers to go fetch some.

"I think we'd like to get down to business," Lee said. "Where is the Trepidation located?"

Max took a seat at the table. "He's holding up in a hotel, located in New York City. It's overlooking Central Park."

"New York?" Toby said surprised. This whole time they were actually heading toward the Trepidation.

"Yes," Max continued. "His guards inhabit most of the hotel. We've sent in people to spy, but no one has ever made it back. We were planning on a full frontal attack. We have the hardware needed, but attaining the manpower has been difficult."

"I can understand that," William said.

"And what about you?" Max asked. "What is your plan?"

"Stealth attack," Lee said. "We're going to sneak into his base and confront him directly."

Max shook his head. "It's a gutsy plan, but I don't think it would work. We've tried it before and failed. Why don't you stick around and help us with our full-scale attack?"

"We don't have a good track record when it comes to full-scale war," William said, not sure how to explain their failures in the past.

"I understand where you're coming from," Lee said, "but we have to try."

"Well, understand that I will still try and talk you out of it, but we will give you everything we have. If by some chance you can sneak in and stop him, we will support you all the way."

INSANITY

Brittany's screams could be heard throughout the hotel. People passing on the streets would have thought that a madwoman was let loose in the massive estate. She had remained in the room for weeks now barely touching the food that Fear had brought to her. She studied the fountain, choosing her path carefully each time. It didn't matter; none of the alternatives brought about desirable outcomes. Fear had considered taking her sword away from her, but she had already examined what would happen if she killed herself.

Fear opened the door to the room just in time to see her slam her fist into the fountain, splashing the water against the wall. She buried her nose into the corner of the room, cradling her hand. She had broken two of her fingers upon impact.

"You haven't eaten in some time now," Fear said. "Please come to dinner with me. I promise that it will be good." He draped a beautiful red and black dress over a chair that sat next to the door.

"I'm not done!" Brittany shouted. "I still need to find the correct path."

"You cannot think correctly on an empty stomach," he offered. "Take an hour to eat and maybe get some sleep, then you can start again."

Brittany looked at him; her eyes bloodshot from sleep deprivation. Black circles had started to form under them. She was on the edge of madness, not sure what she would do next. She nodded, excepting the invitation.

"I'll have someone come look at your hand," Fear said. "They will lead you to the dining room."

After taking a bath and putting on the new dress that Fear had brought to her, Brittany met with the nurse that Fear had sent. As soon as her hand was wrapped up, she was escorted to the dining room. Fear greeted her as she entered. He was not wearing the bulky suit of armor but rather a black three-piece suit with a red button-up shirt.

"I trust you had a good bath," Fear said, touching the wet hair the laid on her shoulders. Despite all of the accommodations, she was still frayed. Her eyes seemed empty and distant as if she was no longer there. "Have a seat." Fear led her over to the head of the table, sitting her down in front of a hot steak with green beans and mashed potatoes. "I hope you do not mind. I searched your memories to find your favorite dish."

Brittany looked down at the dress, which also seemed familiar. "I know this dress."

"It was your mother's. You admired it as a child. You always thought she looked so beautiful in it."

"How do you know all these things?" Brittany asked. "What do you want?"

Fear spoke as he walked to the end of the table to take his seat. "Don't confuse me with a human. I have no emotions or desires. I am simply a tool, used by both sides, carrying out the orders that are given to me. The rest is just an act to benefit you so that you will accept this form. I was told to allow you to gaze into the fountain so that you may understand how to gain the gift of foresight. To read people's actions before they make them."

She shook her head not understanding the meaning. Picking up her utensils, she calmly cut into her steak, moving as if she were in shock. Before she had a chance to bite into the meat, the side door opened. A man in a black leather jacket and blue jeans walked into the room.

"Good evening, Alex," Fear said. "I trust everything went well?"

"Sure did," Alex replied, not noticing Brittany sitting at the table. "That girl was crying and weeping all over that boy. I'm sure she'll end up falling for him."

"And he is unharmed?" Fear wanted assurance.

"He is," Alex said, leaning against the table. "A little electroshock to the head did nothing to hurt him, maybe just his pride."

"Warren?" Brittany asked with her food still on her fork. That story, of Warren's fight with Alex, was still fresh in her mind. It was a story that they would share several times over in the future. She learned it from using the Wellspring, but she never heard Alex's side of that story.

Alex turned to address her. "What happened to you? You look like you haven't slept in days."

"That's probably true," Fear replied.

"You've been letting her use the Wellspring of Foresight?" Alex asked, glaring back at Fear. "That is a dangerous game."

"I do as I am instructed," Fear said. "Both sides will benefit from her using it."

"It must be terrible not to be able to think for yourself," Alex said, turning his attention back to Brittany. "The fountain is not something to be used as a fortune-telling device. Everyone's actions have the ability to change the plans that you lay out and ultimately the King of the Highland is the only one who can know what will happen in the end. The fountain only points out possibilities that could arise. You're supposed to use it to increase your ability to foresee outcomes."

"That's enough!" Fear insisted, standing to his feet. "It is forbidden to tell her the nature of the item."

"It's forbidden to you," Alex said. "As a Law, you must obey your master's wishes, but I am just an administrator."

"An administrator?" Brittany asked.

"Yes, I am an overseer to the Outland. We are there to ensure the world runs smoothly, and that things do not get out of hand." Alex knelt down beside her as if he were speaking to a child. "With the powers of everything in the Outland, I act more like a sentry, guarding the natural order of things. I fight when necessary and remove threatening elements."

"Is that what Warren is to you?" she asked. "A threat?"

"Yes, the greatest threat you could possibly know. But neither he nor your friends understand that now. That is why you were given the fountain so that you can see him and work toward reducing the threat."

"How, by killing him?" She was appalled by the thought.

"No," Alex urged. "That is why we are all here, fighting to keep him alive. You have no idea how far God will go to see everyone saved. The war is going on to ensure salvation. He does care and is eagerly striving to win you to heaven."

"I don't like the future I saw." Tears started to roll down her cheeks. "I want them to live."

"Death is only the beginning," Fear said, joining the two. "The question comes down to, where they will spend eternity? How will you try and get them to that desirable ending?"

Late in the evening, when everything was silent and peaceful, one of the soldiers came and woke up Lee. The hallway where he was asleep was black with the exception of the candle that the soldier was carrying. "The commander needs to see you in the briefing room." Lee looked around the hall, noticing that many of his friends were missing from their beds.

"Where is the rest of my group?" Lee asked.

"They're already in the briefing room. We didn't want to cause a commotion by bringing you all up at once."

Lee continued to the briefing room where his friends were waiting for him. Most of the group was still wearing their pajamas donated by the resistance forces. "So what's going on?" Lee asked, taking a seat.

"We've got a small task for you guys. That is, if you'll take it," Max said.

"I hate small tasks," Toby said while slowly spinning in his seat. "It's hardly ever small and never simple."

"A girl by the name of Alison James has come to us for assistance," Max announced.

"How many people know you're here?" William asked.

"The Trepidation and his Temps are aware that there is a resistance somewhere in this area, but they have not been able to find us."

"And you never thought that this girl might be with them?" William asked.

Max stood as straight as he could so he could address them with authority. "This girl wants you to kill the Temp, Lust." The room remained silent. "Alison says that the Temp is her mother. She claims that her mother is killing the people under her command. Alison wants the violence to end. I told her that I couldn't spare anyone to go after a single Temp. I need my force to hone their skills for the final confrontation against the Trepidation."

"And so you thought of us?" Toby asked, leaning back in his chair.

"Your friend Andre told me how you've already defeated several Temps, and I thought you would be up to the task," Max said. Eyes began to shift onto Andre as he stood nervously against a wall.

"I just recited a few old war stories amongst fellow veterans," Andre admitted.

"I'm not sure what we can do," Lee interrupted. "We've faced Lust once before. We couldn't kill her simply by removing the Sin that she carried."

"Her what?" Max started to ask.

"That's because she doesn't carry a Sin," a girl said entering the room. She was a beautiful girl with long blond hair and a white scarf around her neck. Wrapped in an old ratty, dirty sheet, she was trying to cover up the fancy jewelry and clothing that she wore. With her fancy makeup and her clothes showing through the holes in the sheet, there was no mistaking her for a mere commoner. She was a petite and young lady with an alluring face that held a sense of frailty.

"Everyone," Max began, "this is Alison."

"Typically, the Sin feeds off the person's own life force and their own desire for power," Alison continued. "My mother's

Sin is a parasite that feeds off other people's life force and their desires."

"That's right," Warren said, remembering the time he first saw her. "I remember watching her kill a man right in front of me. I thought that she merely killed him. Now that I look back at it, I think she used his life to regenerate herself."

"That is the nature of the Sin," Alison said. "Though lust is a strong desire for something, this Sin seems to be focused on draining others. But you must be warned, the Sin poisoned her lips too. Most people only need to hear the sound of her voice to become bewitched by her spell. Once under her spell, they become mindless puppets to her every whim."

"What about the few who can resist her?" Lee asked.

"If she kisses them, they too fall to her will," Alison said.

"So how do we defeat her?" William asked.

"The only way to defeat her is to either cut off her head or destroy her heart," Alison said looking away as if the thought was too much to bear.

"Just like a vampire," Toby said, leaning back into his chair again. "Seems fitting for someone who drains the life out of their victims. So why kill her now? Why not wait until we defeat the Trepidation? She might return to normal."

"You sound so confident," Alison protested. "Are you so sure that you can defeat him? Can you stop him before anyone else is turned to dust just so my mother can look at her disgusting body in the mirror? That's the true sin, the addiction she has for her own beauty." Alison held herself, trying to hold back her emotions.

"But why *now*?" Toby insisted with the stares of disapproval pounding down on him. He knew that they were captivated by her sad story and charms, but he smelled something fishy. "Why wait so long, and how do you know that we weren't already coming? You came here at just the right time to specifically request that we kill her."

"Why did you need to make sure we would come?" Warren asked, now becoming suspicious.

"That's enough," William ordered.

"No," Tomas said. "They are right. Why come to us so late in the hour in order to ensure that we go kill her mother."

Lee looked down for a moment before addressing the group. "Tomas agrees. He wants to know."

Alison almost seemed upset yet understanding. "She has my fiancé," Alison said almost in tears. "We ran away when she first gained the power of the Sin, and then one day, she came and took him from me. She uses him as her personal slave, and I fear for his safety."

"If he isn't already dead," Warren said.

Bitterness rolled over Alison's grieving face. "You don't think that I worry about that every day? I do."

"She seems to travel around a bit," Lee said, looking up at her with concerned eyes. "Are you sure she'll be where you say she'll be?"

"I'm sure," Alison said.

Lee scanned the room. "We'll need some time."

As soon as Max and Alison left the room, the discussion began.

"I think we should help," William said. "She needs our help, and we're not doing much good here."

"Speak for yourself," Toby chimed in. "We're running over the blueprints and reports about the Trepidation's lair. Reviewing how to break into the building undetected. We need to study up before we attack."

"You're barely eighteen," William started.

"Nineteen!" Naven corrected. "And you're barely twenty-two."

"What do you know about military tactics?" William said belittling him. "Other than watching too much TV."

"This is getting us nowhere," Warren said. "Some of us have made commitments here, but for every Temp that we defeat, the Trepidation looses a foothold."

"We shouldn't go running recklessly into this," Lee said. "We should leave here, and go directly after the Trepidation ourselves.

No more running around. The quicker we take care of him, the sooner things get back to normal."

"I think the three of us should go," William said, pointing at Lee and Warren. "We've faced her before and won. Now that we know her weakness, we can't lose."

"Don't be so sure," Lee said. "I've got a feeling that there is more to this fight than what meets the eye. Let's just drop it."

William paid no attention to Lee's warnings, making plans without even listening.

"I can't stay here," Tomas said. "No one understands me."

"I know," Lee said.

"I want to go too," Andre said, standing away from the wall.

"We need someone strong to stay behind and help the preparations here," William ordered. "The ones staying behind can help organize the resistance."

Lee stood, knowing that he wasn't going to win this fight. "I propose that we go with William, Warren, Tomas, and myself. The rest can stay behind and help out here."

"I don't know," Kyla said.

"It'll be okay," Warren said, getting to his feet. "I think it's a good plan." Warren walked to the door and opened it. Max and Alison reentered the room.

"So where's this Temp at?" Toby asked.

"They're located just outside of Orlando," Max said. "It's a bit north of here."

"Where exactly is here?" William asked, taking a drink of coffee.

"We're in Fort Lauderdale," Max answered.

"We'll take the job, I guess," Lee said.

The next day proved to be trying on the whole team. Everyone had their own preparations to make, and tension was in the air. Nobody wanted to be left behind, stuck babysitting the resistance. Their biggest jobs would be to hand out blankets and rations. Toby and Naven volunteered to help organize the weapons and do small maintenance on the building, getting them ready for one final battle with the Trepidation's armies, but nobody else wanted to stay. Toby just did not want the group to walk into a trap.

Warren sat on the tail end of a jeep in the loading dock, getting supplies ready for the trip, running through the checklist of supplies that they would need—water, food, ammunition. Max had loaned them the jeep for the drive to Orlando after he had resupplied Warren with two .9 mm pistols and William with a new shotgun. The weapons sat next to the jeep to be loaded in last.

Setting his clipboard to the side, Warren loaded a trunk into the back of the jeep. It mostly contained snacks, power bars, and other travel-sized meals. Toby stood beside the jeep, watching him work.

"I don't like this," Toby said. "She looks like pretty tempting bait to me."

"What do you mean?" Warren asked, picking up his clipboard again, making sure everything was there.

"You know why William was so eager to sign us up for this right?" Toby stopped as he saw Kyla approaching from the maintenance side of the dock. "Incoming," he said softly.

Warren looked up to greet her. "How's it going?"

"Not bad," Kyla said. It was obvious that she had something on her mind. After about five seconds of waiting, Warren decided to finish loading the jeep. Next was the water.

Kyla saw her opportunity slipping by. "So I was wondering what you thought about the upcoming mission."

Warren was at a loss for words. "Okay, I guess," he replied.

"I mean, I think I could be a great asset to the team," Kyla explained. "I work well with Lee, and two Kalymors are better than one. We'll have stealth to our advantage."

"Tomas is kind of like a Kalymor," Warren stated. "He's good at stealth."

"Yeah." Kyla was starting to sound nervous. "But Tomas is a power hitter. You need him for brute strength. It'll be good for the team to have another hidden player."

Warren glanced up, worried about where the conversation had gone. "Right."

"I just want you to talk to Lee," Kyla said. "Get him to see that he could use an extra person on the job."

"Right," Warren repeated.

"Great," Kyla said. "I'm glad we could have this talk."

Toby and Warren watched as she left. "I don't trust her," Toby said.

"Who, Kyla?" Warren asked, knowing to whom his statement was referring.

"Angela," Toby said.

"Alison," Warren corrected.

"It doesn't matter. She's trouble. And all the guys around here are too busy, drooling all over her to see it." Toby shook his head.

"Do you think that is that why Kyla wants to tag along?" Warren asked. Warren was not sure, but he thought so.

"Oh, I'm sure it is," Toby said. "I'm sure both of the girls want to go on this run, just to make sure she doesn't get any bright ideas."

"I think that's why Lee did not invite them to come along," Warren offered. "It might have caused unneeded tension."

Toby shook his head. "Still, Alison is going to be more trouble than she's worth. She's the daughter of Lust! The only reason Max and the others want us go along with it is because she has a pretty face. Now we can be the knights in shining armor."

"What about her fiancé?" Warren asked. "It seems counter-productive to save the man she wants to marry if you wanted to marry her in return."

"Deep down, they're hoping he's already dead. That way they can comfort the grieving girl," Toby scoffed.

"You're kind of cynical," Warren announced, going back to load the jeep.

"Maybe so. But, Warren"—Toby's voice was sobering—"watch out, out there. She's tricky." Toby looked away for a moment. "Do you think she's pretty?" His words were a little alarming to Warren.

"You're more of a human than I am," Warren said, smiling it off. "What do you think about her?"

"I have my standards," Toby said, walking away. "Besides, I think she's more trouble than she's worth."

Warren nodded, stopping what he was doing. He was worried too. He could feel himself becoming more human every day. The safeguards he had once put up around him were slowly melting away. He had to keep his emotions in check. The thought had crossed his mind of why he wanted to go. She was a pretty girl, having inherited her mother's features, but he did not believe that had anything to do with why he was going.

Lee was in an upper room of the building working on their strategy. He had several maps laid out in front of him, studying the lay of the land. He was working on all possible scenarios for when they attacked. This was not going to be another blind hit, like last time. Lee marked coordinates on a whiteboard that laid on the tabletop. He marked the roads with a yellow highlighter and possible footpaths with a pink highlighter. He also had a copy of Warren's checklist, so he knew what equipment they would be carrying and needed to calculate that into the scenario. He wasn't proficient at the job, but he was the only one they had to do it.

Lily opened the door to the conference room. "Hello?" Lily asked, looking to see if she would be invited in. Even after all the time that had passed, she still looked up to Lee like an older brother. He was always kind and helpful, always looking out for others; she admired him for that.

"What's up?" Lee asked in return. His face brightened, but he had not taken his focus off of his work. "Is there something I can help you with?"

"I was wondering about the mission," Lily said. "Do you think that there is room for one more?"

"You want to go?" Lee had a curious look on his face. "Why?"

"I think you guys could use another member. I can be a great help too." Lily seemed a little too anxious to go.

"Your foreman says that you're doing important work here. He said that he needed you. Your powers make you a valuable member of the crew."

"Yeah, but that's Toby," Lily contended. "He doesn't care about the mission."

Lee tossed his marker on the table. It was a serious accusation even if Lee knew she did not mean it. "Are you accusing Toby of falsifying information, endangering the lives of his teammates, just to see this mission fail?"

Lily held her breath. "No, not at..." She did not know where to go from there. "I just..."

Lee was frozen, waiting for her to answer. When none came, he spoke up. "Then what? What are you afraid of?"

"I just don't want you guys to get hurt," she said. "I don't want anything to happen. And if I were there, then I could help."

Lee smiled at her intentions. "Who is it that you're really worried about?"

"All of you," she insisted.

"Sure it is." Lee was playing with her now. "I've known you long enough to know when something is up. I mean, I was your fiancé once."

"That was seven years ago," Lily fired back. "And you didn't even want to marry me."

"I remember you leaving me at the altar," Lee countered. "But it's not me that you're worried about and probably not William either."

"I don't know what you're talking about."

Lee smiled. "Since Tomas isn't *her* type, I'm pretty sure it's Warren." The troubled look on her face was enough to tell him that he was right. "You're afraid Warren's going to run off with Alison?" Silence filled the room. "Don't worry about it. She's not his type either." Lee picked the marker up again, resuming his work, pleased that he could toy with Lily a little.

"What is his type?" Lily asked.

Lee shot a glance up at the sudden question. He was not sure what to do with that one. "Excuse me?"

"What…what do you think Warren's type is?" Lily looked almost embarrassed by the question.

"Don't try and push him too much." Lee figured that this was the best advice for her. "He's just getting over the fact that he's human. He still thinks on the same level as a Warrian, but as long as you're there for him, he'll see how you feel."

Lily took Lee's advice. She spent the entire night preparing a special bow especially for him, making several arrows to take on the journey. The next morning she would present them to him, hoping that he would accept them.

CLOSING RANKS

It was the dead of night; the wind was calm and everything seemed to stand still. Warren and Tomas approached a wall that surrounded the Temp's encampment. She was held up in an abandoned amusement park, a leftover from the devastation that the Trepidation had wreaked upon the land. Warren crouched down next to the wall in his Trial's Level form. He rubbed his nose with his paw and scratched three times in the soft dirt. Tomas covered one ear with his hand and nodded four times in the direction where the guards were. The two of them snuck around the park doing this for hours.

Meanwhile, Lee was sitting up in a tree, half a mile away, in his Kalymor form. William was in the same tree, two branches up, with a pair of binoculars. Both of them were watching Warren and Tomas scamper around the park. "I don't get it," William said. "What exactly are they doing?"

"They're scouting ahead for us," Lee said, looking in the distance. Lee didn't need binoculars to see at night thanks to the Kalymor's terrific eye sight.

"I get that, but why? We've never needed to do this before."

Lee glanced up at William with a look of disappointment. "The last time we tried to invade a stronghold we got our butts handed to us."

"That's not true," William protested.

Lee answered, "What about Sal's?"

"We just got here," William defended. "And I don't want to hear about the Black Castle. We were younger and dumber." William sighed. "What about Envy?"

"How was that a victory?" Lee scoffed. "We were captured, and they threatened to eat us."

"Yeah, but Warren saved us and we totally beat her," William said in celebration.

"What are you two doing up there?" Alison called from the ground. Alison was sitting on two backpacks with a bow and a quiver in her arms.

"Keeping a lookout," William called back.

"Sounds like you're goofing off," Alison replied.

"Sounds like it to me too," Warren said, approaching the rear. "I could hear you all the way over there."

"Sorry, Warren," Lee said. "So what's the prognosis?"

"Thirty to forty guards," Warren replied. "Not heavily armed."

"What's the best way in?" William asked.

"The front gate is the least guarded, but I think that's for a reason. I think the best way in is from the west," Warren said, pointing in that direction.

"He's right," Tomas said still sitting in the shadows, surveying the land. "It has quite a few guards, but they're easy to bypass."

"Okay," Lee said. "We'll head for the west side of the park. We'll sneak in from there and find wherever her chamber room is."

"The main priority is to save my fiancé. Then you can do whatever you want with her," Alison said, reiterating the mission.

"We know," William said in a comforting tone.

Sunrise was only a few hours away when the team approached the western side of the park. The wind was cool and refreshing. It gave everyone a sense of alertness. The group slowly made their way through the park, quickly sneaking around the guards.

"So where is she?" William asked, opening the question to the whole group.

"She's probably somewhere in the center of the park," Warren said. "Somewhere of high status."

"She's the Temp of Lust," Lee jumped in. "She'll probably play that to the advantage of the landscape." William gave Lee an odd look. "Wherever she is, it will have something to do with her beauty or love."

"The Tunnel of Love?" William suggested.

"House of Mirrors?" Lee added.

"She wouldn't be in the Tunnel of Love," Alison said. "The moisture does horrible things to the hair."

"I doubt she would be in the House of Mirrors," William said. "The mirrors usually distort the figure, and she's all about being perfect."

"Then where?" Lee asked sarcastically.

"How about Cleopatra's Palace?" Warren asked with his back to the group.

"That sounds like a winner," Lee said, moving closer to Warren. Warren stood still, looking toward a building with the inscription *Cleopatra's Palace: The Home of Egypt's Wildest Mazes.* "Incredible," Lee said.

"Looks like we found it," William said. "But where are the guards?"

The team took a look around for a moment. "The lack of guards isn't the worst of our problems at the moment," Warren said.

"Warren's right," William said with determination. "Let's kill this old bat, and get back to business with the Trepidation."

"William!" Lee said, looking back at Alison.

"It's okay," Alison said. "I know what needs done. My only regret is that it took losing my fiancé to realize this."

The group quickly made their way through the double doors that led to the main lobby of the building. Inside, there stood two halls that split in different directions. One read, *Hall of the Beautiful*, and the other read, *Maze of Mirrors.* They both seemed to be mazes, but each one had different themes.

"Well, that's nice," Lee said, looking around for another door. "I think we'll have to pick one and run with it."

"Why don't we take both?" William asked. "If we split up, we'll have better chances of finding her."

"Fine, I'll take Alison and Tomas and go through the Maze of Mirrors," Lee said.

"I don't think so," William said. "I'll take Warren and Alison through the Maze of Mirrors."

"What are you two fighting about?" Warren asked infuriated. "It's embarrassing." Alison giggled and blushed as the two boys fought over who would protect her. "I don't want either of you following me. Both of you will take her through the Hall of the Beautiful. Tomas and I will navigate through the Maze of Mirrors." Warren shook his head in frustration. "Give Tomas my bow and quiver." Warren was not going to let the bow out of his sight. Lily had made it and the arrows especially for him. "Let's go Tomas before the senselessness rubs off on us too."

Tomas and Warren followed a sweet and inviting scent through the maze. They had both decided that it belonged to the temptress Lust. "Listen, Tomas, if we get separated, I want you to know that we're both big boys now. We should be able to handle ourselves. We can't risk letting us both get caught."

"That would leave saving the world to the other idiots. The only one I trust is Lee and the job is too big for one little man," Tomas said.

Warren looked down at the ground in sorrow. He was hoping that he would have been able to understand Tomas again. Ever since the night at the cul-de-sac, Warren had wondered why he understood him only that one time. Tomas suddenly stopped and rubbed his nose. He then pointed to a loose floor panel.

"A trap door?" Warren asked himself as he investigated it. He sniffed at the door then transwarped into his human form. He knelt down beside the trap door and pulled out a pouch of herbs and the shotgun shells that William had wasted. Taking out two of the plants from the bag, he then rolled the pouch back up. "Try and grind these for me," Warren asked Tomas. Meanwhile, he took the shotgun shells apart.

As Lee took the lead of the group, William hung back trying to impress Alison with the stories of their exploits. Lee shook his head as he continued to move along the left wall. At one point in the middle of William's story, Alison interrupted him to ask Lee a question. "Lee, what are you doing?" Alison noticed that every hall they went down, they would hit the dead end.

"He doesn't know," William said, hoping to embarrass him.

"If you're stuck in a maze, you should always follow one wall," Lee explained. "A maze is basically two walls with two holes on each end. It may take longer, but we won't get lost."

"I think we are lost," William said. "I've got better navigation skills."

"Really?" Lee asked frustrated with William's attitude. Lee stopped, facing William. "I haven't seen these skills before. Why don't you show them to me?"

"You want to see my *mad* skills?" William asked, preparing to fight. Without warning, the floor dropped out from under them. They all landed on a large slide that sent them flying through the darkness. Screams filled the tunnel as they slid along, finally silencing when the three of them landed in the center of a well-lit throne room. There Lust sat with four guards standing around her. The room was well decorated with tapestries and other decorative pieces hanging from the ceiling. The only part of the room that was not luxurious was the floor. Sitting on top of light blue, topaz, and marble tiles was an eerie powdering of dust and dirt—remnants of her victims.

"What a disobedient daughter," Lust said. "What did I tell you about sneaking boys home?" Lust looked the boys over as they got to their feet. She was intrigued at first until she noticed their faces. "You little traitor!" Lust shouted as she stood to her feet. "You dare to bring the Guardians here!"

"Give it up, Temptress," Lee shouted, pulling out his knifes. "Give back your daughter's fiancé, and we can finish this."

"Right," William said, bringing out his sword too.

"What?" Lust scoffed. "As if you could order me to do anything." Lust opened her hand toward Lee and William as an invisible force threw them back. "I'll deal with you in a minute," Lust said, pointing at Alison who remained on the ground.

Suddenly, Tomas dropped from the ceiling, throwing two paper capsules at the ground. Once the capsules hit the ground, a small bang of gunpowder created a smokescreen. Tomas landed in the smoke and leaped toward the throne, grabbing Lust by the face with one hand then slamming her back against the throne. Suddenly laughter came from behind him. Tomas realized that Lust was not the person he held in his grip; it was one of her guards.

"How in the world?" Tomas asked himself. He knew beyond the shadow of doubt that he had grabbed her. He became confused and let his guard down.

"Kill him," Lust said as if it should have happened already. Tomas took the guard he already had in his hands and swung him, hitting two of the other guards. The fourth guard swung his sword at Tomas who hopped onto the throne and then clung onto one of the tapestries. He was able to easily avoid the guard who was swinging his sword mindlessly. Tomas removed the guard's helmet with his foot and hit him with it, knocking him out. "For crying out loud," Lust said, opening her hand toward Tomas. Tomas was tossed across the room into a wall. "Insolent creature." Lust turned toward William and Lee in order to finish them off. To her surprise, William was directly behind her and shoved his sword into her heart. As she grabbed onto the sword, Lee pulled both earrings out of her ears. Lust screamed from the pain. The scream didn't last for long as her body turned to dust. William took a step back and snapped his fingers, causing the sword to disappear. This way, the body would remain intact. It was his way of showing respect to Alison in case she wanted to do the honors.

"Brad!" Alison yelled, rushing for one of the fallen guards. Alison wrapped her arms around the man and began to weep.

"It'll be okay," William said, walking over to her. Meanwhile, Lee was looking for the Sin that Lust had. He had thrown the earrings down during the commotion, but now he couldn't locate them. "I'm sure he's alive," William said, placing his hand on Alison's shoulder.

In a flash, Alison spun around kissing William on the cheek. William stood there for a moment, stunned at what had just happened. Alison stood to her feet with a renewed confidence. "Seize him!" Alison ordered, pointing at Lee. William wrapped his arms around Lee, keeping him from moving. "Thank you," Alison said, putting the earrings on. "I would have never gotten them any other way. I could have shared the power with her, but she was so selfish."

"What are you doing?" Lee shouted. "What about your fiancé?"

"Are you kidding?" Alison said. "You are so pathetic. There is no fiancé. You just helped me gain the power of Lust itself. Lust is the most powerful temptation of them all." That was her own opinion, thinking only of the temptations that ruled her own life.

"And we played right into it," Lee said, embarrassed.

"And it was so cute," Alison insisted, acting out a cute little pose as though she were innocent. "The two of you fighting over little ol' me even though you thought I was engaged. But don't feel bad. That old fool Max was trying to hit on me too. Men are so predictable."

"What are you going to do now?"

"What else is there?" Alison asked. "I'll make you all my slaves, and then I'll take the other Sins as well. Then I will be the greatest of all."

"Aren't you forgetting about the Trepidation?" Lee asked. "Isn't he the strongest?"

"You have no idea what the Trepidation really is," Alison said. "Now choose. Be my faithful servant by choice or by force."

"Not on your life, you fiend," Lee shouted.

"Men are so predictable," Alison said, reaching out for him.

"Are we?" A familiar voice rang out.

"Warren of Weremore?" Alison asked. "You clever little pup. You never really trusted me, did you?" Suddenly, an arrow shot out at Alison who caught it in her right hand. "Impressive—"

Before she could continue, another arrow shot out. She caught it with her left hand. When Alison's head turned to scan the room, Warren landed behind her with his bow already drawn back.

"You're done," Warren said. "Surrender the Sin, and you won't have to die."

"If you take my power now, I might as well be dead," Alison said, turning to face him. "You're too smart to be here with them. Rule by my side as my king. You will be immune to my Sin, and we'll live forever. I know your true purpose. We will rule the universe."

"I don't think so," Warren said, pointing his bow at her heart. A small pouch was tied to the tip of the arrow. "You can't dodge the arrow this time."

"I can force you," Alison said, raising her hand toward him, dropping the arrows. "You can't resist me." That was when Warren felt a sharp blow on the back of his head.

"Here, Warren," Lily said, handing him a bow. "I made this for you." Lily then handed him a quiver full of arrows. "This is a special gift, so make sure you bring them back in one piece."

"I will," Warren said, pulling them around his shoulder. "I will return."

Lily wrapped her arms tight around him. "I want to go with you. You can't protect me if you're gone."

"You don't need me to protect you," Warren said, pushing her back a little. "But I will always be by your side."

"You mean it?" Lily asked with tears in her eyes. "You won't leave?"

"Come on, Warren," William called out.

"I'll see you soon," Warren said as he walked away.

"Warren's got a girlfriend, Warren's got a girlfriend," William teased.

"Warren," a voice called. Warren's vision started to turn black. "Warren. Warren?" Warren's eyes fluttered open. He was on his back under the afternoon sky as Lee and Tomas knelt down over him. He had been knocked out, dreaming about the day he left the resistance's base. "You're awake!" Lee shouted.

"Where am I?" Warren asked as he sat up. "The last thing I remember was leaving the resistance's stronghold." Warren sat there for a moment, his body rocking back and forth in the wind. "Wait, Alison betrayed us."

"That's right," Lee said. "You blew her up."

"Along with yourself," Tomas followed.

"What did you put in that little bomb?" Lee asked. "It went off like a grenade."

"I don't understand," Warren said, trying to stand and failing. "I remember getting hit."

"That's right," Lee said chuckling. "You had Alison standing in front of your arrow when one of those mindless goons of hers came up behind you and clocked you in the head with his helmet. As soon as he did that, you released your bow, striking her down. Your arrow blew up on impact. Tomas had to carry the two of you back up."

"Two?" Warren asked looking around. Lying behind him, about twenty feet away, was William under the cool shade of a tree.

"He's okay," Lee said. "He's got a killer headache. Apparently, whatever was used to control the people has a harsh side effect when that person dies."

"Like a drug?" Warren asked, remembering Addiction, and the affects he had when they first arrived. "He's going through withdrawal?"

"Something like that," Lee said, helping Warren to his feet. "He'll be okay."

The journey back did not seem to take quite as long as it did to get there. It felt sad, going back minus one. They were supposed to return with at least one extra person. Despite that, they were grateful that no one else was lost on this mission. Arriving back home, they were greeted warmly by their other companions and several other members of the resistance. Toby took time to gloat about his suspicions of Alison. After their brief homecoming, Max invited Lee and William to the manager's office for a debriefing.

"So she was just after her mother's Sin?" Max asked, sorrow briefly showing on his face. "Such a waste."

"Now that this task is complete," Lee started. "I think it would be wise for us to move on."

"You know, your help would be greatly appreciated here. We could use a couple more hands. It's been a relief with your friends here."

"Sorry," Lee said. "Now that we have our maps and now that Toby has had a chance to make up a plan, we need to leave."

Max simply nodded his head. "I understand. I wish you well." Lee and William both could tell he did not mean it. He was bitter about losing valuable resources.

"Once we take down the Trepidation, things should loosen up around here," William offered.

"If you actually take him down," Max said, doubting their ability.

Lee gave a small bow, exiting the room with William close behind. Tension remained high as they got ready to leave. It was clear to see that the people wanted them to stay, to help them with their fight against the Trepidation, but the Raven Clan needed to continue their mission. This group was not prepared to fight against the armies of the Trepidation, and if the Raven Clan had stayed there, they would have lost their lives.

Fear stood on the balcony of his suite, overlooking Central Park. Everything was slowly coming together. Nothing was unforeseen. The Wellspring of Foresight had correctly depicted all of the results. All he needed to do now was to wait for the Warriors to enter the building. He had delectable treats waiting for them. They would leave understanding the skills it required to survive in the real world.

"Does something bother you?" Brittany asked from within the shadows.

"Nothing much." Fear turned to face her though he could not see her. "I'm preparing for my central act on stage. The last scene is the most important. A story is nothing if the ending is not just right."

The doors opened, and a soldier walked into the room. "Sir, the preparations are ready. We have the Colfount in the chamber as directed."

Fear turned his back to the soldier, signaling him to leave.

After he left, Brittany began to speak again. "A Colfount, why do you have one of the legendary water dragons? What are you planning on doing?"

"Nothing is as it appears to you." Fear turned toward the park once again. "Remember, I am a tool used by both sides. One side wants to get them home, the other wants to train them to fight as Warriors."

"We still have a deal, right? You're not going to kill my fiancé."

"It is not my intention to kill anyone," Fear answered. "I am to instruct the Warriors on how to survive the coming apocalypse and to make their resolve stronger."

"And the Colfount isn't going to hurt them?"

"We never said anything about hurting them."

Brittany almost wanted to cry. "Why did it have to be them?"

"Random," Fear offered. He could hear her stop breathing, obviously upset at his words. "What? Would you like me to lie to you? Say that they are special? That they have a special hate in their heart which makes them attractive? They do not. The only thing that made them attractive was the fact that they wound up in the Outland. Only the Christ can stop it if they would ally themselves with Him."

"They will," Brittany insisted. "I'll die to make sure they do."

Snow gently fell from the sky. In the distance, thunder rolled as flashes of lightning stretched across the sky. The weather in New York seemed to be displeased with the day and its newest arrivals. The Raven Clan marched through Central

Park on their way to face the Trepidation. The group had swiftly moved north after defeating Lust and her daughter. They were now ready to face the tyrant that held a cloud of fear over the world. The wintery blast of air did little to discourage their trip.

"Is that normal?" William asked, pointing to the lighting. "Is it supposed to lightning in the wintertime?"

"Why not?" Lee asked. "The principles are still the same. Electrons in the air..." Lee started to go into a long explanation before Warren stopped him.

"Maybe it's normal for lighting to strike in the cold, but how about that?" Warren said pointing at the lightning. Every time the lightning flashed it only struck at a single building. It was an antique of a hotel, sitting across the street from Central Park. "That has to be it," Warren said. "He's in there."

The hotel itself was built after the Trepidation had gained his power, but it was constructed with an older feeling about it. The Victorian motif was on a grand scale, one that would compete with the best architecture in the country. Nothing in the entire city could compare to this magnificent structure. Sculptors spent years on the carvings, which were floating over every window and door. Some sculptures were of angels and of sirens. Others were merely of leaves and wreaths. Though the sculptures made for interesting pieces by themselves, they did an exquisite performance accenting the twenty-eight floors of the hotel.

In the front of the building, the main entrance offered revolving doors with wooden style frames. Above the doors sat arched windows, offering as much natural light as possible. A crystal chandelier hung from the main lobby, warmly inviting the people into the resort. Everything in the hotel felt natural and solid. There was almost nothing made from plastic in the entire building, inviting the wealthiest of individuals to the estate. Even though the Trepidation lived out of this hotel every time he visited the New York area, it was a viable piece of real estate. He would entertain his guests and rent out rooms to the highest bidder.

William, Lee, and Warren made their way around to the back entrance where the help were supposed to enter; Lily joined them. One of the greatest conveniences for the residents of the hotel was that they did not have to watch their lowly help scurry about, coming and going. The servant entrance, as they liked to call it, was located in the rear of the building next to the kitchen. William's half of the team entered there because they had hopes of surprising anyone inside. The rest of the group entered in the front door, hoping to offer a distraction if needed. The building appeared empty though it was supposed to have occupants. There were no signs of life anywhere. Even the help had disappeared. William and his group came out of the kitchen into the dining hall.

"Where is everyone?" Lee asked.

"Maybe they have the day off?" William suggested.

"Maybe to ensure they don't set off any of the traps," Warren said, standing still. "I don't like this. I think we should get the others out of here."

"I agree," William said, moving back to the door slowly. "Now that we know the building is empty, we can regroup and make a better plan." Just before William could get back to the exit, the door slammed closed. "No!" William said, jumping back. "I knew—" Just then the floor opened up, swallowing them down into its abyss.

The group fell fifty feet, landing into a large pool of water. The massive room below was the size of a football field and made entirely out of a blue and white decorative tile. Light emanated from recesses in the ceiling and in the floor. Though no lightbulbs or flames could be seen, it was obvious where the light was coming from. Also to their surprise, the entire room was lit up.

The group surfaced out of the water coughing. "This is horrible!" Lily said, spitting the water out of her mouth.

"It tastes like saltwater," Warren added.

Lee ran his fingers through the water. "It feels denser than normal water," Lee said. "I don't like this." Lee began to swim, heading toward a ladder in the corner of the room. It led to a hallway that sat close to the ceiling about fifty feet up. The ladder itself was carved into the tiles and stone.

"I found a ladder!" Lee called out just before getting sucked under the water.

"What just happened?" William asked.

"We shouldn't be here!" Warren yelled trying to swim toward the ladder that Lee pointed out. A stream of water began to rise out of the water like a snake out of a basket. The taller the tube of water got, the more the water level dropped. Lee was able to grab a hold of the wall with his Kalymor claws, breathing heavy as he pulled himself out of the water. Once the stream of water had finished rising out of the pool, the water level had settled at their chests. The tube of water had reached the top of the room, snaking forward, as if to stare at them. Two arms formed and a head pulled itself from the tube, giving it an appearance of a dragon. The dragon was made entirely of water, hovering over them, moving back and forth in a slow swaying motion. The creature had used the water in the pool to form its arms and head, leaving the water level at just below their ankles.

"What is that thing?" William shouted. It was like nothing he had seen before.

"It's a Colfount," Warren answered, forming a fireball in his hand. Warren launched it at the creature. The ball of fire sizzled out as it landed against the water.

The dragon laughed at him with its eyes at such a pathetic attack. It opened its mouth with shocking speed as water shot out like a cannon, hitting Warren in a fury. The blast of water relentlessly pushed him into the corner and didn't stop. Lee threw his knife at the creature, and watched it get sucked up into the current of the water.

"What do we do now?" William cried. "We can't fight water."

"Sure we can," Lee said, getting down on all fours. "Water has no definite shape." Lee started to chip away at the stone tiles with his knife, trying to break the seal in the pool.

"I get it," William said, thrusting his sword against the tiles, hoping to break them. This caught the attention of the dragon. It stopped its attack of Warren and turned its sights on William. "If you have another plan then now is the time to speak up!"

Warren gasped for air as he came out of the water, his body soaked. He had almost given up on surviving. His breath had been stolen for so long that it took him a moment to register what was going on. Once he regained his bearings, he stretched his hand toward the monster, hoping his fire could have an effect but nothing happened. Then Warren realized that his bracelet was gone.

"Oh no!" Warren turned, looking for where it might have landed. A grate caught his eye, and he put his head under water in hopes of finding what he had lost. Sure enough, it was there. The bracelet was caught, located behind a set of bars which was used as a filtering system. Warren held his breath as he reached through the bars in hopes of retrieving it.

Lily was on the other side of the room, stuck back in a corner. She had tried to throw a few daggers at the creature, but the current of the water just caught them up, pushing them through its body. William charged the creature, hoping that his sword would do damage if he could land a blow to the Colfount's body. But before William got close enough, a wave, which looked like a tail, knocked him back into the wall, cracking it. Water began to run from the ceiling like rain.

Lee jumped at the Colfount with his claws ready, hoping that he could do some damage. He was wrong. Lee slashed at the Colfount's body and was sucked inside as he connected. The current inside the body pulled Lee up and down like a washing machine. He tried his best to break free, but there seemed to be no hope. William got to his feet, but before he could do anything, the dragon snatched him up in its claw.

Meanwhile, Warren was still struggling to reach the bracelet. He was running out of time. He needed to regain his power. It was then that time seemed to stop for him.

What are you doing? a voice asked. It seemed like the voice of the flame inside of him. The fire was asking him, *What are you doing?*

I need the bracelet. It is the key to my power, Warren answered.

Whose power do you seek? the flame asked rhetorically. *Do you honestly think that a piece of leather holds any power?* Warren stopped reaching for a moment, listening to the voice. *Who gave you that power?*

God? Warren thought to himself.

If God allowed you to use my power, then let me work through you. I am not constrained by the use of such weak things. Leather will burn and silver and gold will melt. My fire cannot be quenched by water or rain but only by blood.

Warren closed his eyes, letting go of his pursuit for the bracelet. He emerged from what was left of the water with his will to fight renewed. Fury empowered him as he saw his friends in pain. "Let them go," Warren said. The dragon looked at Warren in disdain. The creature quickly noticed, after the deathly stare, that the water had slowly stopped leaking from the ceiling. The Colfount looked up. Flames had covered the ceiling, racing back and forth on it, drinking up the water before it could feed the beast. The Colfount looked down at Warren, not impressed. "I said now!" Warren didn't hesitate. A massive pillar of fire ripped through the middle of the water. William fell from its clutches, and Lee slipped through the hole that the fire had made. The dragon toppled for a moment before falling over, returning to a massive puddle.

Lee coughed and hacked for a few minutes before William helped him get to his feet. "Are you okay?" William asked.

"Yeah, thanks," Lee answered.

"That was amazing!" William said. "What took you so long to pull that off?"

"I needed to find my power within," Warren said. "I needed to realize my own strength.

Lee stopped, not knowing what to make of Warren's comment. *Find the power within?* What power was he looking for? It was obvious that he had power, but from who? He seemed arrogant as if it was *his* power. Lee always thought that God gave Warren the phoenix fire, that it was somehow God's power working through him, just like the transwarp tunnel.

Toby and his group walked down a hallway on one of the top floors, hoping to find the Trepidation. "If I were a megalomaniac, where would I hang my hat?" Toby asked himself aloud.

"You'd probably want someplace big," Andre suggested.

"With a view," Kyla added.

"And food!" Naven jumped in getting excited.

"Please be quiet," Tomas said. "I'm tired of hearing you talk."

"Tomas is right," Toby said. "He probably wants to be somewhere fancy, like the king's suite or something."

They all stopped as an evil cackle came from behind them. They turned to see a man in a dingy white straightjacket with a deranged smile on his face. The man clung to a cleaver in one hand.

"What's up with him?" Toby said, looking him over. Toby had remembered stories that Lee and William had told him about a crazy man wielding a knife. With a twisted laugh, he charged them. Tomas stepped in the way, grabbing the man with one hand as he came into reach, throwing him back. Tomas was able to strip the knife away from him. He had it only for a second before Toby kicked it out of his hand.

"What are you doing?" Tomas yelled.

"Don't be foolish," Toby said. "That blade is his Sin. I don't see any other items on his body, do you?" The man ran for the blade laughing hysterically, but Toby tackled him first. Andre tried to break them apart, but the crazy man was too strong. The man had Toby by the throat, choking him.

"Die, die, die, die!" the man yelled, followed by hysterical laughter again.

It took the whole group to get the man off Toby and then he clung to Tomas's arm. The man clung on tight as if he had become part of the arm. He swung the man violently trying to get him off even to the point of beating the man against the wall. He continued the assault against the wall until the man finally relented. Tomas then took hold him and threw him down the hall.

"That guy's crazy!" Toby said, peeling himself up off the floor. Toby was shaken. "What's wrong with him?!"

"He's crazy," Tomas replied, rubbing his arm. "Or didn't you notice?"

"How are we going to deal with him?" Andre asked, looking to Toby for answers.

The group did not see the crazy man land or who walked up to him once he came to rest. The tall Native American, Jealousy, stood over the crazy man's body, holding the cleaver in his hands. He looked down at the crazy little man who chuckled nervously.

"Murder?" Jealousy asked. The man smiled and nodded continually. A wild smirk filled his face as he nodded. The crazy man had no idea what was about to happen. Jealousy raised his foot and stomped on the man's chest. It only took one blow for the crazy man to turn to dust, scattering across the floor. Jealousy looked up at the others with a new taste for vengeance in his blood. They all could see the murderous look that had befallen him.

"Yeah, that's bad," Toby said. Toby and Naven turned, running down the hall. Toby stopped when he realized that the others weren't following. Toby whistled at them. "Come on!"

The group ran down the hall, making blind turns hoping to get away from the man. Toby had no intentions on fighting someone that big with the murderous intent that the crazy man fought with. The little guy was hard enough. Toby wasn't watching in front of him, literally running into William. Both of them cracked heads, tumbling to the ground.

"Dude, what's wrong with you?" Toby said, grabbing his forehead.

"I was going to ask the same question," William said getting to his feet. "What happened?"

"We're running away from Comanche Joe," Toby said as William helped him to his feet. "Hey, look!" Toby pointed to a set of double doors, which they landed in front of. It was the presidential suite. "I bet he's in there."

"Let's hope you're right," Lee said, pointing down the hall behind Tomas. There stood Jealousy, enraged more than ever.

"Go on," Tomas said. "I'll take care of him."

"And he's not alone," Toby said, stepping up beside him, calling for his sword. He was not thrilled about this fight, but he was not about to leave Tomas to fight alone. This would have to be their last stand. The Trepidation was right in front of them, and Toby knew he had to buy them some time.

"Me too," Naven insisted. "We won't let you down."

"Are you sure?" Lee asked, knowing that they could all die.

"It has been an honor," Tomas said, knowing their fate as well. Lee swallowed his feelings and pressed on into the room leaving Tomas, Toby, and Naven to fight. "I know you don't understand me, but let me fight him first. I will weaken him, and then you can come in and finish the task."

"Not a chance," Toby said, rushing for Jealousy. Jealousy swung the knife at Toby but he swung too soon. Toby didn't even have to dodge the attack. He cut along Jealousy's leg and spun around to strike his back. Jealousy was able to block the attack and kicked Toby through one of the walls.

"Toby!" Naven cried.

Furious, Tomas rushed the man. He was able to knock the knife out of Jealousy's hand and force him to the ground were they began to wrestle for their lives. Jealousy was able to kick Tomas off. Once he was free from Tomas's grasp, Jealousy picked him up and tossed him into a wall, continually beating his head against the wall. He was only able strike three times before Naven sunk his teeth into the man's arm. Jealousy grunted in pain as Naven dug his claws into his abs. Jealousy wasn't able to throw Naven off, thanks to Tomas biting onto his shoulder. Tomas was holding on for dear life. Toby jumped out from the hole that he was just thrown through. With sword in hand, he charged

Jealousy. In a last ditch effort, Jealousy spun around throwing his arms in the air. It worked. He was able to toss both Tomas and Naven off. However, Toby was still able to plant his sword in Jealousy's stomach. Jealousy reached back and punched Toby in the ribs, sending him back about twenty feet. Blood flew out of Toby's mouth as he landed on his back. Pain raced through his body as the tears ran down his face.

"Toby!" Naven cried, rushing to him. Naven stood over him to check on his condition when a great quake rocked the entire hotel. Naven toppled over beside Toby. That was when a white light rushed over them all.

END GAME

Cecil opened the door that led into a pure white room where Amos was waiting with Jonas and Harper. Jonas and Harper were sitting at a table while Amos rested against it.

"They're on their way," Cecil announced. "As of right now, things are moving according to plan. They have finally arrived at the Trepidation's room and are preparing to be transported back to where they belong. How are things moving on your ends?"

"All the preparations have been made," Jonas reported. "But the struggle has only begun."

"How should we proceed?" Harper asked.

"Cautiously," Amos said. "We may be out of the enemy's backyard, but we've moved onto the big playing field now. Baccale has pressed us hard, operating on the clan already. The enemy will press us heavily, trying to turn the Warriors to their side, convincing them to kill off the Guardians."

"They are currently trying to convert the Guardians to their side as it is," Harper added. "Surely they will try to remove any unsympathetic people from the playing field."

"Let's keep in mind that there are a lot of factors to this endeavor," Cecil urged. "There are a lot of cogs moving in this machine, and the enemy is watching every single one of them. They are not as asleep as some like to speculate, and the moment we forget that is the moment that they win."

"So you still think there is hope?" Amos asked. "Even the Wellspring of Foresight predicts the worst kind of ending."

"That is because the fountain cannot account for everyone's decisions nor can it account for ours," Cecil reminded. "This can still work."

Lee and the others entered a long room. It was as black as night; a cool breeze brushed by. "Welcome to my home," a deep, dark voice said. "I am the Trepidation. You cannot defeat me." The Trepidation stood from his throne and began to walk toward them. His footsteps were loud and hard as his armor banged against the floor. He stood eight feet tall with broad shoulders and a wide chest. "Why have you come here?"

"We want to get our home back," William said. "So get lost."

"Why do you want your homes back? It was a favor, sending you to the Outland. Lee, there you were seen as a man of God, a prophet. At home, you're just a putrid geek, an insufferable know-it-all."

"I would have been a fraud!" Lee shouted.

"William, you were a hero on your way to becoming one of the greatest Guardians, like Amos. Isn't that what you wanted?"

"Not anymore," William said.

"And how about poor Toby?" the Trepidation asked. "He wanted Naven to come with him, but you know what will happen. The government would take him away, kill him, and cut him open. He is such a sweet animal. Together, in the Outland, they are famous. They would live happily there. Apart, they will wither and die."

"That's not your call," Warren said.

"Oh, yes, Warren. How about you? Do you know anything about your history? I'm sure you've realized that you're not just a Warrian by now. I know the dirty secrets that are hidden in your past and what waits for you in the future."

"Don't be afraid," Warren said. "If you fear him, he'll only grow stronger."

The truth hit Lee like a powerful force. Feelings flooded him, overwhelming his senses. He wasn't sure if he wanted to throw up or shout for joy. Suddenly, Lee started to laugh. "I get it now." Everyone looked at him; their faces worried at his onset of delirium. He just continued in his spout of laughter. "Trepidation. Fear. It means to be afraid. You're nothing more than a Temp, the Temp of Fear." Lee chuckled a little more in order to get it out of his system. "We've been doing this all wrong. We had to beat the temptation, not the Temp. We've been fighting flesh when we should have been fighting spirit."

"It's impressive that you made it this far without figuring it out sooner," the Trepidation said. "But you are wrong about me. I am not a Temp and you are too late."

"But it's not too late," William said. "You *are* a Temp, and that means we can still defeat you."

"Don't be so sure," a female voice said from the shadows. "He is not a Temp, and you will not be fighting him. You have to contend with me first, love."

"Who is that?" Warren asked.

"Let me shed some light on the situation," the Trepidation said, raising his hand to the ceiling. The building quaked under foot, knocking them all to their knees.

Warren looked out the window. He could see that the building was rising. "What's going on?"

"A little going-away present," the Trepidation said. Pieces of the ceiling began to fly off and erode away, filling the room with the morning sunlight. The building was rapidly rising into the sky.

A flame surrounded Warren's hand as he readied himself to fight the Trepidation. Suddenly, a second darker flame shot out of the shadows striking him. Warren was thrown across the room, bouncing against the far side wall. As he climbed to his feet, the wall was sucked away into the sky, almost taking him with it. Warren held on to the edge of the floor as the wind tried its hardest to push him off.

Lily ran to his aid, trying to pull him back into the room. Andre joined her and successfully pulled Warren to safety.

William stood in shock as he saw their attacker. It was his partner from the Outland, Brittany.

"Brittany, how could you?" William cried. "We're your friends!"

"You don't know what I've seen," she demanded, "the horrors that will be committed. I have the true phoenix fire, and I will stop it somehow." She looked at William with tears in her eyes, doing her best to hold back her emotions. "Only you can stop this."

"You wanna bet?" Warren said, standing to his feet, unleashing fire in the palms of his hands.

"Now, now," Brittany said, smiling through her pain. "Your fire is fueled by something other than passion."

"It's not too late," Lee said. "Help us defeat him so we can go home."

"Why would I want to do that?" Brittany asked. "He is not our enemy. He is trying to help us."

Warren snapped his fingers, forming his fire whip in a violent furry. "Now stand down."

"Never! You'll need to defeat me if you want to get home!" Brittany unleashed a column of fire at Warren who added his own fire against it. The two struggled to gain control over the tower of flames. Warren pushed with all of his might. It was clear that Warren had more power to his flame, but Brittany had more skill.

Warren struggled to overcome his handicap. He was starting to wish that he had used his flame more. He pushed one last time, the struggle ending in a violent explosion. Brittany was flung back through the air, knocking her through a wall. Warren dug his heels into the ground only being pushed back a little. He clasped his hands, concentrating on his fire wings and a small sword for his left hand. Brittany suddenly shot out from a different wall, tackling Warren facedown into the ground. She did not need any fire wings, understanding the nature of her flame and using that to her advantage. Brittany pounded Warren's head into the floor.

"You won't destroy it!" Brittany yelled. "You won't kill him!" After the third hit, Warren's wings wrapped around Brittany, tossing her off his back.

Warren hopped to his feet, forcing himself to look through the haze that settled over his vision. The rest of the clan could only look on in horror as the battle between fire users raged on. Warren snapped his fingers, setting off an explosion next to Brittany's feet. The explosion was at least five feet off center, but the power behind it was strong enough to send her flying again. Warren took a second to catch his breath, letting his vision straighten out before a pillar of fire rocked him to the ground.

"Come on!" Lee shouted, throwing a knife at Brittany. Brittany turned her flame into a giant Chinese fan. She dug her heels into the floor, pulling the fan back. With a grunt, she swung in the direction of the attack, blowing the knife off course.

"Why are you doing this?" William asked.

"I'm doing this because it needs done," Brittany said. "I am protecting our future. I know what will happen if things are left the way they are. You have no idea, but this is only the beginning. It gets harder from this point on."

"We're finished!" Warren shouted from behind her. Brittany barely had time to turn as Warren rammed into her. Her fan disappeared as they crashed through it. Brittany twisted Warren onto his back as they crashed to the floor. She wildly swung at him. Warren formed a fireball close to her stomach, blasting her off him.

"Warren?" Lee yelled, coming to his aid. "Are you okay?"

"Toby would be disappointed," Warren answered Lee, wiping the blood from his face. "My face feels like hamburger."

Lee looked up in time to see Kyla and Andre rush to Brittany only to get pushed back. Brittany grabbed Kyla by the collar of her shirt, slamming her into the ground and tossing her off the edge. When Andre came to her rescue, swinging at Brittany, she set off an explosion near his center, sending him flying in the other direction.

“What can we do?” Lee asked desperately. “We need to stop her.”

“We have two choices,” Warren said. “We need to either drain her of her power or knock her unconscious.”

“Leave it to me,” William said standing by them, watching the fight rage on. “Just keep her busy.”

Warren climbed to his feet. He wasn’t ready to take another hit, but he shook the pain away. Warren smiled through the hurt, letting rage and madness wash over him. It was the only way he could fight at this point. “Hey!” Warren shouted. Brittany turned her head just as she had knocked Andre off the ledge.

“What?” Brittany asked with authority.

“I hear your mama was a Snog,” Warren said chuckling. Brittany gave him a confused look. “That’s okay, Will isn’t the brightest either. You’ll make a nice couple. You wouldn’t want to be smarter than the man you want to marry, right?” Brittany sneered at Warren.

Lee was so embarrassed that he wanted to cover his face. He had no idea what Warren was thinking. Most of the insults that he was hurling did not even make sense.

Warren started to get louder and more obnoxious. “Then again, you won’t have any smart children, not at this rate.” He was trying to think of what Toby might say next, after all, Toby was the best at distracting people.

Brittany raised her hand to form a fireball. Anger had taken control of her. She prepared to fire when she was struck in the head with the hilt of William’s sword. Brittany’s eyes rolled up into her head, her body falling limp to the ground.

“Sorry,” William said, clenching the blade of his sword. His hands were bleeding from where he had gripped. William dropped his sword, kneeling down to check on her. “Brittany?” William picked her head up and rested it on his lap.

“Nice work,” Lee said to Warren as he passed by.

“Right,” Warren replied, ready to fall over.

“What’s going to happen?” William asked Lee as he approached.

"I don't know," Lee answered.

"We might crash," Warren said, pointing to the clouds. "We're starting to fall." Once Brittany had been incapacitated, the building started to descend.

"Look!" Warren said, pointing toward the edge. The floor itself was being ripped apart from the edges. "I don't know if we're going to make it."

"Are we all going to die?" Lily asked.

"No," Lee said, unsure in his own heart.

"I don't want to die," Lily said, backing away from the group and the edge that she watch erode away.

"Lily!" Warren yelled, running for her. She was so worried about falling off one side, she went right off the other. Warren formed his fire wings and dove after her.

Lee and William remained silent as Warren went off the edge, not sure if this was going to be their last moments. Then something caught the attention of Lee, who stood alone watching something hanging out just over the eroding floor's edge. Lee stepped forward to investigate. It was a wind chime from the porch of his house. Lee remembered it so clearly. He then looked up and began to talk with someone that none of the others could see.

William began to call for him to come back, but Lee seemed like he did not hear him.

"Hello, Amos," Lee said, looking up at him as he stood out on the open sky.

"Hello, Lee. Are you ready to go home now?"

Lee looked around. "I think I am."

"Will you miss any of it?" Amos asked.

"Just my friends," Lee said.

"I'll let you go whenever you are ready," Amos said, taking a step back. "Just remember your promise. Look after William."

Lee looked down and saw that the floor was now gone and he too was standing in midair. He turned to look at William. "It's time to go," he shouted back. "Don't be afraid. Good-bye." Lee leaned back and began to gently drift back and fall with peace.

William remained in the center of what was now just a floor, Brittany in his arms. He looked down at her as she slept. Sadness riddled over her face. "At least you won't be awake to feel it." He leaned down to kiss her on the forehead when a powerful gust of wind swept them off the platform, pulling them apart. William was now free-falling in the air. He saw the ground approaching fast, and he closed his eyes, preparing for the impact.

William hit the ground hard, cracking his head on concrete. The pain surged through his entire body. William lay there for a moment before slowly reaching up to feel his forehead. He could feel a stream of warm blood running down the side of his face. Behind him he could hear the sounds of laughter echo through a tunnel. William staggered to his feet. He found himself in a small, five-by-twelve cement room with a solid steel door. William staggered to the door and peeked out of a small window mounted in the center. His vision was too blurred to see out of the piece of glass so he turned back to his room. Against the left wall was a cot hanging from the wall. It looked like a prison cell. "What's going on?" William asked himself, searching the room for answers. "Where am I? Brittany? Warren? Lee?" He was left alone with nothing but this empty cold cell.

ENDNOTES

1 Romans 3:23
2 Romans 6:23
3 Acts 3:19
4 Romans 5:8
5 Revelation 3:20
6 James 2:19
7 2 Corinthians 10:12
8 Job 1:7
9 Ephesians 2:8-10